Thank you

To all the people who beta-read this manuscript over the years – too many to name! – and gave me their valuable feedback. You've made Rocky and particularly Bernadette, the characters they are today.

Judith Hudson

TEMPLE OF THE JAGUAR

A Rocky and Bernadette Murder Mystery

J.M. Hudson

Chapter 1

The plane circled over the Yucatán jungle on its final descent into Cancun. From her cabin window, Bernadette Mallow searched the lush undergrowth for signs of an overgrown temple, but no crumbling stone pinnacle disturbed the flat landscape below. She knew they were out there, ruins hidden in the jungle, but why the ancient Maya had abandoned their cities was exactly the kind of mystery Bernadette loved to solve.

"On vacation, dear?" her maternal seatmate asked.

Bernadette sat up straighter. "No. I'll be working."

"At one of the hotels?"

Bernadette shook her head, tried to be cool but couldn't hide her excitement. "I'm a writer. I'm heading into the jungle—to Ox B'alam."

The woman's eyes widened in alarm. "I hope you're not going alone, dear."

Bernadette smiled. "I'll be travelling with my new partner—a photographer—and a tour guide. It's my first assignment with a magazine," she confided.

Her seatmate patted her hand on the armrest. "I'm sure you'll do just fine, dear."

"I hope so," Bernadette murmured, turning her gaze back to the window. She'd finally gotten her old friend Jen, now an editor at *Let's Travel!* magazine, to give her a chance. Now she had to blow her away with the finished piece if she wanted Jen to give her more work.

The 'fasten seatbelt' warning chimed, and Bernadette stowed her book in the carryon tote bag at her feet, then stuffed the whole thing under the seat in front of her.

Leaning back, she closed her eyes and her hands lightly gripped the armrests. A prickly sensation ran up her arms like a current as she registered the buzz of excitement from the passengers in the crowded cabin. Her senses were often exceptionally acute, especially in enclosed spaces. And they were seldom wrong.

She was particularly excited about visiting the Mayan archaeological sites listed in the itinerary, including the partially excavated ruins in Old Ox B'alam, the community where they were posted for the week. It was ten years since she'd worked a few digs in the Middle East, right after university. But when her son Colin was born, she'd given up the nomadic life and returned to Vancouver where she'd taken a safe, stable job transcribing archeological field notes for her old professor.

Now she was finally getting out of the office and back into the field. Digging in the dirt had never really been the allure—it was the people who caught her imagination. These were the stories she wanted to tell, but, she realized, not really the stories *Let's Travel!*'s readers wanted to read. So on this first assignment, she was determined to do the job Jen had hired her to do: write a tourist piece on an ancient city in the heart of the Yucatán jungle. Her anthropology degree, archeology background and writing experience had convinced Jen to give her, a novice magazine writer, a chance on this feature article. That, and the fact that her old friend's back was to the wall. The original writer had pulled out at the last minute. Jen had made it clear that this piece was for tourists and travellers, not academics, and Bernadette was determined to get it right. This was her big chance.

The plane landed smoothly and a few minutes later, Bernadette descended the stairs to the blistering tarmac. Heat rose in waves and the acrid aroma of hot asphalt seared her nostrils. Inside the terminal building, the temperature wasn't much better.

The line to customs and immigration snaked on interminably and as Bernadette inched forward, she pulled a compact mirror out of her shoulder bag. She wanted to appear cool and professional when she met her new partner, photographer Rocky Falconi, but after six long hours on the plane from Vancouver, her nose was shiny and her shoulder length, blondish hair—always prone to erratic curls in the humidity—was already beginning to frizz. She wiped the worst of the shine off her nose with a tissue, wound her hair into a knot on top of her head and then, giving up in defeat, tucked the mirror away.

The immigration officer barely glanced up as he stamped her passport and waved her through. Across the no-man's land between the gate and the iron railing holding back the hotel drivers and tour guides, she spied a man holding a sign with her name on it.

* * *

Rocky Falconi picked his new partner out of the crowd the moment she walked through the gate. She'd fixed her eyes on the sign he held at his chest and towing her suitcase behind her, headed toward him like a heat seeking missile. Halfway across the open space, her suitcase fell on its side and one wheel rolled away across the marble floor. She blew the hair up off her forehead but, undeterred, picked up the case and soldiered on.

Stopping in front of the sign, she looked up at his face for the first time and stuck out her hand. "Bernadette Mallow."

Tall and classy, not at all what he expected, Rocky pushed the aviators up on top of his head, but before he could respond, she added, "The writer."

Slowly, he reached for her outstretched hand. "Rocky Falconi." He paused. "The photographer."

She paled slightly as she shook his hand, and he hoped it wasn't from the heat because it was only going to get hotter when they got into the jungle, away from the ocean breezes. "Let's go. They're waiting for us at the bar."

He reached for her suitcase, but she grabbed it first. "Thank you. I can manage."

He nodded—fine with him—and plunged into the churning sea of people, heading back to the terminal bar where he'd left the other tour members. But when he glanced back over his shoulder, she was already falling behind, lugging her damaged suitcase.

He stopped and shifted his camera case to his other shoulder while she caught up, then took the suitcase out of her hand.

She raised her eyebrows and snatched back the case. "I can manage."

Feisty. He shrugged. "Suit yourself." He wasn't in the mood to argue. In fact, he'd rather not be here at all—but that had nothing to do with her. It had been a hell of a month, straight from one job into another and now, to top it all off, his old partner Schuster was on the disabled list.

They forged their way through the crowd to the terminal bar where Rocky happily handed the writer over to Manuel Ferrara, the leader of the Cultural Tour. A stocky man with the round face and smooth facial features typical of the Maya people, Manuel stood a few inches shorter than Bernadette, but he greeted her with what seemed to be his usual boundless enthusiasm.

The two men waiting with Manuel clambered to their feet to greet Bernadette. Hank, a jovial bear of a man in a Hawaiian shirt and plaid shorts, towered over Arthur, who looked more like a mouse in a three-piece suit.

Arthur ran a hand nervously over his vest before holding it out to Bernadette. *Money belt*, Rocky thought. An obvious tell.

When Bernadette took Arthur's hand, her eyes widened, and Rocky could have sworn she paled again, sweat popping out on her upper lip.

Just great. Mexico in the rainy season and the writer couldn't handle the heat. They'd better get her into the air-conditioned van before someone had to carry both her *and* her suitcase.

"You are the last one," Manuel told her with a smile. "The van is waiting outside." He picked up the broken suitcase and headed for the exit with Bernadette and the others trailing behind. Rocky grabbed the duffle bag he had left with Manuel and followed.

A few feet outside the terminal door, a passenger van shimmered in the heat. Rocky dropped his sunglasses back down on his nose. While Manuel stowed the suitcases in the rear compartment, the others climbed in through the sliding side door.

Rocky left his duffle bag with Manuel but kept his cameras. Stopping at the side door of the van, he surveyed the remaining choice of seats. Arthur had appropriated the front passenger seat, and boxes of supplies filled the two seats behind him. Hank's vast girth took up most of the rear bench, and Bernadette sat on the seat opposite the side door, tight against the far window.

Hank seemed like a nice guy, but rather than squeeze in beside the big man, Rocky dropped his camera cases onto the seat beside him and sat next to Bernadette. She gave him a quick smile and shifted slightly closer to the window, wedging her carryon tote bag between her legs. As the van pulled out of the airport parking lot, she fixed her gaze on the scenery outside the window.

Rocky rubbed the back of his hand across his mouth.

According to Jen, his old partner Schuster had fallen off a roof, breaking his leg in three places. He was out for at least six months and there was nothing Rocky could do about it.

He studied his new partner. "So, Bernadette. Have you done any writing before?"

She turned to face him, a ready smile on her face. "Yes, some. Mostly transcribing field reports for scholarly journal articles."

She shifted in her seat and his eyes dropped to her legs. Nice legs—but it was the book peeking out of the basket between her knees that caught his eye: *Writing Travel Articles That Sell.*

Kee-rist. Raising his shades, he squinted at her. "And you know Jen how?"

"We worked together at a travel agency—"

Rocky dropped his shades back in place, tipped his head back and closed his eyes.

Seriously, Jen. A rookie?

Chapter 2

Bernadette woke with her cheek pressed to the darkened window. Checking her watch in the van's dim light, she saw they'd been on the road for two hours. The van's headlights illuminated a narrow, paved road ahead with a solid screen of vegetation on each side. She pressed a hand to her chest. Enclosed spaces didn't bother her, not when she could see outside, but now, with night closing in, it was a little difficult to breathe.

Surreptitiously, she studied her sleeping partner's reflection in the glass. Rocky Falconi wasn't anything like the suave, worldly photographer she'd imagined. Call her naïve, but in her mind's eye, he'd looked more like Harrison Ford, with that Indiana Jones smile that quirked the corner of his mouth. Reality was not so kind. Dark and swarthy, a day's worth of stubble covered his jaw and the bare arms crossed over his chest writhed with an eclectic collection of tattoos. The small gold earring glinting through the tangle of wavy black hair that fell past his shoulders made him look more like Antonio Banderas than Harrison Ford—and more Desperado than Zorro at that.

Aviator sunglasses hid his eyes. Even now, asleep in the seat beside her, heat and tension crackled off him like static electricity. When they'd shaken hands at the airport, like sparks between live wires, a sharp frisson of current had jumped from his hand and hers. It had raced up her arm and down her spine, coiling in her belly and hissing like a snake.

But that spark had been nothing compared to the jolt she'd received when she shook hands with Arthur. His touch had made her skin crawl and sting like she'd stumbled on a nest of fire ants. She had wanted to jerk her hand away but had forced herself to remove it slowly. Even now she could feel a residual prickle.

Her Granny had told her their second sight was a gift, but to Bernadette it had always been more of a curse. In her experience these episodes rarely foreshadowed anything good. In fact, the ones like the one from Arthur's handshake, the ones that felt like a Taser sting, always seemed to foreshadow death, like the death of her dog and the death of her grandmother.

These episodes were something she didn't understand, couldn't control and definitely did not want to talk about, but she had a feeling that two shocks in one day didn't bode well. And then there was the mother of all shocks she'd felt at the restaurant last week when she'd met Jen for lunch. When her old friend offered her the job, Bernadette had told herself that, for once, the shock might predict something good—a new job, a fresh start—but now she wasn't so sure.

Rocky stirred beside her and she shifted closer to the window. She really hoped they could get along and thought that if she could just get a decent meal in her stomach, and maybe a good night's sleep, she could embrace their new partnership. She was certainly going to try, because she had a feeling that Rocky's endorsement was crucial to her getting more work with the magazine.

This assignment wasn't the same as working at an active archaeological dig, but it was a way to get out of Professor Kristofferson's office, and maybe be able to do more than just keep a roof over Colin's head. His father sent support payments whenever he could, but working on grants at digs as he did, the payments weren't much and weren't often.

The van slowed to a stop. Outside the window, a string of garish lights hung over the veranda of a roadhouse restaurant where two people sat on plastic chairs at a small table. No other lights were visible making it difficult to tell if this was a town or just a stop on the road.

Bernadette felt a palpable shift in the atmosphere the moment Rocky awoke. His body remained still, but his eyes flew open. He patted his pockets, twisted in his seat to check his gear and only then did he relax.

"We must be almost there," he said, peering past her out the window.

The van turned to the left, into the darkness. The headlights illuminated jungle foliage lining one side of the road and, on the other, an almost-full moon reflected on the still water of a small lake.

The van lurched over rocks and into potholes for about a mile, then Bernadette's hopes soared when the lights of an imposing hotel entrance lit the windows on the jungle side of the van. The hotel looked much better than Jen had described it, but then the van lumbered past.

A hundred feet further along, they turned in at a smaller, unlit gate in a walled complex. At the end of a tree-lined drive, the van rolled to a stop in front of a long, two-story, white stucco building. Light spilled from the open doorway, down the wide front steps.

Manuel switched on the interior van lights and turned to his passengers. "Leave your bags. Our men will retrieve them."

Bernadette rolled gratefully out of the van and stretched her aching back. Her agenda for the evening was dinner, maybe a drink, and then bed. It had been a long day, she was exhausted and wanted to be fresh in the morning for their first outing with the Cultural Tour.

Manuel led them inside, saying, "Welcome to my home, Hacienda Ek B'alam." His voice echoed off the lobby's peach-colored stone walls. In the corner, a white marble staircase rose to the rooms above. Beside the staircase, an arch in the wall opened to the dining room, and Bernadette could see another stone arch on the far side of the room, leading to a dimly lit outdoor terrace.

Behind the reception desk, a man with a curling handlebar moustache beamed a warm welcoming smile. Manuel stepped up beside him. "This is my father, Senor Ferrara. He will check you in. Then, *por favor*, meet the rest of the group in the terrace bar for a quick orientation before dinner."

Two men in white cotton uniforms, laden with bags, scurried past them and up the stairs. A few minutes later Bernadette dragged herself up the marble staircase, key in hand, heartened to see her room number on the door directly across the hall at the top of the stairs.

Her room was large and airy, with rush mats on cool terracotta-tiled floors, locally-carved masks on the walls and a hand-embroidered bedspread with a rich flower border. The bed looked soft and tempting, but she knew if she lay down now she might never get up. First, she needed to eat.

Sliding open the glass door in a wall of windows, Bernadette stepped out onto the dark balcony. Like a picture postcard, the lake glittered in the moonlight. The hot, humid air was steeped in the heady scent of night-blooming blossoms, ghostly in the darkness below. Leaning over the balcony rail, she inhaled the intoxicating fragrance. She'd landed in paradise.

Revived by the thought, she went inside and took a quick shower. She put on the one dress she'd brought, a practical floral sheath, and wound her wet hair in its customary knot on top of her head. She piled the three heavy tomes on Mayan culture that had weighted her suitcase on the bedside table and, eager to get started, slipped a fresh notebook into her shoulder bag.

She sensed Mr. Falconi did not have much faith in her ability. But Jen believed in her, had given her a chance, and Bernadette owed it to her to do the best job she could. She'd prove to Rocky she could handle the job. The week would go more smoothly if they could work together, and she was determined to do everything in her power to get this right.

Chapter 3

Bernadette's stomach was growling as she locked her bedroom door and started down the stairs, her hand riding the cool marble bannister. She paused at the landing to look down on Señor Ferrara who was still at the desk, checking in a young couple, and Manuel, who stood in the entranceway talking to a new arrival, a tall sandy-haired man with two bulky suitcases.

Bernadette descended to the lobby and went into the dining room. Trying to ignore the enticing aromas drifting out of the swinging kitchen door, she crossed the room and stopped under the arch to the terrace to survey the scene. Overhead, ceiling fans languidly churned the hot sticky air without seeming to do much to alleviate the heat. Potted palms and rattan furniture flowed seamlessly through the covered lounge onto the outdoor patio, where the pool glowed an unearthly blue in the darkness.

On the terrace, ten people stood stiffly in clusters, drinks in their hands. Hank's deep laughter rolled across the room. He was hard to miss, standing a head above the crowd, dressed in a fresh Hawaiian shirt. Rocky sat at the bar between two buxom women. Not wanting to interrupt their cozy threesome, Bernadette headed across the room to join Hank. He was talking to two women and introduced them to Bernadette as Meredith Richards and her daughter Annie. He offered to get Bernadette a drink from the bar since he was going for a refill, and although a glass of wine sounded good, she wanted to stay sharp, so she opted for club soda.

While Hank got their drinks, Annie explained that she and her mother were from Toronto, and that she was in her third year of university studying indigenous Mexican history. She then launched into an enthusiastic lecture on the sophistication of the ancient Maya.

As she spoke, Bernadette nodded. She'd used the few days she'd had before the trip to cram Mayan and Mexican history, but some of the details were still blurry. Like the dates, and the names. Pretty well everything really. Annie could be very helpful.

Manuel called for the group's attention and the small talk subsided. Holding out his arms to include them all, he said, "Welcome to the Cultural Tour of Hacienda Ek B'alam. I, Manuel Ferrara, will be your guide to the wonders of the Yucatán. We have a busy week planned with visits to the ruins at Chichén Itzá, Tulum and here at Ox B'alam."

Pulling out her notebook, Bernadette jotted a note, that Manuel pronounced Ox as *Osh*.

"Let's start by introducing ourselves. We have some new friends and one old friend returning." He swept an open palm in Arthur's direction.

The little man nodded, rose to his feet, twitching his jacket and fussing with his cuffs. "I am Arthur Bickenbaum." His voice cracked in a rough falsetto. He cleared his throat and the tone dropped a few notches. "I am an accountant from New York City and interested in Mayan historic sites." He blinked once through eyeglasses as thick as tumbler bottoms, then sat down, pulling a white handkerchief out of the breast pocket of his suit jacket and wiping his damp brow.

Manuel didn't let him off the hook that easily. Arthur ran a finger around his buttoned shirt collar as Manuel said, "Arthur is quite the Mayan scholar. This is his second trip with us this winter."

Hank, Annie and Meredith introduced themselves next, followed by an older couple from New York, Phyllis and Bernard Morris.

Then one of the women sitting beside Rocky hopped

off her bar stool, her ample bosom spilling out of her skimpy sundress. Bernadette guessed her to be in her late thirties. She had a friendly smile and in a thick Australian accent, introduced herself as Eloise and her shorter, quieter but just as buxom companion on Rocky's other side as Celeste. They were nurses from Brisbane and like most of the other tour members, were here on holiday, had an interest in archeology and were looking for something a little different on their vacation, maybe a bit of adventure.

Rocky slid off his stool to speak next. He had cleaned himself up, put on a fresh white shirt, rolled the sleeves up to the elbow and left the top three buttons undone. He'd shaved, pulled his hair back into a neat ponytail and looked surprisingly respectable. An interesting transformation from the vagabond she'd met at the airport.

He beamed a megawatt smile at the group. Bernadette would have sworn it sparkled like a toothpaste commercial against his tanned, olive complexion.

"Rocky Falconi from San Francisco. I'm a photographer." He nodded in Bernadette's direction. "Ms. Mallow and I are doing a story on the tour for *Let's Travel!* magazine. I'm glad to see such an attractive group. I hope you will all agree to be in my photographs." Cue the smile. Twitters of pleased laughter ran through the room.

So, he could be charming after all.

Suddenly Bernadette realized that while she'd been ruminating on the intriguing Mr. Falconi, all eyes had turned in her direction. A blush crept up her neck as she quickly got to her feet.

She'd always had trouble meeting new people, so she fell back on the tips she'd learned at Toastmasters and gave everyone, Rocky included, a wide smile, being sure to make eye contact with each person in the group. "I'm Bernadette Mallow, from Vancouver, and as Rocky said, I'm writing an article about the trip. I'm looking forward to getting to know you all and to an interesting week."

She sat down, and Manuel took the floor. "Once again, welcome to Hacienda Ek B'alam."

"What does 'Ek B'alam' mean?" one of the Australian women asked, her voice already shrill with wine. Bernadette checked her notes. It was Eloise, the tall one.

"Ek B'alam means 'Black Jaguar' in the Mayan language. B'alam was, and still is, one of the most powerful gods of the Maya people. But don't worry," Manuel hastened to add. "We don't see many jaguars here anymore. I must warn you, however, to beware of the crocodiles."

Nervous laughter skittered around the room, but his tone was serious. "I mean what I say. There are many crocodiles in the lagoon across the road."

Discussion broke out among the members of the tour, forcing Manuel to raise his voice over the tumult. "Do not worry. To our knowledge, they have never killed a human. They are small crocodiles, but dangerous nonetheless."

Silence descended on the room until finally, Annie asked, "How small?"

"Ten to thirteen feet, nose to tail, although a few are longer."

Meredith gasped.

Eloise looked at Celeste and laughed. "That's just a baby. Back home we grow them twice that big."

Arthur's eyes grew round behind his thick glasses. "Do they ever kill anyone?"

"Sure do," Eloise said, in her best Aussie brogue. "A couple of times a year at least."

Manuel interrupted. "That is Australia. Here in the Yucatán, the crocodiles are much smaller. They have never attacked a human, although a few dogs have disappeared. I warn you against teasing them, though. And definitely—no swimming in the lagoons. The pool behind the hacienda is much cleaner and there it is easy to spot a stray croc." Manuel's face remained serious as he looked around the table, then it collapsed into an infectious smile. "I am joking. Do not worry about crocodiles in the pool. We have perimeter fencing."

Bernadette noticed Rocky didn't join in the discussion—probably too tough to let a few crocs worry him. She tried to laugh off the threat, too, but couldn't help glancing across the terrace to the swimming pool, glowing like an enchanted jewel in the darkness. She half expected to see a primordial head rise up out of the water.

True to his word, Manuel kept the introductions short. "Now, let us push the tables together and get to know each other better over dinner."

* * *

Rocky sat at the bar, still sandwiched between the two *very* friendly Aussie women. As he nursed his beer, he glanced left and right. They made a scary tag team, and although their abundant cleavage would make the kind of photos he knew would sell, he hoped he didn't have to listen to their chatter all night.

He pulled himself up. They were probably very nice. He was just generally pissed off. First the business with Schuster's fall—that sucked—and now he had to break in this new partner, who was standing in the doorway across the room drinking club soda, for Christ sake. Jen had been vague about Bernadette's qualifications over the phone, but he had hoped for someone with a little experience. Someone who knew the ropes. Someone he wouldn't have to walk through every damn step of the week.

And then there was that business with his girlfriend, Samantha. She'd left his place last night pissed as hell that he was leaving again. Granted, he'd been working a lot lately—too much, really—but he didn't feel they'd been together long enough for her to have a say in what he did. And, come on, it was his *job*.

He emptied his glass and put it down on the bar with an emphatic smack. The sound brought him back to the moment. He was here, and so was Bernadette, and if he was smart he'd go over and patch up the mess he'd made of their introduction at the airport. It wasn't her fault they were stuck with each other this week. If he could mend some fences, the week was bound to go more smoothly.

Pushing himself away from the bar, he ignored the Aussies' entreaties to stay and walked over to where Bernadette stood in the dining room doorway. He leaned against the doorjamb. "Hello."

"Hi," she replied, her eyes on the flurry of activity in the dining room as the staff pushed the tables together.

He frowned. "Something wrong?"

She pulled herself up to her full height, turned to face him with a smile. "Absolutely not."

She was tall; they were almost eye-to-eye. Rocky peeled himself off the door jam and stood up straighter. Her lips were pursed, her delicate brows raised and her brilliant blue eyes shot sparks everywhere she looked. Right now, she was looking at him.

"Sorry if we got off to a bad start at the airport." He dragged a hand across the back of his neck and glanced at the floor. "I'm just used to working with my regular partner Schuster, and the idea of working with a rookie—"

Catching his mistake, he glanced up in time to see her nostrils flare. *Not her fault.*

He tried again. "This whole arrangement just caught me off guard. Can we start over?" He shot her his brightest smile, the smile that got him through almost anything, and held out his hand to shake. "Rocky Falconi. Nice to meet you."

Bernadette's eyes flashed. *Irish.* He'd bet his last dollar.

She crossed her arms on her chest and took a moment to give him a visual once-over he wasn't used to getting from women.

Her eyes narrowed on his ponytail. He stiffened. He'd tied it back especially for the meet-and-greet.

Her gaze traveled down and stopped at his upper arm where the bicep tattoo peeked out from under his rolled shirt sleeve. A clean white shirt, he wanted to point out—but held his tongue.

Her eyes settled on the eagle on his forearm, and her brows inched higher. His jaw clenched. *You're not exactly my type either, sweetheart.* He liked a woman with a little edge, a little warmth, not one as chilly as a glass of chardonnay.

She reached out and took his outstretched hand. "Bernadette Mallow. Nice to meet you. I'm looking forward to working together this week. I will try not to get in your way."

Rocky pushed his charm into overdrive. "Can I get you a drink?"

She smiled politely. "Thank you. Club soda."

He tried not to cringe. Schuster she wasn't, but as he headed to the bar he swore to himself he'd have her drinking tequila before the week was over.

Chapter 4

By the time Rocky returned with her drink, the hacienda staff were carrying platters mounded with food in from the kitchen and arranging them on the dining room buffet tables. Inhaling the mix of savory aromas, Bernadette almost sobbed. All she'd eaten since dawn was a dry airplane sandwich.

"Thank you," she said, accepting the peace offering from Rocky. "Let's see what they're serving."

Rocky followed her to the buffet and surveyed the platters of food. "Could be the fifty-first state."

"Not exotic enough for you?" she asked as she piled her plate with rice, fried fish, small tortillas and salad, relieved that she could identify almost every dish.

He dug into a big bowl of salsa in the center of the buffet. "I can spice it up."

Under wrought iron chandeliers hanging from the high beamed ceiling, the long table of the Cultural Tour dominated the dining room. As Bernadette settled into her seat, a young Maya waiter in a white cotton uniform approached with a jug of ice water in one hand and a decanter of red wine in the other. Clean cut and smiling, his almost-black eyes sparkled in his smooth, broad face.

"*Hola*. I am Luis, your waiter tonight. May offer you some red wine?"

"Yes, thank you. What kind of wine is it?"

"Some of our best Mexican wine."

Bernadette had never tried Mexican wine, but at this point she'd have drunk anti-freeze. She accepted the glass and took a sip. Pretty good. And why not? Mexico had the climate for grapes and a history of Spanish expertise to go with it. Pulling her notebook out of her shoulder bag, she made a note about the wine.

Manuel walked into the dining room, his hand on the arm of the sandy-haired man she'd seen him talking to in the lobby. Addressing the group, Manuel said, "Tonight we welcome another returning guest. First Arthur, now Jason. Everyone, meet Jason Caruthers. He was with the tour last week and now has stopped in for one more night before returning home."

He turned to Caruthers. "Please join us for dinner."

Caruthers nodded a brisk acknowledgement to the assembled group, but said, "No, thank you. I don't want to intrude."

He scanned the room, then went to the buffet. A few moments later, Bernadette heard him settle at the table behind her. When Luis offered him some wine, he declined.

Bernadette turned around and, sending Caruthers a friendly smile, said, "It's surprisingly good."

"No, thank you," he replied curtly.

He obviously didn't want to be part of their group, so she turned her attention back to Annie who had continued with her explanation of the fine points of Mayan loose stone construction.

Just as Bernadette reached for her wine, she heard the scrape of wood on stone behind her and without further warning, her chair pitched forward. Burgundy liquid sloshed over the rim of the glass in her hand and a bright red stain oozed over the pristine white tablecloth.

She spun around. "What the—"

Caruthers, whether in clumsiness or haste, had bumped into her chair and, without stopping to apologize, was making a bee line for the bar by the terrace arch where the bartender had just appeared.

Bernadette turned back to mop up the mess and saw Rocky watching from across the table. Even though the accident wasn't her fault, her cheeks burned. He just had that effect on her— made her feel like a klutz. Like the suitcase episode at the airport. Way to make a good impression.

Luis appeared at her elbow with fresh napkins. He shrugged off the mess as he wiped up the spill. "Don't worry. No problem."

After thanking him for his help, Bernadette tried to put the incident out of her mind and turned back to Annie. "You were saying?" Annie jumped into her lecture without missing a beat. Although Bernadette thought she might be able to use some of this background information in her piece, the hours of travel had taken their toll and it was becoming increasingly difficult to concentrate.

After the meal, Manuel stood up at the head of the table and tapped his spoon against his water glass. "Your attention, please. If you look at the itinerary you will see that tomorrow morning we go to the archaeological site here at Ox B'alam, less than a mile away around the lagoon. We will wake you early —" Bernadette stifled a groan, "—to take advantage of our proximity and visit Old Ox B'alam before the tour buses arrive. Only a few buses come here from Cancun each day, but even so, it is best if we go early. You will thank me later in the day when the heat rises and you are already back in our hotel swimming pool.

"Later in the week, I will escort you to the temple at the top of the pyramid to watch the sun rise. Tomorrow, though, we will explore the ruins. Breakfast is at seven and the bus leaves at eight. And now, *buenas noches*, thank you for your attention and enjoy the rest of your evening."

Manuel hustled off and the other tour members began to drift away. Revived by dinner, Bernadette no longer wanted to return to her room. Instead, she was eager to begin gathering information for the article. For instance, she could talk to one of the previous tour members about their experiences. Jason Caruthers had already vanished, but she could always talk to Arthur. She rubbed the faint heat rash on her arm. He didn't seem very talkative, but then neither did Caruthers.

She wandered out to the terrace where she found Rocky and Hank already seated at the bar. The overhead fans stirred the humid air.

Hank immediately moved to the next bar stool leaving an empty seat for her between the two men. Rocky nodded a greeting as she slid onto her seat.

"What would you like to drink?" Hank asked.

A door behind the bar swung open and the bartender she'd seen at the dining room bar strolled through. Apparently, the dining room bar and the one on the terrace were back to back, connected by the swinging door. The bartender was strikingly handsome and knew it. He was tall and slender and didn't really look Maya. Although similar in coloring, his face was narrow and his cheekbones too sharp, slashing diagonally across his angular face.

His eyes, intense and hooded, slid over Bernadette. "What can I get for you, Señorita?" he asked, his voice low and familiar. Placing his elbows on the bar, he leaned toward her. The urge to lean back was strong, but she managed to smile coolly and order red wine.

Rocky indicated his empty glass. "Another *cerveza, por favor*, Salvador."

Eloise and Celeste bounced into the room and surrounded Rocky at the bar, nudging Bernadette out of the way until she had to grip the bar to keep from falling off her stool. She leaned into Hank and when he gave her a playful poke in the ribs with his elbow, she laughed, shaking her head in exasperation.

When Annie and Meredith arrived, Hank excused himself to join them at a table on the terrace, leaving Bernadette alone at the bar with Rocky and the Aussies.

Feeling like a third wheel—or maybe in this case a fourth—she stared into her drink as the other women regaled Rocky with tales of their exploits in Mexico City the week before.

She could always go and sit with Hank and Annie and her mother but, useful and well-meaning as Annie might be, Bernadette had had enough of her lecturing during dinner. Swallowing a yawn, she signed for her tab and headed for her room.

In the lobby, a new man stood behind the reception desk. With a smile, he introduced himself as Jose. The lobby was quiet at this late hour and he was clearly eager to talk. After hearing all about his cousin in Los Angeles, Bernadette was finally able to get away.

The clock on the lobby wall said ten thirty, which would only be eight thirty in Vancouver, before her son's weekend bedtime. Instead of going straight upstairs, she slipped out the front door, hoping to find a strong cell signal.

The night air was heavy. The exotic perfume of tropical flowers pressed in around her, and the shrill insect chorus provided yet another reminder that she was far from home. Pulling out her phone, she called her son. She missed him already. Her mother, who lived in the apartment below them in the old house they shared, was taking care of Colin for the week. Although the lack of privacy sometimes grated, Bernadette didn't know what she would do, as a single mother, without her mother's unwavering support. For starters, she could never have accepted this opportunity.

Colin answered.

"Hi, Sweetheart. Are you having a good time at Gramma's?"

"We went swimming at the community center. It was great. Can you swim in the ocean at your hotel?"

Bernadette told him about the crocodiles and his

response was, "Awesome!" He'd wanted to come with her, but luckily there was no way he could miss school. Maybe someday, but on this first trip she had to focus on the work.

The call was short and as Bernadette disconnected, Caruthers came out of the hotel, grunted an acknowledgement and hurried past her down the stairs. She briefly considered calling after him, asking if she could buy him a drink and talk to him about his tour experience the week before, but really, she was too tired to formulate any coherent questions.

Anyway, he was already gone, hurrying down the shadowy lane. Unlike her, he was obviously on Yucatán time, probably off to experience the nightlife, if there was any nightlife in Ox B'alam.

Too tired to even wonder where he was going, Bernadette dragged herself up the stairs to her room and to bed.

Sunday, Day 1

"... within this secluded region may exist at this day, unknown to white men, a living aboriginal city, occupied by relics of the ancient race, who still worship in the temple of our fathers."

J.L. Stephens, <u>Incidents of Travel in Yucatán, 1842</u>

<u>Chapter 5</u>

The next morning, Bernadette awoke to a pre-dawn knock on her door. Groaning a response, she rolled over and cracked one bleary eye to check the clock. Six thirty. She struggled not to do the math, but she couldn't fool her body-clock. It would only be four thirty a.m. in Vancouver.

Once awake, though, the gears started grinding in her head. The ruins at Old Ox B'alam awaited them this morning. Her first assignment. A burst of adrenalin propelled her out of bed and into the shower.

After dressing, she lay her equipment out on the bed: pad, pens, her phone—because even if the internet was spotty or, she feared, non-existent, the voice recorder might be handy. She threw in two water bottles she'd picked up from the stand in the lobby the night before and a small spray can of mosquito repellant. A liberal coating of sunscreen on her face and arms was a must. Her pale complexion—another 'gift' from her grandmother—was a sunburn waiting to happen. Her new hat was a green canvas Outback with a broad brim.

Pulling it on, she put her hands on her hips, struck a jaunty pose and grinned at her reflection in the mirror. Intrepid Travel Reporter, ready for any jungle adventure, grinned back.

As she entered the dining room she was greeted by a buzz of voices. Taking one of the last seats at the tour's long table, Bernadette greeted the Morrises, who were dressed in matching linen safari suits that only highlighted the fact that the missus was stick thin and he was rather plump.

Luis, the waiter, appeared, carrying a pot of coffee, filling her cup with a friendly, "*Buenas dias.*"

At the buffet table, cooks in tall white chef's hats fried eggs on a griddle for *huevos rancheros*. She loaded her plate with tortillas and beans and cool green salsa. Who knew how long the tour of the ruins would take and when they would eat again.

When she got back to the table, Rocky swung into the last empty seat, beside her.

"Should get some good shots today," he said, slathering both the red and green salsa onto his eggs. "Apparently Old Ox B'alam is still almost totally overgrown."

His good mood surprised her, but if he wanted to start fresh, she was more than happy to oblige. He glanced at her plate. "How is it?"

"Good." She shoveled a hearty spoonful into her mouth.

Seconds later, like steak on a barbeque, her palate burst into flame. Eyes bulging, she clutched a hand to her throat and looked frantically around for somewhere to spit, but there was nothing at hand. Besides, Rocky was watching, so without even chewing, she swallowed the fiery mouthful.

Barely bothering to hide his amusement, Rocky poured a glass of ice water from the pitcher on the table and handed it to her. Tears streamed down her face as she grabbed the glass out of his hand and drank it all in one go.

"Hot?" he asked.

Squinting teary eyes at the sarcasm, she poured herself another glass.

Rocky scooped up a forkful of eggs piled with both red and green burning salsas and shoveled it into his mouth, somehow managing to grin as he chewed.

She wanted to smack him, but instead slowly drank the second glass of water. Over the rim of her glass, a flurry of activity in the lobby caught her eye. Manuel and his father conferred at the front desk. They called over one of the bellmen, barked an order at him in Spanish, and he scrambled up the stairs.

She took another sip of water and watched as, moments later, he ran back down.

Scraping all the salsa off her eggs, she went back to her breakfast but kept an eye on the drama unfolding in the lobby. Manuel was next to dash up the stairs, only to race back down moments later. He hurried into the office, followed by his father.

Very interesting.

A few minutes later Manuel appeared in the dining room, walking along the table, encouraging the tour members to hurry. "You will thank me later when the sun is high and the heat is rising."

As he passed Mrs. Morris, she touched his hand. Bernadette's ears perked up as the older woman asked, "Anything wrong, hon?"

"It is probably nothing," Manuel replied, but Bernadette thought his smile looked forced. "Has anyone seen Mr. Caruthers this morning?" he asked of the table at large. "He was supposed to leave early for his flight home from Cancun, but he did not come down. I checked, and he is not in his room, although his car is still in the lot."

"Maybe his flight is delayed," Mrs. Morris suggested. "Or he might have gone for a walk." She patted Manuel's plump hand with her bony fingers. "I'm sure he'll be back soon."

Manuel forced a smile. "You are probably right," he said, but he didn't sound at all sure.

Bernadette thought back to the night before, when Caruthers had passed her on the front steps. She opened her mouth to mention it to Manuel, but Rocky shot her a sharp look. She lowered her eyebrows in question, but he shook his head. Although he obviously didn't think she should get involved, she felt uncomfortable withholding the information, even though at this point it might all be nothing.

Before she could make up her mind what to do, Manuel was gone and people began to drift away from the table, preparing for the trip to the nearby ruins.

A few moments later, Luis returned and refilled their glasses with a shaky hand, spilling water on the table and cleaning it up in a flurry of nerves. When he leaned down to take her plate, Bernadette asked in a low voice, "What's going on, Luis?" She nodded towards the lobby. "Not trouble, I hope."

Everyone at the table shifted slightly forward to hear his reply. Everyone except Rocky, who sat back in his chair as if trying to distance himself from the discussion.

Luis's ears turned pink and he glanced uncomfortably at the empty lobby desk. His eyes dropped to the table as he continued to load dishes onto his tray. "They found a body—in the lagoon."

Chapter 6

Annie's hand flew up to cover her mouth. "A body? Whose body?"

"They are not sure," Luis answered, his voice low as he glanced towards the lobby again. "It is often hard to say after they have been with *los cocodrilos*." He whisked the last glass up from the table and, hefting the heavy tray onto his shoulder, hurried back to the kitchen.

The group was silent as the meaning of his words sank in. Bernadette's gaze swept the table, registering the reactions of those still seated. Their facial expressions varied from confusion to shock to outright horror.

Annie screwed up her face. "Ew-w-w."

"Yes," Arthur said. "The crocodiles." He had come up quietly behind them, his ghoulish tone sending chills down Bernadette's back. "They are scavengers, and while they might not attack a live human, they would happily take advantage of the situation if they found one who was already dead." His owlish eyes blinked impassively behind his glasses as he studied their horrified faces.

Hank spoke first. "I didn't know crocodiles existed in Mexico until Manuel told us last night."

"There aren't many lakes in the Yucatán so here, inland, it is usually not an issue," Arthur replied. "The lagoons around Ox B'alam are an unusual geological formation. Quite fascinating really."

Annie's round eyes made her appear even younger than her twenty years. Bernadette searched her mind for a topic to take the girl's mind off the death so close to home. "Annie, I see images of jaguars everywhere throughout the literature about the Maya. Do you know their significance?"

Annie blinked like she was waking from a daydream—or maybe a nightmare. Still, she began to speak, seeming glad of the distraction. "Jaguars are the top of the food chain in Central America and were given many literal and mythical roles by the ancient Maya. Many priests and rulers incorporated 'jaguar' into their names—sort of like Richard the Lionhearted did."

Her eyes cleared as she picked up steam. "Also, the Maya thought each person had a group of animal soul companions who guided them through life. They were called *way* in the Mayan language. Farmers had animals like possums and weasels as their *way*, but the rulers and priest had jaguars—or crocodiles." A shudder ran through her and her eyes flashed to the lobby, but she valiantly continued. "Priests and rulers, who could be one and the same, often wore robes made of jaguar skins, sometimes complete with the cat's head sitting on top of their own. They thought they could draw the strength and power of the jaguar from the skin."

"Fascinating," Bernadette said, rummaging in her bag for her pad and pen.

"The jaguar, B'alam, was famous for his stealthy silence and the ability to disappear in any terrain," Annie said. "The Maya believed he could pass on these skills to those he protected."

"They still believe," Arthur added emphatically, pulling out a chair and joining them at the table, his eyes disturbingly bright behind his glasses. "Ek B'alam, the Black Jaguar, is feared and respected as the Night Sun God of the Underworld."

"In ancient times," Bernadette suggested as she wrote down the name.

"Not only then," Annie said. "Even today the old myths remain active in remote communities."

"Who is to say," Arthur challenged, "that the old stories, or 'myths' as you call them, are any less valid than the 'religion' the Spanish imposed on the people?"

Bernadette looked back and forth between the two. *Interesting.* They were head to head on this, both Mayan scholars but with differing viewpoints: Annie the academic versus Arthur the romantic, a mystic who seemed to believe in the powers of the jaguar.

"Night Sun God," Bernadette repeated. "Is that like the moon?"

"Not at all," Arthur said, leaning toward her as he warmed to his subject. "When the sun dips below the horizon at sunset, the Sun God must cross the underworld through the hours of darkness. For this extremely hazardous journey, he becomes the Night Sun God, taking on the body of the strongest fighter—the black jaguar."

"I see." Bernadette scrambled to get it all down, but it didn't sound quite right. "Ek B'alam is a black jaguar? Aren't jaguars gold? With spots?"

Annie answered. "Usually, but there is another variety that are very dark, almost black. They are rare, however, and considered sacred."

Arthur's eyes had glazed over and he continued his story in a haunting voice as if unaware of the interruption. "Then, in the morning, when the sun rises, an exhausted Ek B'alam returns, demanding a sacrifice of blood."

"But in return he gives the people rain," Annie added.

"All jaguar legends are tied to blood," Arthur said, putting an unsettling emphasis on the final word.

Arthur's intense interest in blood-sacrifices felt a little weird to Bernadette, considering someone had recently died an apparently violent death.

Manuel appeared in the arched doorway to the lobby with the Morrises and the two Australian women behind him. The final tour members took their seats at the dining room table and silence descended on the group as they waited for Manuel to speak.

He didn't seem to know where to start, but finally he began. "There has been a death in the community. A body was discovered this morning in the lagoon. So far, the police do not know who it is."

Manuel's face was unusually pale. He had to be thinking of Caruthers. That had certainly been Bernadette's first thought.

After a moment, he continued. "While it is extremely unsettling—Ox B'alam is usually a safe and friendly community—the Police Chief has given his okay for us to continue this morning with our tour of the ruins, as planned."

No one spoke, just looked guardedly at each other for their reactions. Bernadette tried to remember who had been at the table when Manuel had told them Caruthers was missing. Rocky. The Morrises. Perhaps that was all.

"There is nothing we can do here," Manuel continued. "We are already late to begin our day, so let us gather our belongings and meet at the van in fifteen minutes."

Rocky gave Bernadette a pointed look, then excused himself and went up to his room to get his equipment. All she could discern from his unintelligible looks was that he didn't think they should get involved. She decided to accept his more experienced judgment. She didn't know it was Caruthers they had found—didn't really know anything about the situation—so until they had further information, she'd keep her thoughts to herself. To be honest, she didn't want to get drawn into any trouble on this trip, either.

It was already past eight o'clock, nearly time to leave. Slinging her bag over her shoulder and putting her hat on her head, she went out the front entrance to wait for the others.

She met a wall of balmy air at the door, with the

promise of heat to come. Birds called, hauntingly unfamiliar songs, from the flowering bushes surrounding the entrance. Halfway down the front stairs, a wave of dizziness washed over her. Heart racing, she grabbed for the handrail. She had experienced this sensation once before, years ago, when she was a teenager. Terrified, she had asked her Grandma Bernadette what it meant.

"Relax and see what happens," the old woman had said. "It's an opportunity to see what's coming. A message from beyond. Open your senses to anything unusual you might think or feel."

Remembering her grandmother's words, she tried. Still clutching the handrail, she closed her eyes and let the sensation wash over her. A fizz of adrenalin raced down her arms. Her body seemed weightless, as if floating in vapor—then suddenly the air cleared, and she sank back onto solid ground. The twitter of birds resumed, and once again she could smell the dank morning mist.

She blew out an exasperated breath. She'd almost had it. That was the closest she had ever come to being in the zone. Was it a premonition? If so, of what?

If only she'd had more time with her grandmother, she might have learned how to interpret these spells. She clung to the idea that these recent ones were manifestations of her excitement, although that was getting harder and harder to believe. But even the discovery of a body in the lagoon couldn't totally quash her excitement about spending the day at the ruins in the jungle.

The rainy season usually began in March and, right on schedule, the rains had begun the previous week. Today, however, the sky was clear. The morning sun glinted off the dew-laden foliage that lined the hacienda drive. Tropical fragrances ripened the steamy air but, underlying it all, she could detect a cloying odor of decaying vegetation that she hadn't noticed the night before.

When she got to where the vans were parked, Annie was already waiting, foot tapping impatiently. "Where is everyone?"

As if on cue, Celeste and Eloise burst out the front door, followed by most of the rest of the party. They all piled into a larger van than the one Bernadette had arrived in the previous day. She took the seat across from the side door again and at the last minute, Rocky ran out of the hotel entrance and climbed in beside her.

Manuel paused the van at the end of the driveway, just beyond the hacienda walls. Across the road that skirted the water, a narrow verge blended with the shoreline in a thick bristle of reeds. The van turned right, back the way they had come the night before, and started around the lagoon.

They passed the elaborate stone entrance of the resort next door and then left the hotels behind. As the van made its way over the rough pitted road, jostling the passengers from side to side, dense foliage pressed in on the road from the right while the lagoon washed up through the reeds on the left. Only one grass-roofed hut stood by the water on the entire stretch of shore back to the restaurant intersection.

As he drove, Manuel spoke to the group through a microphone he wore on a headset. "There are no lakes or rivers in the Yucatán. The water drains through the porous ground into underground caverns. Sometimes the roofs collapse to expose pools below. These we call cenotes.

"The five lagoons around Ox B'alam are all cenotes that have overflowed their banks. Underground rivers connect them to each other. The edges are marshy but the centers of the lagoons are very deep."

So beautiful in the moonlight the night before, the lagoon took on a sinister cast now that Bernadette knew about the crocodiles and the floating corpse. Searching the silver surface of the water beyond the reeds, she made out dark backs riding silent and low, cruising for their next meal.

Rocky leaned forward to look past her out the window. "Grisly," he said, as if reading her thoughts.

Her shoulders convulsed in an involuntary shudder. Manuel wouldn't have to warn her twice to stay out of the water.

At the roadhouse restaurant, the bus turned right and left the lagoon behind. Dark tropical foliage lined the narrow road. Ninety miles from this remote jungle crossroads lay the glitzy resort world of Cancun. The Ferraras did their best to make the hacienda comfortable, but there was no internet for research, no bright streets or flashy nightlife.

Remembering the long ride through the darkness the night before, Bernadette realized for the first time just how cut off from the outside world they were in this small jungle town.

Chapter 7

Bernadette didn't have much time to ruminate on their isolation because almost immediately, Manuel turned the vehicle into a white gravel parking lot carved out of the forest at the side of the road. At this early hour, only a pair of dusty rental cars were parked in the lot.

As she clambered out of the van, the morning sun crested the trees and glinted off the tin roofs of the souvenir huts that surrounded the open space. The vendors were just opening their stalls and called out to the group as they passed, but Manuel shepherded everyone past the hawkers, saying they would have time to shop later.

He spoke briefly to the ticket-taker at the gate who waved them through into the archeological site, a cool green realm alive with the chatter of unseen birds. Here, away from the lagoon, the earthy aroma of the primeval undergrowth was cleaner, fresher, renewed by the recent return of the rains. A gentle energy whispered through the trees and the history of the ancient city hung almost tangibly in the air, reminding Bernadette of the feel of abandoned cemeteries and other historic sites she'd visited.

The branches of the forest canopy met in a gothic arch over a wide trail of white gravel that stretched into the jungle. According to Manuel, this unusual white material was the remains of ancient coral reefs which had been pulverized by the waves and then used by the ancients to build their roads. Bernadette pulled out her phone and activated the voice recorder, determined to catch his every word.

Manuel held up his hand to get the group's attention.

"As you see, the hotel is not far from the ruins. You can walk here later if you wish to explore on your own, but let me warn you not to wander into the jungle. What we will see today is only a tiny portion of the ruins. Old Ox B'alam was a city of one hundred thousand people. The ruins cover many square miles. Most of the site is unexcavated. The local people hunt deer in these forests and trails run for miles in all directions, but there is no outer fencing. If you lose your way we will search for you, but I can not promise that you will be found. Stay on the well-marked paths and you will be safe."

He started walking backwards down the trail as he talked, and they fell into a disorderly line behind him. "Ox B'alam means 'Jaguar Paw'. B'alam, the black jaguar, is a very important god to our people. We think the ancients called the city this because of the jaguars who drank from the lagoons at dawn, the time when B'alam returned from his nightly journey through the underworld. We rarely see the big cats anymore. Their territory has been lost to agriculture, and the farmers have killed so many jaguars that they are now endangered."

Bernadette knew large predators need room to hunt, but it was amazing that even in this remote region, development had such an impact on the wildlife.

They followed the straight trail through a valley, with low hills covered in trees and vines rising on either side. Remembering her research, Bernadette said, "Manuel, I thought the land was flat. This seems quite hilly."

"The mounds are actually ruins of buildings that the jungle has reclaimed."

With his words, the blinders lifted from her eyes and she discern huge piles of square-cut blocks of light gray stone beneath the thick undergrowth, the remnants of colossal buildings now blanketed by shrubs and ferns. Ropey tree roots ran over the stone, somehow managing to get a foothold in the miniscule pockets of soil between the rocks. Most of the trees were small enough to circle with your hands, but here and there stood a mahogany giant, a survivor of the original hardwood forests.

Half a mile along the trail, Manuel led them onto a smaller path, and they stopped at a restored, multi-story stone edifice that rose majestically from the forest floor. Vegetation, ferns and saplings, rolled up the white limestone steps, blurring the line where the jungle ended and the building began.

As the sun rose, burning off the morning dew, ancient vapors seeped out from between the rocks. Smoke from a smudge pot burning somewhere nearby mingled with steamy jungle scents. Perspiration collected on Bernadette's forehead and she regretted having worn long pants into the jungle. Shifting her bag to the other shoulder, she wiped her sleeve across her forehead. Rocky was standing right behind her. She didn't want him to see her sweat.

"Fantastic," he said, whipping the tripod off his shoulder and setting it on the ground. He clamped the camera body firmly on top, aimed the lens at the structure and put his eye to the viewfinder, his hand working the big lens with unconscious precision. Suddenly, he was the consummate professional, shooting tree roots strangling the stone walls and leafy vines cascading through sunbeams from the platform above.

Bernadette climbed a narrow flight of stone steps to the arched opening of a tunnel and peered into the shadows. Although the archeological site was a public place, she felt the hint of ancient spirits lingering in the ruins.

Inside the tunnel, a shadow shifted. Her pulse spiked and, in her imagination, a priest in full regalia emerged from the shadows, waving an incense burner.

But it was only Arthur. He walked out into the dappled sunshine, blinking behind his round glasses as his eyes adjusted to the light. "This is what I loved from the last trip," he said, before scuttling away.

Bernadette smiled. Arthur was a man of few words, but she totally understood his eagerness to return. The archeological sites she'd studied in university and since had always intrigued her. She'd pour over pictures of enigmatic stone sculptures and couldn't help wondering about the people who had carved them. Now that she was actually here, the otherworldly atmosphere was bewitching. The feeling could easily become addictive.

Shielding her eyes from the dazzling glare of the rising sun, she looked up at Rocky who was teetering on a stone platform far outside the roped-off safety zone, photographing their group, clustered below. The sight of him working snapped her out of her reverie and she scrawled a few notes on her pad on her impressions of the feel of the place as she hurried over to where Manuel was standing in the shade, speaking to a circle of tour members.

"This building was a temple. Of the thousands of buildings that dot this archeological site, the largest were temples. One thousand years ago the ancient Mayan cities housed the priests and royalty, as well as the most highly regarded artisans and scribes."

As Bernadette followed the group along the path, a soft breeze brushed by, like a whisper of spirits. The next building was little more than a pile of stones with a dozen steps leading up to a platform high above the ground.

The group spread out to explore, most studying the eroded carvings of sculls around the base. Trees sprang directly from the detritus and it was impossible to tell whether their roots held the stones together or tore the steps apart. Bernadette started up the stairs. Ferns grew from cracks in the rocks and in places the steps dissolved into piles of rubble.

When she reached the top step, a familiar rattle sounded behind her, like the crackle of autumn leaves underfoot, and a primal chill slithered down her back.

Chapter 8

She had heard the rattle years before and would never forget that sound.

When Bernadette was a child, her grandfather had killed a rattlesnake under his cabin in the dry hills of central British Columbia. He'd felt badly about having to kill it, and perhaps the incident would not have left such an impression on her if he could just have sent it on its way. But now, when she heard that raspy sound, her blood ran cold.

Turning slowly on the platform, she caught sight of a movement a few steps below. The snake lay in a patch of sunlight, his pattern of gold diamonds on a gray background camouflaging him against the debris. At his thickest, he was as meaty as a man's upper arm. Looking straight at her, he rattled his tail again.

Swallowing a shriek, Bernadette stepped backwards on the platform. The space was the size of a small room and at one end stood a pile of stones that at one time could have been an altar. She looked back at the snake. It flickered its forked serpent's tongue at her as if he were the temple guardian and she the intruder.

She peeked over the nearest edge of the platform. It was a steep, twelve-foot drop to the ground. Quickly, she checked the other two sides but found they were the same. Perspiration beaded her upper lip and she wiped it away with the back of her hand. She couldn't go back the way she'd come, yet hated to draw attention to her predicament. Looking down, she considered the drop. Broken rubble littered the ground below, but she'd take her chances jumping rather than walk down those steps past the snake.

Rocky and Hank came around the corner of the

foundation. She smiled down at them through clenched teeth. "There's a snake on the steps. Can you help me down?"

The men hurried over and stood beneath her.

"What kind of snake?" Rocky asked, aiming his camera up at her.

She could see he thought she was over-reacting. "A rattlesnake."

"Really?"

"Yes, really."

"I don't think there are rattlesnakes in the jungle," Hank said.

This from the man who the night before hadn't thought there were crocodiles in the Yucatán.

She glanced back at the staircase, half-expecting the snake to slide over the top step and onto the platform after her.

Manuel appeared below her. "A rattlesnake? Where?"

Pleased to be vindicated, Bernadette hurried back to the top of the stairs, suddenly worried that with the noise everyone was making, the snake had taken off into the jungle, leaving her looking like a fool, but it was still coiled right where she'd left it, dozing in the patch of sunlight halfway up the staircase.

Manuel picked up a branch from the ground and began to speak in a low voice. "Tzabcan, the rattlesnake of the Yucatán, is revered by our people as a messenger from the gods."

He prodded the snake gently with the branch. The lazy serpent turned its head, flickering its tongue in protest and slithered up a step, toward Bernadette.

Her breath caught in her throat and she took a step back. "Is it poisonous?"

"Extremely."

Bernadette hopped back again, glancing over her shoulder to make sure she wouldn't fall off the other side of the structure. Manuel approached the snake from a different angle and finally the rattler slipped down the stairs, as effortlessly as running water.

When it had disappeared into the jungle, Bernadette blew out a breath and sucked in another. Her knees were weak as wet noodles and she wasn't sure she could negotiate the steps right away, so to give herself a minute, she pulled out her notebook. "So, the snake, Sabacan, is a messenger from the gods? How do you spell that?"

Manuel spelled it out. "Seeing Tzabcan is a good omen."

"As long as no one gets bitten," Hank observed.

Manuel's expression turned serious. "That is why we do not encourage them around this site."

Bernadette put her pad away, glad to feel the strength return to her legs. She made her way down the crumbling staircase and as she started up the trail after Manuel, Rocky fell into step beside her. "You okay?"

He wasn't laughing any more, but their conversation from the previous evening came back to her—the one about dragging a rookie around in the jungle—so she pasted a smile on her face and lifted one shoulder in a half shrug. "Sure. No problem."

Manuel was back in lecture mode. "Ox B'alam was already in ruins, reclaimed by the jungle, when the Spanish Conquistadores reached the Yucatán five hundred years ago. No one knows why the old city died. The city's descendants remained because of the lagoons—water is precious in the Yucatán—but until the new roads came, Old Ox B'alam was so remote that the village lay undiscovered by the outside world until well into the twentieth century."

He stopped at a carved stone slab protected by a tiny thatch-roofed pavilion. "In the old days, hundreds of these stone *stelas* would have decorated the city. A few still remain but, over the past hundred years museums and collectors have stolen the best ones with the most beautiful carvings. Today the Mexican government is working to get some of them back."

Hank walked over to study the carved four-foot slab sheltered under the thatched roof. "This must weigh a couple of tons. How could they get it out of the jungle?"

"They cut them up," Bernadette said. "Sometimes into pieces as small as two-foot square. They reassemble them later but butchering the artifacts like that destroys the meaning and integrity of the image."

"Like the Elgin Marbles," Annie added.

Bernadette nodded. "Originally, they were a frieze on the Parthenon. Lord Elgin was really nothing more than a high brow looter for the British Museum."

"We saw them," Mrs. Morris said. "Didn't we Bernard? You remember, when we were in London. All cut up in little pieces and then stuck back together. Nice, but I think you're right, dear, they did lose something up on the museum wall like that."

"The magic," Arthur said. "They lose the magic."

A smile twerked the corner of Bernadette's lips. No doubt about it, Arthur was a romantic. Despite the tweed suit he insisted on wearing even in the jungle, the ruins had him under their spell.

Bernadette understood how he felt; she felt the magic too as she walked in and out of the dappled forest light. Although other tourists were just a few feet away, she could imagine the thrill the explorers must have felt one hundred years ago when they first stumbled on these buildings hidden in the jungle.

What mysteries did these buildings hold? The Mayan language was the earliest written language in the Americas, but it was only in the last thirty years that archeologists had began to make progress in unraveling the ancient script. Bernadette was almost sorry they were figuring it out. The romantic in her appreciated the mystery.

It soon became clear that very few buildings in the site had been restored, probably less than a dozen scattered through the acres of forest. Ferns and broad-leafed trees had taken over the wide courtyards where people once gathered. At intervals along the main trail, narrow tracks led into the undergrowth, offering enticing glimpses of crumbling arches or broken stela.

Manuel led his posse off the central trail onto a broad path off to the right, stopping between two well-restored parallel walls built of cut stone. Each was twenty feet long and they were fifteen feet apart, with a large stone ring set high in the center of each wall.

"The ballcourt," Manuel said. "We cannot judge the ancient Maya by our own standards. All we can do is try to understand. Their ball games were not sport. They were ritual. A contest. Played to the death. We know someone died at the end of the game, but we do not know who—the victor or the vanquished."

Bernadette stared at the stylized images carved into the walls and as Manuel spoke, the pictures came into focus. *Men chasing a ball through the court, bouncing it off the walls.*

"They could not touch the ball with their hands," Manuel said.

A man kneeling in the dust.

"The game was over when one side got the ball through the ring."

One man standing with a ball in his hand.

"And in the end, one man lost his head."

Bernadette sucked in a sharp breath. He wasn't holding a ball at all. It was a head, and a river of blood flowed onto the ground from a kneeling man's severed neck.

"Oh, my goodness, would you look at that," Mrs.

Morris said, stepping back from the glyphs.

"Some argue it was the loser who was beheaded," Manuel continued. "As a sacrifice to the gods. Some say, the winner."

"Then what would be the incentive to win?" Hank asked, walking up to one of the walls to get a better look at the carvings.

"Perhaps the one who gave his blood was blessed and would return as a high priest. Or even become a god himself. The answer is lost in time."

The pictographs continued along the wall and now that Bernadette could read them, she was intrigued and followed them to the end of the ballcourt wall where the path disappeared into the trees between two mounds of rubble. To the left, a partial wall arose, vines trailing down its face, saplings growing along the top, the roots like fingers tensing, ready to tear the stones apart. A few feet further down the path, a large relief carved into the wall peeked out from behind the veil of vines.

Bernadette walked over and gently pulled the green vines apart, uncovering a carving, the simplified face of a jaguar in a two-foot square, stylized glyph, set into the crumbling wall. She was about to call Rocky over to take a shot when, a few feet away, a shadow separated itself from a crevasse in the wall. A man in green and brown camouflage clothing, strange garb in this land of white cotton, stepped toward her. Black streaks highlighted his cheek bones like the faces she'd seen in pictures of fierce guerrilla warriors.

Speaking in heavily accented English, he said, "Do not…go off…trail."

"Why?" she asked, thinking he must be a park guard. "Is this area restricted?"

His hand shot out and grabbed her arm.

Her chest constricted. She couldn't breathe, couldn't call out. "Let me go," she insisted, although her voice was not as strong as she would have liked.

She tried to pull her arm away, but his grip was like iron. She glanced over her shoulder for help, but the ballcourt was empty.

The group had left her behind.

Chapter 9

The black eyes of her assailant pinned her down as securely as his hand. A vision of herself floating face-down in a cenote flashed through Bernadette's mind.

He repeated his message, emphasizing the words with a shake of her arm. "Do not…go off…trail."

Her heart hammered in her chest and she flinched when she heard herself ask, "Why not?" But she had a million questions. Was it because of the poisonwood trees? Or so she didn't get lost? Was this guy a guard to keep nosey tourists out of the restricted areas?

Or did he have something to do with the body in the lagoon?

She didn't ask anything more though, because he threw down her hand and pointed back toward the ballcourt. The thought crossed her mind that he might not speak English. She remembered *por que?* or something like that from high school Spanish but wouldn't have understand his answer if he'd given her one.

She rubbed her wrist where he'd held her. He was very strong, and not giving an inch. Retreat was definitely the wiser course. She backed away. The camouflaged man held his ground, still pointing as he watched her go. Finally, when she'd put ten feet between them, she turned and ran.

Back in the ballcourt, she looked over her shoulder, but camo-man had vanished, as if the jungle had swallowed him up.

The ballcourt was empty, and now the vibrations were so strong she could see waves rising from the ground like heat off a sunbaked road. Her heartbeat sped up even more and her vision blurred. She took off again, through the court, down the path, after Manuel and the group.

At the main trail she looked left and right, gasping with relief at the sight of Hank's loud, print shirt far ahead. She sprinted toward it down the wide, empty trail. A few minutes later, she burst into a clearing. The sight of the central pyramid, blindingly white in the glare of the sun after the dim light of the forest brought her to a screeching halt. Limestone steps built for giants rose into the sky, and a small, crumbling temple sat like a crown on the summit.

By then sweat was running down her face, but her panic had subsided. She bent at the waist, hands on her thighs, catching her breath. Now that she was back in the safety of the group, she was embarrassed at having wandered away after Manuel had specifically warned them not to. And now she'd fallen behind. Clicking on her recorder, she hurried over to where the rest of the group stood in the shade at the edge of the clearing, listening to Manuel.

"This was the tallest pyramid in the Yucatán," he was saying. "Far taller than the one at Chichén Itzá. You will not be allowed to climb at the other ruins we visit, so I urge you to climb the steps here. If you reach the top, you will feel the power the priests felt hundreds of years ago when they stood there, surveying their land."

Bernadette tried to focus on what he was saying but she couldn't get the image of camo-man out of her head. He hadn't hurt her, but still, she felt violated. The incident on top of the death that morning had left her shaken.

When the others began to climb, she hung back and said to Manuel, "I saw a man, just beyond the ballcourt."

Manuel's eyes swivelled from watching the climbers to Bernadette's face, but he didn't respond.

"He told me not to go any further. Was he a site

guard?"

"Possibly." Manuel looked back at the pyramid. He didn't seem to want to discuss it. Maybe it was nothing to worry about. The encounter would make colorful content for her story—the man was certainly an unusual character—but she was uncomfortable with the way he had responded to her.

"He had black stripes of paint on his face. I thought he might be paid by the park…"

"Only the gatekeeper is paid by the park. He was probably a hunter. Local people hunt on these lands. It is best to stay with the group."

"I know, and I will, but I just thought I should tell you that he was rather—rough. He grabbed my arm."

Manuel looked at her sharply. "Were you hurt?"

"No, he didn't hurt me—"

"I will report the incident. No one is supposed to interfere with the tourists."

"Yes, but do you know what he was doing there? He told me to keep away."

"He was probably just concerned for your safety. I will report it to the authorities." With that, Manuel headed to the base of the pyramid.

Not entirely satisfied, Bernadette followed. She could see Rocky, already half way up.

"How many steps?" she asked Manuel, peering up into the brilliant sky.

"One hundred and twenty."

She closed her eyes in resignation. Heights had never been a problem for her, but in this ancient city her internal radar, always delicate, seemed completely awry. The last thing she needed was an attack of dizziness halfway up the steep, stone staircase.

But how could she write about visiting the pyramid, possibly the pinnacle of the trip, if she didn't scale the darn thing? So, throwing her shoulder bag onto her back, she started to climb.

The blocks were enormous. Each step was a stretch. A heavy rope ran up the center of the broad staircase, connected to the steps at intervals by giant screw eyes. Some of the group held onto the rope and pulled themselves up, hand over hand, but Bernadette felt more confident climbing on all fours.

The blistering sun beat down on her back and soon sweat trickled down her face. A quarter of the way up she passed Hank, who was sitting on a step, getting his breath, talking to Meredith who smiled up at him. Eloise and Celeste had taken the stairs at a good clip and were on their way down by the time Bernadette reached halfway.

She stopped once to wipe her forehead and another time to roll her pant legs up to the knee. Looking down didn't bother her. It was looking up at the skewed perspective of the narrowing pyramid that made her woozy. Perhaps this was part of the test designed by the ancients—only the strongest could reach the summit.

Two thirds of the way up, she sat on a step, opened her water bottle and took a long drink. Here, high above the treetops, a breeze blew in, deliciously cool on her overheated cheeks. None of the other buildings they'd visited that morning were visible through the verdant foliage that rolled in a sea of unrelenting green to the horizon. The ballcourt was swallowed up completely and even this tall structure, from a few feet away, would be masked by the jungle canopy. Manuel was right. It would be easy to lose your way in this flat land with so few markers to guide you.

Rocky had reached the temple at the top, taken his shots and now stopped on his way down. He sat on a step a few feet away, aimed his camera at her and looked through the viewfinder.

Bernadette held up a hand to hide her face.

"Seriously?" She didn't want pictures of her, flushed and sweaty, gracing the pages of the magazine.

"No, this is perfect." He reached out and moved her hand aside. "Sometimes editors want photos of the writer at the sites."

She grimaced grudgingly at the camera as he fired off three shots. Then he went down six steps and shot up at her again.

"Get some good stuff?" he asked from behind the lens.

"Manuel's a font of information."

Looking down, she picked out the other members of the group assembling in the dusty plaza with Manuel a bright white spot at their center. How did he manage to stay so clean? She felt grimy and sticky and ready for a shower—and it wasn't even noon.

Rocky moved up beside her, scrolling through the shots in his camera. "Quite a morning."

You don't know the half of it. First the body in the lagoon. Then the snake. Now camo-man. She couldn't get his forbidding image out of her head, or shake the feel of his hand on her wrist.

"What do you think about the murder?" she asked.

Rocky didn't look up from his camera screen. "I think we keep out of it."

"I saw Caruthers leave late last night."

He glanced up. "No need to tell anybody about that, yet."

"I feel I should. If I have any information, I feel I should tell them."

"We're in Mexico. You don't want to get involved with the local authorities unless you absolutely have to. Wait until they ask."

She chewed on her lip for a moment, then decided to take the plunge. "Something funny happened at the ballcourt."

Rocky kept his eyes fixed on the pictures on the screen.

"I was looking at a plaque on a wall just beyond the court and a man came out of the forest and grabbed me."

"What?"

He looked at her sharply. *Now* she had his attention. "He didn't hurt me," she added quickly. "But it was kind of scary. He grabbed my arm and told me to keep away."

Rocky frowned. "Away from what?"

"I don't know."

"He was probably just concerned for your safety. Manuel told us the same thing."

"He looked like a guerilla—dressed in camouflage, with face paint."

Rocky processed the information. "Weird. Well, don't wander off again."

"I didn't wander off." Her voice rose indignantly. "I was twenty feet from the end of the ballcourt."

"Even so." He shook his head and started down the steps. "I can't be watching you all the time. We'd better get down."

She had no choice except to follow him down. Nothing annoyed her more than being dismissed. Between the heat, the insult and the embarrassment, she felt like a cartoon character with steam shooting out its ears.

Except, she wasn't laughing.

Chapter 10

It was hard to stay mad at Rocky. There was just too much to see. He may be a jerk, but, if she had to, Bernadette could write the story alone.

Camo-man was harder to dismiss, but she tried.

As the morning progressed, the group explored the over-gown paths of the archaeological site, finding secret spots where other buildings seemed to grow directly out of the jungle floor. At one point she glimpsed a small lagoon through an impenetrable tangle of trees. Finally, when the sun rose high in the sky and shade was becoming hard to find, everyone agreed it was time to go.

Exiting the park, they spread out into the vendors' stalls that ringed the parking lot, mixing with customers from a tour bus parked in the lot. Most of the huts sold souvenirs, but a few kiosks sold water and snacks. Bernadette joined Meredith, following Annie from stall to stall.

Bernadette wanted to buy some mementos, gifts for her son and her mother, and maybe a keepsake for herself, too. Apparently, this was the only place in town to shop but with over a dozen booths the selection was surprisingly good. She'd pass on the blankets with gaudy pictures of Montezuma and the word 'MEXICO' woven in bold letters, but some stalls carried items that looked like they might be locally made: small onyx sculptures, woven hammocks and the heavily embroidered clothing worn by the Maya women.

Colin had asked her to bring him a sombrero, and she was sizing up the colorful collection of hats hanging on the wall of one large stall when Rocky sauntered in.

"Try one on," he suggested. She shook her head. He

had already treated her like a child at the pyramid today and she wasn't about to let him do it again. Pressing her lips firmly together to hold back a rude reply, she checked the prices, wondering if the hats would be cheaper elsewhere.

"You will not find a better price anywhere," the vendor interjected, as if reading her mind. Placing one hand dramatically over his heart, his wide smile, exposing a set of nicotine-stained teeth, did nothing to lessen the alarming impact of a raised scar that ran from his right ear to his collarbone. "I am Ricardo Gonzales, proprietor of this establishment."

Bernadette's lips quirked in a smile at his obvious pride in the three-sided, tin-roofed hut.

"I have everything you are looking for, local carvings, beautiful silver jewelry." He passed a hand laden with silver rings along a plank shelf where striped onyx chess sets snuggled up to black stone jaguars.

The jaguars caught Bernadette's eye right away, but when she looked at them closely, she realized that the carving was crude and the eyes were painted on. Any one of them would seem cheap once she got it home.

A dusty glass case housed a limited but appealing display of jewelry. She was immediately attracted to a pair of silver earrings, disks the size of her thumbnail engraved with a Mayan calendar.

"Wonderful choice," Ricardo said, retrieving the earrings and handing them to her. With a flourish, he produced a hand mirror.

Holding the silver disks to her ears, she turned her head from side to side and smiled. "I'll take them."

Ricardo smiled broadly in return. His eyes darted into the dim corners of the stall for more items with which to entice her. "Something else perhaps?"

"Not today," she said briskly. "And may I please have a receipt?"

Ricardo's smile stiffened. How much of what he sold did he declare? She didn't really care, but with the always nerve-wracking moment at customs in mind, she insisted on a bill.

Eventually he produced a cheap dime-store pad from beneath the counter, stamped his name at the top and scrawled 'earrings' and the price, below. Good enough. She filed it in a pocket of her shoulder bag.

Meredith and Annie had moved on, but Rocky stuck by her side. As they stepped out of the booth they were hit by heat pulsing off the white gravel parking lot. The rest of the group were already waiting in a small patch of shade by the van.

As Bernadette and Rocky approached, Celeste pointed skyward and shrieked, "Look at that."

Overhead, a man whooshed past, strapped to a zip-line that ran out of a wooden lookout tower at the edge of the parking lot. He swooped off on a gentle downhill glide across the lagoon toward the hotels on the far shore.

Manuel frowned. "They are crazy, flying over the crocodiles." With his hands, he mimed the snapping mouths of hungry crocodiles, leaping out of the water.

A trio of young British tourists, walking across the parking lot toward the ticket window beside the rickety tower, overheard his comment and cried, "No, it's brilliant. We're going again."

The empty harness slowly made its way back along the line to the starting point. Bernadette waited with the group by the van while the Brits zigzagged up the wooden staircase between the legs of the tower. Then, in total silence, the Cultural Tour held its collective breath until the first maniac burst out of the hatch, screaming gleefully.

"Crazy," Manuel said, his forehead creased with worry.

The scream faded away as the Brit sailed effortlessly across the water to the small hut on the far side of the lagoon.

"I don't know," Hank said, shaking his head, the hint of a grin quirking one corner of his mouth. "I might have to try it."

Manuel regarded him in horror. "It is for crazy people."

Hank hitched up his plaid shorts. "I might just be crazy enough."

Eloise stepped forward. "I'm with you. You only live once."

Manuel was beside himself. "But the crocodiles!"

Hank patted his enormous stomach. "It would take a big croc to mess with me."

As Hank and Eloise marched across the parking lot to the ticket office, Rocky took Manuel by the arm. "If they want to do it, there's really no way you can stop them."

Manuel's gaze followed the retreating figures as Rocky steered him toward the van.

"Let's meet them at the other end," he said, taking the keys out of Manuel's hands and opening the big side door of the van for the others.

That broke the spell. Manuel grabbed his keys from Rocky and raced around to the driver's seat. Rocky slammed the side door after the others and jumped into the passenger seat. Before he could close the door, Manuel was gunning the engine.

The last of the British fliers hit the air, racing past them in a downward trajectory across the lagoon. With a spray of gravel, the van sped out of the ruins' parking lot, flying over potholes in the road, everyone bouncing like lottery balls in the back. Moments later the van arrived at the zip-line landing zone, the small shed Bernadette had noticed that morning on the shore near the hotel. A typical Yucatán thatched-roofed structure, bales of straw lined the back wall to soften the impact should the zip-line rider fail to stop.

The British kids stood on the platform, holding onto each other, doubled over with laughter.

"Brilliant," screamed the one who had landed moments before. Two attendants quickly unleashed him from the harness and flipped the switch, sending it back across the lake. The Brits rolled down the road to their hotel, their laughter fading as they turned in at the gate.

Bernadette found herself laughing too, just watching them. It looked exhilarating, but too far out of her comfort zone to try. She would be content to live vicariously through Hank and Eloise.

Rocky set up his tripod on the landing platform and aimed his camera out over the water towards the tower. She had to hand it to him; he was a pro. He'd gotten them to the landing pad in time to shoot Eloise and Hank's rides.

The group waited in tense silence as the empty harness inched its way to the launch station. Shading her eyes, Bernadette followed the line out over the lake until it disappeared against the dazzling sky.

Minutes later, a hoot that had to be Eloise, echoed across the water. Bernadette laughed with excitement as the screams got louder and the tiny bundle came into view over the lagoon. When Eloise was halfway across, Celeste stepped forward and screamed, "RIP—IT!"

A crocodile sunning itself on the bank of the lagoon directly in the path of the zip-line twitched his tail like a cat but didn't leap into the air.

Eloise hurtled toward the hut at an incredible speed, Rocky taking shot after shot as she sailed in, feet first, over the croc. The two attendants leapt into action, jumping onto the landing pad ready to catch her, their feet braced against boards nailed to the floor.

Considerably taller and heftier than either of the Maya attendants, Eloise dangled from the harness laughing hysterically as they fought to release her. As she fell into Celeste's arms, she cried, "Amazing."

Catching the excitement, everyone started talking at once, but soon they all fell silent, watching the harness inch its way back across the lake.

Annie let out a nervous giggle. "Do you think Hank…?" She didn't finish the sentence, but Bernadette knew exactly what she was thinking. Hank was BIG. He would strain anything, never mind the one thin cable that stretched across the crocodile lagoon.

Manuel covered his face with his hands. "I cannot look."

Another hoot, deeper this time, echoed across the lake. Then Hank, clearly visible in his Hawaiian shirt, was coming toward them growing larger by the second. He was travelling at break-neck speed, much closer to the water than Eloise had been, the zip-line straining under his weight.

Soon he was skimming in over the lagoon. Everyone shrieked with excitement. Bernadette's hands started mimicking jumping crocodiles snapping at Hank's royal-sized butt as he sailed in, barely skimming the surface of the water.

Manuel watched, his eyes wide in horror as one by one the entire group started doing crocodile leaps with their snapping fingers. Hank's booming belly laugh filled the air as he sailed into the hut.

When the dazed attendants had freed him from the harness, Hank only had one word to say. "Brilliant!"

Soon after, the grin still on her face, Bernadette walked back to the hacienda beside Rocky, his tripod slung jauntily over his shoulder.

"Going to try it, Mallow?" he asked, leaning in to nudge her with his shoulder.

He meant the zip-line—and he was only half joking. "Are you?"

"Unfortunately, no. I have to be waiting to get the shot of you sailing in over the lagoon."

"Oh sure. With crocodiles snapping at my butt."

He laughed, and she glanced at him out of the corner of her eye. He could be funny, and nice, when he let down his guard. His eyes were still sultry, black lashes thick as brushes, but his mouth had relaxed into a lopsided grin that was really quite—appealing.

Shaking her head, she laughed out loud.

No possible way.

Chapter 11

The sun beat down mercilessly and although it was only a few hundred yards to the hacienda, Bernadette was melting like candle wax by the time they got back. Luckily, there was time for a quick swim in the pool before lunch.

After changing into her bathing suit, she returned to the terrace to find Rocky sitting on the edge of the pool in his trunks, his hair pulled back in a ponytail. She tried not to stare, but a fascinating collection of tattoos covered his muscular back and shoulders.

Of course, she'd noticed them before, they were impossible to miss, peeking out at the neck of his shirt and coiling down his arms, but until now she had never seen them in their full glory. She walked up behind him and pulled her sunglasses down on her nose for a better view.

He turned and looked up at her. "What?"

"What possessed you to get so many?"

He surveyed his arms and pointed to a traditional pattern of ribbons and roses around the word "Angelina" on his right bicep. "I got this one when I was sixteen and wanted to be a longshoreman. Angelina's my mom's name. I thought she wouldn't be too angry if I dedicated the first one to her." He looked up at her with a boyish grin. A smile tugged at the corner of her mouth and Bernadette was sure his mother had caved when he turned that grin on her.

He pointed to the eagle on his forearm. "Then I got this one with the guys for high school graduation." He looked over his arms and chest. "I don't know. After that it kind of became a hobby."

"Are you planning to get more?"

"I don't think so. Sometimes, though, when I go somewhere where tattoos are part of the culture," he turned his back to her again and pointed over his shoulder at the geometric, tribal tattoo on his back, "I just can't help myself."

Stepping closer, she examined the bold design that covered half his back. "Where did you get this one?"

"It's Maori. I got it in New Zealand on my first assignment."

A small lump in the skin was worked into a spiral of the design and without thinking, Bernadette ran her finger over it.

Rocky jumped as if he'd been shot. He whirled around to face her.

She stepped back. "What's that?"

"Childhood injury."

She didn't think so. In fact, it looked like a bullet wound. Not that she'd ever seen a bullet wound before. A chill ran over her. What kind of life had he led where he could have been shot? Possibly part of a gang. Her gaze followed the trail of symbols over his shoulder and onto his chest.

His hands grasp her upper arms and her eyes flashed up just in time to catch the glint in his eyes before he threw her into the water.

* * *

After lunch, everyone assembled in a shady spot on the pool terrace to listen as Manuel outlined the upcoming activities. "This afternoon we will go into Ox B'alam pueblo and visit a few of the Maya families who live there."

A low murmur issued from the group.

"I know, you may feel uncomfortable at first, going into the homes of strangers. But it is the Maya way to invite guests to the community into our homes."

When he finished, a few people went up to their rooms to prepare for the outing, but Bernadette stayed at the dining room table, finishing her coffee. Annie was prattling on about early Mayan architectural styles while Meredith looked on with what Bernadette was beginning to recognize as the blank mask she wore whenever her daughter was lecturing.

From her seat at the table, Bernadette could see two strangers standing at the lobby desk. Their uniforms identified them as police officers. The older man was heavy set with a broad face, bushy eyebrows and a moustache to match. The younger officer was tall and thin, and from the way he twisted his hat in his hands and shifted from foot to foot, she could see he was agitated.

They must be here about the body. Her stomach began to grind.

The older man was obviously in charge. He leaned over the counter, speaking quietly to Manuel's father. Señor Ferrara signaled for one of the staff in white to approach—Jose, she thought—and whispered briefly in his ear.

As Señor Ferrara ushered the police officers into the office and closed the door, Jose ran across the lobby and up the stairs. Moments later Manuel raced down, crossed the lobby and hurried into the office.

Very interesting. Bernadette looked across the table for Rocky's reaction. He seemed to be following the action in the lobby too, but she couldn't read the expression in his eyes.

The other members of the group began trickling back to the terrace, waiting for Manuel to return. As time ticked on and word of the police visit spread, an unusual hush fell over the group.

Finally, the office door opened, and Manuel and the

two officers emerged. They spoke briefly together in the lobby, then crossed the dining room to the terrace where they stopped in the doorway.

Tension crackled like heat lightening in the heavy air. Beyond the shaggy palapa roof, the noonday sun rode high in the sky.

Manuel's face looked unusually haggard. "We are devastated to tell you that one of the guests of our hotel has been found dead. Sadly, a member of the Cultural Tour."

Bernadette scanned the room, quickly counting heads. When sure no one from their group was missing, she exhaled a relieved breath.

"Not one of your group," Manuel assured them. "Mr. Caruthers, from the previous tour, the man who arrived last night. The man I introduced to you at dinner…" His voice trailed off, his gaze dropped to the ground and he shook his head sadly. Then pulling himself together, he continued. "My friends, this is Police Chief Pacho. He has requested your help with the investigation into the death of Jason Caruthers."

Chief Pacho addressed the group. "We have now seen the coroner's report. Jason Caruthers' death has officially been designated a homicide."

A gasp flew around the room. Bernadette's heart hammered in her chest. Although she had hoped for a different outcome, Chief Pacho's announcement was not entirely unexpected.

The Chief continued. "Since you were among the last people to see Caruthers alive, later I will want to ask you some questions. Please do not leave the hotel." With that, he nodded at the assembled group and walked out the arched doorway into the dining room.

Goosebumps rose on Bernadette's arms. Suddenly she knew what the chill that had enveloped her that morning when she stood on the front steps had meant.

She'd been sitting on those same steps last night when Caruthers had breezed by. If only she'd known, she could have warned someone.

However, this morning had probably been too late. And what could she have said? The feelings were never easy to explain.

Manuel made an obvious effort to pull himself together. "We will continue with our plans as best we can, but unfortunately we must postpone our trip to the village for now. Chief Pacho has requested that you stay at the hacienda until he can speak to each of you individually to verify your location last night."

Everyone had something to say about that.

"What do you mean?"

"What location?"

"Why would he want to talk to us?"

"We were all here. Where else would we have been?"

Manuel broke in and at the sound of his voice, the terrace became still. "That is the point, I am afraid. Chief Pacho wants to question everyone who was at the hacienda last night. He will speak to the hotel staff first, then later this afternoon to each of the guests."

Fabulous, Bernadette thought. What if they were sequestered for the rest of the week? What would that mean to their assignment for the magazine? She looked at Rocky, but his face was a blank mask.

When Manuel left the room, everyone began to speak at once. Everyone except Rocky. He took his drink to a table near the pool where he quietly observed the room from behind his mirrored sunglasses. Bernadette watched him for a minute, then left Annie to her mother and went over to join him.

He didn't invite her to sit down, but neither did he object when she did. With a hot, exasperated breath, she blew the hair up off her forehead. "What will this mean for the assignment? And what do the police expect to learn from us?"

She was just venting, thinking he'd understand how she felt. She didn't expect him to answer and was surprised when he did.

"It's standard procedure when they suspect foul play. The key could come from anywhere. Any one of us could have seen something that may not have seemed unusual at the time but might not fit when they put it together with the other pieces of the puzzle. It could be as simple as someone being in the wrong place at the wrong time."

Bernadette raised her brows at him. "Watch a lot of crime dramas? I can never follow them, myself. The ending is always a total surprise." She shook her head. "We didn't even really speak to him. Caruthers, I mean. I spoke to him briefly about the wine, but he didn't seem to want to talk."

"He had the red beans and rice for dinner."

Bernadette turned to him in surprise. "I didn't notice that. But I did notice that he was interested enough by something at the bar that he didn't stop when he banged into my chair."

After a moment, Rocky started to speak, as much to himself as to her. "What does he mean, 'local police'? If they're from Tulum or one of the other large towns, that's one thing. But if they're from Ox B'alam, they'll know everyone in town. That will either speed up the investigation or kill it completely."

They were both silent for a moment, mulling over the ramifications of that, then Rocky said, "I need a drink." Pushing himself up from his chair, he headed to the bar where most of the group had assembled.

Bernadette followed him over. She didn't usually drink in the afternoon, but murder seemed like a good reason to start.

Chapter 12

Bernadette found a spot at the bar, crowding in with Rocky and the rest of the group. The atmosphere was unusually silent.

"Why can't we at least go into town and do a bit of shopping?" Celeste asked in her breathy child-like voice.

"They don't have anything good there," Eloise replied. "I want something really special, not cheap commercial junk. I suppose I could get one of those lovely embroidered dresses."

Bernadette coughed to cover a snort of laughter at the mental picture of tall, buxom Eloise in a dress designed for a small, softly rounded Maya woman. She caught Rocky's eye and his mouth twisted as he suppressed a smile. "Maybe an embroidered tablecloth," she suggested.

"Or a relic," Celeste said, her eyes widening.

Eloise brightened. "Something really old."

"With mystical powers," Celeste suggested.

Eloise laughed as Salvador set a tall drink in front of her. "You'd pay dearly for that."

Rocky held up two fingers and the bartender opened two Coronas and set them on the bar in front of him and Bernadette. She virtually never drank beer at home but she was anxious enough now to accept it without question.

Arthur spoke up from his seat on the far side of Eloise. "There is a dealer in Tulum who has a few antiquities for sale, along with some good reproductions and souvenirs."

"You can't take relics out of the country, you know," Annie said, leaning in to look at Arthur and Eloise from the far end of the bar. "The Mexican government has laws against taking antiquities out of the country, and treaties with other governments, including the U.S., to stop the smuggling and to begin the repatriation of artifacts already in collection and museums outside of Mexico."

"I wasn't going to steal them," Arthur said pointedly, his voice rising in an insulted squeak. He stood up and grasped his glass of club soda. "I am fully prepared to pay for them." Walking stiffly to a distant table, he sat down with his back to the group at the bar. Obviously, as far as he was concerned, the subject was closed.

Eloise was also clearly offended. "I wasn't going to steal anything either."

"No one's suggesting you were," Bernadette said quickly. "I think Annie's point is that taking sacred treasures out of the country, even if you pay for them, is, in a sense, stealing from their rightful owners. Their community."

"The local people measure the value of these relics in ways other than money," Annie added. "Trade in illegal artifacts goes on all the time and collectors don't seem to have any conscience."

Bernadette had to agree. Antiquities collectors were robbing people with few resources, but there didn't seem to be any way to stop them. In the interest of peacemaking, she said to Eloise, "I'm looking for a nice souvenir, too. Something a step up from what the vendors in the parking lot sell. Maybe when we're in Tulum we could see if Arthur's dealer has any nice reproductions."

Her statement was followed by a moment of silence, then Rocky voiced the thought on everyone's minds. "Assuming the police let us go anywhere at all."

***

As the afternoon wore on, silence descended on the terrace bar where the members of the Cultural Tour had dug in. Although the group had been a unit for less than twenty-four hours, they instinctively drew together for comfort.

Under the desultory ceiling fans, the Morrises were playing gin rummy at a table in the corner, and Meredith had started a game of backgammon with Annie, no doubt trying to keep her daughter's mind off Caruthers' murder.

Celeste and Eloise changed into string bikinis—sure to go over great when the police got around to questioning them—and were sunbathing by the pool. They appeared undisturbed by the death, but maybe as nurses they were inured to the shock.

Arthur sat alone at a table, still as a statue. Although he had a book open in front of him, he didn't turn any pages. He only moved to wipe the perspiration from his face with a limp white hanky. He still wore the suit and vest but had gone almost native and left off the jacket.

Bernadette moved to a table and took out her book. After a few minutes, Rocky followed her over but didn't say anything.

An hour later, she had given up the pretext of reading and was playing with the drops of condensation running down the side of her second bottle of beer when Manuel hurried out onto the terrace, followed by the two police officers.

Bernadette's shoulders stiffened, and she glanced across the table at Rocky, hoping he would know what to say, but he was keeping his ideas to himself behind the impenetrable shield of his mirrored glasses.

Looked like she was on her own.

Chief Pacho nodded to the group, then walked briskly across the terrace to the swinging door that led to the kitchen. The young officer, who followed him across the room and through the doorway like a puppy, bounded back out moments later.

"Arthur Bickenbaum," he called, his voice heavily accented. The rest of the group watched in silence as Arthur stood up and crossed the room to the kitchen door.

"Surely the interrogations are only a formality," Bernadette said softly to Rocky. "After all, we'd all just arrived. What could any of us know about Caruthers' death?"

Rocky just grunted from behind his sun glasses, but Bernadette couldn't think about anything else. There must be a reason the police thought it was murder. Rocky was right, they must suspect foul play.

Foul play. She was beginning to sound like a detective novel herself, but *foul play* was much easier to swallow than *murder*. The fact that it was a homicide, though, explained the chill she'd felt on the stairs that morning.

Her premonitions had never foreshadowed murder before, but they had portended death. Like the day her mother phoned to tell her that her grandmother had died. As soon as Bernadette touched the telephone, she had felt the shock and started to cry. That time the meaning was clear; today on the stairs it had not. Not at the time. But now the death, coming right on the heels of that incident on the stairs, was too much of a coincidence to deny. The increasing frequency of the episodes had her spooked. She pulled a paper napkin out of the holder on the table and tore it in half. Then in half again.

"The police are taking their own sweet time," she said to Rocky.

No reply.

"I wonder if they plan to interview us in alphabetical order from the tour list. Bickenbaum. That would explain why Arthur was first."

Silence. Rocky obviously didn't feel like talking. She, on the other hand, couldn't seem to stop. "Strange that Arthur would have made the trip again so soon. Manuel said he was here just over a month ago. Caruthers death really seems to have upset him—he was sweating like crazy out here."

"Maybe he wouldn't sweat so much if he didn't wear that stupid suit."

"I don't think his trips overlapped with Caruthers'," Bernadette mused. "But I wonder if they knew each other."

"Unlikely."

"Not that weird on a trip like this. An archeology club? Arthur said he came from New York City. Where was Caruthers from?"

"I don't know."

He was definitely testy. Idly, Bernadette drew a skull and crossbones in the condensation on her almost-empty bottle, and then realizing in horror what she'd just done, quickly wiped it off. She frowned. "I've heard that sometimes, in some small towns, the cops are corrupt. I guess it applies here as much as at home."

"Small towns, big cities, anywhere," Rocky said. "And here, it's probably even more likely. If it's one of their own, they could easily look the other way. A poor villager in an altercation with a rich tourist? How hard would they investigate? And what will they do if they find out the murderer *isn't* someone local?"

"He must be a local," Bernadette objected. "What reason would any of us have to do something like that? We had just arrived." She pictured the floating body and her shoulders twitched as a shudder ran through her.

"We might never find out," Rocky said quietly. "I don't trust these guys. Why did this have to happen in Mexico?"

Bernadette didn't think Rocky expected an answer,

but she knew exactly what he meant. Everyone had heard the stories of the corruption that ran through all layers of the Mexican judicial system. Gruesome gang murders from south of the border were in the news at home all the time. What hope did they have of a fair investigation in this remote community? How long would the investigation continue? Would they be stuck here until the murderer was found?

Melting in the afternoon heat, she held the wet bottle to her temple, closed her eyes and tried to picture the scene from the previous evening. Arthur had not seemed to pay any particular attention to Caruthers when Manuel had introduced him to the group, but then, she hadn't been paying much attention to Arthur. "Caruthers wasn't very friendly. I tried to talk to him about the wine, but he didn't want to talk."

"It happens."

Smart ass. Still, she couldn't stop talking. Her vocal cords seemed to have contracted a case of Montezuma's revenge. "And why did Caruthers come back? Manuel said he was on his way to the airport."

"Ox B'alam isn't on the way to the airport," Rocky said softly, almost to himself. "It isn't on the way to anywhere. It's a dead-end road, halfway between Chichén Itzá and Tulum. A bad road to nowhere."

Arthur slipped out of the kitchen and hurried across the terrace to the dining room door, not making eye contact with anyone enroute. Bernadette's shoulders tensed. What had the police asked him? She'd find out soon enough.

The junior officer appeared at the door, barely suppressing his excitement. They probably didn't get many chances to interrogate foreigners in Ox B'alam.

"Celeste Bright."

Definitely alphabetical.

Celeste pulled a towel around her voluptuous curves

and padded quickly on bare feet to the kitchen door, giving the young deputy a shy smile as she swept past him. His eyes bulged in their sockets, then he gulped and followed her into the kitchen, closing the door behind him.

What if, when Bernadette's turn came, she said the wrong thing? Her pulse quickened, and more perspiration popped out under her arms. The terrace was hot and still as a sauna. She wrapped her hair into a tight knot and stuck a pencil through to hold it on top of her head.

Looking at Rocky for reassurance, she found him staring at the kitchen door, clenching and unclenching his fist on the table, the expression on his face hovering somewhere between furtive and belligerent. She sucked in a horrified breath. *He looked guilty.*

She gave him a kick in the shin under the table and when he turned and scowled at her, she followed it up with her strongest, raised eyebrowed, *what-the-hell-are-you-doing* look.

He held her gaze for a few seconds then relaxed his features, but she could have sworn it was by force of will alone. Regardless, it was just in time.

"Rocco Falconi."

Her eyebrows shot up almost to her hairline, this time in surprise. She had assumed Rocky was a street name. Who called their kid Rocco?

Obviously Mr. and Mrs. Falconi.

Rocky walked toward the kitchen door, passing Celeste on the way, his swagger even more pronounced than usual. What was with this guy? You don't fool with the police. Certainly not in Mexico. Hadn't *he* been the one who told her that?

Bernadette's throat was parched, and she considered ordering another drink, but if she wanted to keep a clear head, it shouldn't be another beer. She should probably have thought of that before having the second one.

Pulling her pad out of her shoulder bag, she went through the list of last names of everyone on the tour. Her chest tightened, and she wheezed in a breath when she realized she was probably next. Better not drink anything more or she'd have to go to the bathroom first and that might look suspicious.

Her paranoia would have been hilarious if she'd had any breath left to laugh.

After a few minutes, she realized she was tapping her pen loudly on the patio table. Stopping abruptly, she looked around to see if anyone had noticed. Hank gave her a reassuring smile and, sheepishly, she grinned back.

Just as she stood up to join him, Rocky sauntered back out through the kitchen door. This time there was no cocky grin, as his walk would have suggested. She had no idea what he was thinking but she didn't have time to ponder the mysterious Rocko Falconi since the young officer was calling her name.

Chapter 13

Bernadette lifted her chin, tugged her shoulders down from somewhere up around her ears, and blew out a long breath. As she walked across the terrace to the kitchen door, she took the pencil out of her hair, letting it fall to her shoulders.

What made police questioning so harrowing? And why was she so worried? She didn't know anything about Caruthers' death.

Inside the kitchen, Chief Pacho had set up a makeshift office on the central stainless-steel island. He stood when she entered and reintroduced himself, this time introducing his deputy Officer Perez, as well. He motioned for Bernadette to take the empty stool across from him and once she sat down, he resumed his seat. The deputy closed the swinging kitchen door and stood in front of it, arms crossed on his chest, feet wide like a TV cop.

Bernadette folded her hands in her lap and waited for Chief Pacho to begin. He looked at his notes for a moment, glanced up at her, then went back to his notes and kept reading.

Senses tingling, her mind felt unnaturally alert. The slightest movement seemed to echo in the hard-surfaced room. The minutes stretched out like taffy. Her eyes glazed over, dry from not blinking. She had no idea what to expect. She would just try to hold it together, answer the questions but not offer anything extra. That's what they said to do on TV—when you don't have a lawyer.

Christ! Why would she need a lawyer? She took a deep breath, willing herself to calm down.

"Ms. Mallow," Chief Pacho said, startling her out of her ruminations. "When did you meet Mr. Caruthers?"

"Last night, when Manuel introduced him to the group."

"Where did this take place?"

"In the dining room."

"How would you describe his mood?"

She thought for a moment. "Distracted. Possibly worried or upset."

"Why do you say that?" Chief Pacho probed.

"I don't know, maybe because he didn't seem very friendly. Of course, I didn't know him. Maybe he was always like that, but he didn't want to sit with Manuel and the group and he spoke rudely to the waiter, who offered him wine, and to me when I spoke to him."

Chief Pacho looked at her for a moment without blinking. He shifted his eyes to his papers, lifted his pen and wrote a line. When his eyes came back up to hers, they narrowed. "Why did you speak to him?"

Bernadette failed to see the importance of this and shrugged, shaking her head. "Just being friendly."

"What did you say to him?"

"Nothing really. Just a comment on the wine he had turned down."

"He turned it down? He was not drinking?"

"He did go to the bar for a drink a bit later. He knocked my chair as he went by."

"Did he have a drink with him when he returned?"

"I don't know. He was sitting behind me. I didn't see him go back to his seat."

The Chief sat silently, hands clasped in front of him on the stainless-steel table. Bernadette felt a twitch develop in her jaw but fought it. Finally, he said, "When did you see him next?"

"He passed me, later that night, on the front stairs."

"Was he coming or going?"

"Going."

"Where?"

Her shoulders twitched at his non-stop bombardment of questions. "I have no idea."

"Where had you been?"

"Nowhere. I was sitting on the step, talking to my son on the phone."

He stopped to make a note on his page and she glanced around the kitchen. It was beginning to feel small.

"What time was that?"

"Ten thirty. Maybe closer to eleven."

"Did you speak to each other?"

"No," she said firmly.

Chief Pacho gave her a long steady look and then said, "Do you wish to add anything? Anything at all?"

She thought for a moment, then shrugged. What could she say? "No. I can't think of a thing."

He continued to stare at her, his hands steepled on the table. Her nerves were beginning to fray. Finally he stood up, indicating the interview was over and she collapsed slightly in on herself in relief. "If you do not have anything more to add, you are free to go. If you think of anything else, we will be around the hotel for the next few days. Thank you for your cooperation."

Bernadette stood up, surprised to find her legs like jelly. Although the kitchen was cool, her clothes were damp with perspiration. Officer Perez held the door for her and she escaped to the terrace. Although she had nothing to hide, a guilty feeling of relief coursed through her, as if she had gotten away with something.

As she walked away, a chill ran down her back. Glancing over her shoulder she saw Chief Pacho standing in the doorway, watching her go, an impassive look on his face.

Suddenly the full extent of the possible consequences of their isolation became clear. She was so far from home, from the world she understood. In Ox B'alam there weren't many ways to contact the outside world. With no car, no bus service, no wifi, they were at the mercy of this man, this police officer about whom she knew nothing.

As she crossed the terrace, Officer Perez called Eloise next. Unconcerned, she sashayed toward him, spilling out of her bikini, a towel wrapped low on her swaying hips. Bernadette glanced back again to see Perez's reaction, and the look on the deputy's face almost made her smile.

Not knowing what else to do, she headed up to her room. At the top of the stairs, another officer sat on a chair in front of what she guessed had been Caruthers' room, the first door on the left at the top of the stairs, directly across from her own. At least she assumed the man was police. The only part of the uniform he wore was the black brimmed hat that he'd pulled low on his forehead.

Balancing on the back two legs of a dining room chair, arms crossed over a substantial belly, he watched her carefully as she crossed the hall, but did not acknowledge her presence with a word or a gesture. She concentrated on keeping her footsteps even as she walked to her door, but at the last minute she veered away and kept walking. She didn't feel like being alone.

Rocky's room was down the hall, next to Caruthers'. Tinny video game music and sound effects emanated through the door. Stopping in front of it, she knocked.

"Who is it?" he called.

"Me."

She took his grunt as an invitation and opened the door.

His room was large, similar to her own, but looked out to the rear gardens of the hacienda instead of toward the lagoon. He sat on the bed, a computer hooked up to the small TV with a long cable, playing a video game with crashing cars racing through downtown streets. He pressed 'pause' and looked up, then ran his hand down his face in a vain attempt to wipe away the worry. "What's up?"

Stepping inside, she closed the door and smiled faintly. "Well, I survived the interrogation."

"Yeah, it's different when they're asking the questions."

"Yeah," she said, then frowned. "Different from what?"

"Hard. I mean hard to concentrate." He pressed a button and went back to his game.

"And I don't even know anything." She shook her head in bewilderment. "Imagine how hard it would be to keep your cool if you did have something to hide."

He kept his eyes on his game, but said, "That's just what they're counting on." After a minute, he glanced at her again. "Want to sit for a while?"

Strangely relieved, she accepted his offer.

* * *

That night at dinner, conversation was subdued. Afterwards, Manuel told the group that he had received the okay from Chief Pacho to continue with their itinerary, so the following day they would be going to Chichén Itzá as planned, to take advantage of the bigger, more comfortable bus he had booked for the daylong trip.

Although they had missed their visit to the local village that day, he assured them they could easily fit it in later in the week. His assurances relieved Bernadette's mind. She didn't want to be cold, thinking only of the job in the face of a murder, but since there was no way she could help the police, the story was still her number one priority.

After dinner, most of their group drifted out to their regular gathering spot at the terrace bar. Bernadette took the last empty stool, next to Arthur, at the end of the bar. He had his back to her and was talking to Celeste, who had managed to get next to Rocky again but had lost his ear to Eloise on his other side. Salvador was fixing fancy drinks with tiny umbrellas stuck in the top for the Aussies, and something on the rocks for Hank at the far end of the bar.

Luis came through the door behind the bar to help Salvador with the drink orders. Apparently in this small family-owned hotel most of the staff performed double duty.

The afternoon had been a bust as far as work on the article was concerned, so when Luis brought Bernadette her glass of white wine, she thought she'd try to get some background information from him.

"Where are you from, Luis?"

"I was born here in Ox B'alam. I'm lucky to have such a good job and not to have to go to the coast and work in the big hotels."

"Do you live with your family?"

"No, I live in the staff bungalows by the perimeter wall. I share a room with my cousin Salvador."

Hearing his name, Salvador looked up, his white teeth flashing in a smile, and walked over. "You want me, Señorita?"

Definitely not. "Luis just mentioned that you are cousins."

Salvador glanced at Luis. "That is true. I have been in Ox B'alam for four months now. I have family here," he said, giving Luis a paternalistic pat on the shoulder. Salvador waited expectantly, but Bernadette couldn't think of anything to say. What she wanted was to talk to Luis, but he was doing a disappearing act through the door to the dining room bar. Not knowing how to end the conversation with Salvador, she finally asked, "Do you like living here?"

"It is quiet. The big city is better." He leaned both elbows on the bar, thrusting his smiling face well into her comfort zone. "But we can find fun even here in Ox B'alam."

Bernadette shifted back in her seat. Hank came unknowingly to her rescue by holding up his glass for a refill at the far end of the bar. Sending one final smile in her direction, Salvador drifted over to help him. Bernadette breathed a sigh of relief and wondered if he ever had any luck finding lonely women on holiday who were looking for a little action.

Arthur still had his back to her and while she didn't really want to talk to him, either, the thought of standing at the other end of the bar was not appealing. Suddenly her phone vibrated on her hip. Taking it out of her pocket, she saw it was Colin. She smiled as she started toward the door to the empty dining room.

"Hi, Sweetheart."

The call was a reassuring reminder of her real life, far from police questioning and unexplained death. She decided on the spot not to tell Colin about Caruthers' death. No reason to worry him since her part in the affair was probably over.

As she'd predicted, he was having a great time. His grandma was spoiling him rotten. She took a seat on the cool marble stairs in the foyer, rubbed the knot of the anxiety at the back of her neck and tried to enjoy the chat. The conversation was short but sweet. He didn't seem to miss her and while she knew that was a good thing, she felt a gentle pang anyway at the thought that he didn't need her quite so much anymore.

"Don't forget my sombrero," he said, just before he hung up.

After ending the call, she peeked into the bar from

her perch on the stairs. Everyone was still sitting where she'd left them. Exhausted by the heat, the walk at the ruins and the police interrogation, she decided to go up to her room rather than back into the bar. Caruthers unfortunate death notwithstanding, she had to get her story back on track. She had notes to write up from their excursion to Old Ox B'alam today. They had risen early is morning and tomorrow they would be up earlier still to go to Chichén Itzá. But that was okay. She had studied the famous site in archeology class years ago and was buzzed at the prospect.

As she trudged up the stairs she vowed that, unlike today's fiascos, the snake and camo-man, tomorrow she would impress Rocky with her solid professionalism.

She'd show him she could take care of herself.

* * *

Rocky's ears perked up when Bernadette answered her phone with, "Hi, Sweetheart."

But she quickly walked out of the bar so that was all he heard.

Must be her husband. Or boyfriend. Whatever.

This week was certainly one for the books. His spidey sense had told him right away that Caruthers had been murdered, but he was not about to offer an opinion to the police. He didn't trust Pacho and his band of merry men. The deputies were a bunch of buffoons and the jury was still out on Pacho himself. He'd heard stories about Mexican police and it stretched the imagination to think this guy could be legit.

Manuel seemed to like Pacho, though, even respect him, and Rocky intuitively trusted Manuel. He had looked for signs of coercion when Manuel spoke of the Chief, but his trust did not seem motivated by fear.

Even so, Rocky planned to keep his distance. The last

thing he needed was to get involved in a murder investigation in Mexico.

Monday, Day 2

"The discovery … gave rise to the exciting idea that the great mounds scattered over the country contained secret, unknown and hidden chambers …"

J.L. Stephens, <u>Incidents of Travel in Yucatán, 1842</u>

Chapter 14

The rap on Bernadette's door next morning came even earlier than it had the day before. Determined not to do the time zone tango, she squeezed her eyes shut and groaned an acknowledgement. The only consolation was that Chichén Itzá, their destination today, the premier archeological site of the Yucatán, was worth the struggle.

Once she had forced herself out of bed, she had to admit she was glad to be getting away from the hotel for the day. Waiting in the heat for the interviews yesterday had been nerve-wracking—too much time to think and wonder about how Caruthers had died and the condition he was in when the police found him.

She gave herself a pep talk in the bathroom mirror as she applied a liberal layer of sunscreen. Yesterday hadn't gone as smoothly as she'd hoped, but today would be better. She would take control of her story and no snakes, animals or men with greasepaint on their faces would get in her way. She would stick with the group and do her job.

Rocky had seemed pissed when she told him she'd run into trouble at the ballcourt. She was pissed that he was pissed, but a pissing match wouldn't do her any good. She needed this job and sensed she needed Rocky to vouch for her to Jen. So today she would be strong and in control—and keep out of Rocky's way.

Then she opened her door, saw the screaming red police tape on Caruthers door across the hall and her spirits deflated like a ruined soufflé. Excitement about today's outing had pushed Caruthers death out of her mind. *A psychologist would have a field day with that.* At least the paunchy deputy teetering on his chair was gone.

Hurrying past the crime scene, she trotted down the stairs. In the dining room, the atmosphere was quietly giddy; everyone seemed glad to be getting away from the hotel and the disturbing police presence.

Manuel had rented a full-sized bus for the day, and although Rocky could have chosen a seat by himself, Bernadette was pleased when he climbed into the seat beside her. It was still dark outside when the bus pulled away from the hacienda. Manuel turned off the interior lights and quiet murmurs rustled through the bus, but as they turned onto the road around the lagoon, a hush fell over the group.

Bernadette couldn't take her eyes off the silver sheen of moonlight on the water and a shiver ran through her as she pictured hulking reptiles circling a body floating in the still water. Finally tearing her eyes away, she turned her head and saw Rocky staring intensely at the scene.

"I'd rather meet a guy with a knife in a dark alley than a croc in that water," he said softly.

It wasn't until they passed the restaurant and turned onto the road out of Ox B'alam that she blew out a breath and her shoulders relaxed. The bus's headlights created a tunnel of light in the darkness and the monotonous blur of jungle foliage on either side soon lulled her into a restless sleep, punctuated by disturbing dreams of thrashing water.

She woke to the sun streaming in through the window as they pulled into the Chichén Itzá parking lot. It was almost empty, but even before they climbed out of their vehicle, another tour bus pulled in beside them.

Manuel hurried their straggling group through the turnstiles. "There are two reasons we come so early," he said. "To miss the heat and some of the crowds."

Looking back over her shoulder, Bernadette saw another bus roll in.

Although regarded as a national treasure, Chichén Itzá remained in private hands. On either side of the entrance lane, tables piled with garish souvenirs flowed in a steady river of changing color: painted masks, colorful pottery, black obsidian carvings and thousands of tiny white pyramids.

Within seconds, Bernadette was surrounded by a sticky web of peddlers, all vying for her attention and tourist dollars. A tiny old crone, barely four feet tall, came at her as aggressively as any of the men. Wearing traditional dress, heavy with colorful embroidery, she thrust a white pyramid in Bernadette's face.

The farther she walked, the more persistent the vendors became. Clutching her shoulder bag to her chest, she kept her head down and tried not to make eye contact, but the crowd, mostly men, called out for her attention as they jostled against her arms and shoulders. Over their heads, she caught sight of Hank and the others.

The Spanish phrases she had practiced for just such occasions deserted her now in her time of need. She raised an arm in front of her face like a shield and twisted away from one particularly aggressive vendor, only to bump into another.

A devil's face swooped in from one side and although

she knew it was only a shaman's mask, in this chaotic river of people it seemed startlingly real. The devil grabbed her arm, pulling her toward his display and, try as she might, she couldn't pull free. Excited people pressed in on her from all sides.

When the masked man jerked her arm again, she thought, *enough is enough*. She turned to face him, fist swinging, ready to fight, and made satisfying contact with someone's shoulder.

"Hold on there." It was Rocky, pulling the man off her arm. Rocky wasn't much taller than Bernadette, but he was taller than most of the Mexicans and every stocky inch was solid muscle. He tossed the man aside like an offending gnat and took her by the elbow. Miraculously, the sea of vendors scattered before them as he propelled her straight down the dirt road.

"Thank you," she said stiffly. "But I could have handled it."

"I'm sure you could."

She didn't detect any sarcasm in his tone, but she pulled her arm free and straightened her shoulders. "I'm fine now. They just caught me off guard."

"In places like this, a woman alone is a target," he said seriously.

She knew that. She was embarrassed to make such a rookie mistake. She'd been too long in the safe halls of academia, had lost her traveller's savvy. The key was to walk with assurance, not look like a victim. Psychology was half the battle. In future, she would be more careful.

But Rocky's attention had already shifted to the wide green space that opened before them. Bernadette's breath hitched at the sight of the monolithic pyramid rising in the center of the open field. Even though she'd seen it in countless photographs, standing in the presence of the real thing momentarily took her breath away.

Rocky snapped his camera on top of the tripod. "This is perfect. When the sun gets too high, the light gets harsh. There's too much glare and these great shadows disappear."

Following his lead, Bernadette clicked on the voice recorder on her phone, lifted it to her lips and spoke. "Gleaming white in the morning sun, the limestone monument stands alone and majestic in the still-empty common. The low sun casts strong, angular shadows on the steps that rise to the sacred alter at the top. The contrast between the riotous road of souvenir stalls and the silence surrounding the pyramid makes the stone structure even more imposing. The size, the symmetry, the grandeur. It took my breath away."

What a string of clichés! Writing this was going to be harder than she thought. Harder still because all the clichés were true.

Regardless, she continued her recording. However trite, her notes would bring back these first impressions when she started writing her piece.

As always, the group assembled around Manuel as he started to speak. She held the recorder over their heads, trying to catch his words.

"Chichén Itzá means, 'Well of the Water Magicians.' We will see the well, a cenote, later this morning."

He led the way to the foot of the pyramid where crumbling, roped off, stone steps rose to meet the sky.

"The Maya built the temples high to get closer to the gods. They called this one, 'Pyramid of Kukulkán', but the Spanish renamed it *El Castillo*, The Castle."

Arms gesturing like a windmill, he went on to explain that the pyramid was a form of calendar, precisely oriented to the four cardinal directions. "Unfortunately, we can no longer climb these steps, but later this week we will climb the pyramid in Ox B'alam again to watch the sun rise."

And this time, Bernadette silently vowed, she would make it to the summit.

Manuel stood by the central stone staircase beside one of the waist-high stone snakeheads that flanked the lowest step. With fangs projecting from their open mouths, they were eerie reminders of the snake Bernadette had seen the previous day on the steps at Ox B'alam. As Rocky moved in for a shot of Manuel with his hand on one of the snake heads, she decided to use yesterday's episode in the article, to go with this picture.

"At the top of the staircase, instead of a tail, there is another head," Manuel said. "The two-headed snake brought the knowledge of the gods to the priests and the people who filled the square below."

As he spoke, Bernadette saw in her mind's eye, the pyramid as it had been in ancient times, decorated with murals and intricate carvings painted red, ochre and black. Each year on the equinox the high priest, his body painted blue and decked out in a ceremonial costume of iridescent feathers and tawny skins, descended the steps in time with the setting sun to present the message of the gods to the multitude assembled below.

Eloise's voice shattered her vision. "Kind of like Stonehenge. You remember Celli, out in the middle of a field like this…"

Celeste nodded in agreement. "With all that stone."

"These pyramids were built layer upon layer over older buildings," Manuel continued. "Ancient temples like this dot the Yucatán jungle. Most are in ruins, and the structures above them have never been restored. But some are still used by the Maya for worship or, in times of political unrest, for meetings. Luckily for us, we can visit this old temple."

He led them to an inconspicuous doorway built into the side of the staircase wall. It stood open but was roped off. Bernadette peered uneasily into the dark narrow corridor that led to the heart of the pyramid. Beside her, Annie twitched with the excitement of a racehorse at the starting gate. When a guard arrived and removed the rope, Annie plunged into the dim stone passage.

Arthur followed with the stiff-legged gait and the wide eyes of a convert about to receive the grail. He was normally such a mousey man that his passion always surprised Bernadette, although it probably shouldn't have, considering this was his second visit in as many months.

Bernadette followed more slowly into the narrow corridor, telling herself she had to go in. These experiences were vital to her story.

A few feet into the damp, airless tunnel, the walls on either side began to press in. Needing a focus other than the long narrow corridor before her, she fumbled for the voice recorder. When the red light blinked on, she began to speak. "Thirty feet down the corridor beneath the pyramid, the air is heavy and it's getting hard to breath. The corridor itself is narrow at the floor, widening at my shoulder, then narrowing again with a flat narrow ceiling overhead, like an upright coffin."

She cringed. Bad image, but true. Shaking it off, she started again. "I'm climbing the stone stairs behind Arthur. He stopped at the entrance to a small room that holds two statues. One, a recumbent figure with traditional Mayan features, is looking toward the door, as if it's a guard."

Low-wattage bulbs hanging in the corners of the chamber cast harsh shadows on the rough stone walls. At the back of the room in a roped-off square stood the second statue, a cat.

Beside her, Arthur inhaled an audible breath.

"What is it?" she asked.

"The jaguar throne," Arthur breathed. "We weren't allowed in here last time I came."

He hurried across the chamber to the statue and, as she followed, Bernadette recorded her impression of the cat. "At least three feet high at the head, the stylized jaguar's body is painted bright red, possibly with cinnabar, and spotted with inlaid spheres of translucent jade. His back is flat, and he stands firmly on all four feet, staring at us as we enter the chamber through haunting jade eyes."

The statue had an eerie presence and she had the disconcerting feeling that it was displeased that they were disturbing him after centuries of silence.

Annie was standing next to the throne, her camera raised. A guard pushed past Bernadette and put his hand on Annie's arm. "No pictures, *por favor*."

Rocky stood at the edge of the chamber with his pocket camera palmed inconspicuously in his hand. Bernadette wouldn't have put it past him to be taking a few illegal shots.

Eloise squatted in front of the statue and looked it in the eye. "The face is kind of cute. Round, like a pussy cat."

Bernadette stared into the face of the jaguar. Perhaps the spherical cheeks and little round ears sticking up from the top of his head could be described as 'cute', but the white fangs protruding from the snarling mouth told a decidedly different story.

In the dimness of the cramped room, the jade eyes seemed to glow from within. The low-ceilinged chamber was hot and stuffy, and a sickly flush washed over Bernadette. Blackness crept into the edges of her vision until all she could see were the jaguar's pulsing eyes.

He was the temple guardian and was warning them that they were not welcome in this sacred space.

Chapter 15

Someone—in her daze, Bernadette wasn't sure who—took hold of her arm and pulled her out through the chamber door. After the episode with the pushy vendors, her instinct was to fight, but as she shook her head to clear it, she realized it was Rocky, again, pulling her against the stream of people pouring in, up the passage to the entrance. Stumbling, almost falling, she followed him out of the temple, into the blinding sunlight.

The air fresh on her face felt wonderful. Her sweat-dampened shirt clung to her back and she gasped, inhaling deeply, finally able to breathe.

Rocky took her hand and pulled her into a small patch of shade. She shook her head again, struggling to clear it, and ran the back of her other hand across her dry mouth. Manuel was there too, offering her water. She drank. The panic slowly subsided and her heartbeat gradually returned to normal.

"You are so white, a *fantasma*," Manuel said, concern written on his face.

Rocky's response was not as gentle. "What were you thinking, Mallow. Going in there if you're claustrophobic?"

She slumped on the ground against a stone wall in the last remnant of shade. In a few minutes, even that would be gone as the blinding Yucatán sun reached its zenith. Her eyes rolled up. Three vultures circled overhead. Sickly sweat coated her skin and she groaned as she realized she'd had another episode.

Her eyes swiveled to Rocky's face. He was watching her closely, waiting for a response.

"I'm not claustrophobic." Her eyes darted left and

right as she searched for an answer he would accept.

He looked questioningly into her face. "Too much sun? I don't want to have to worry about you all the time. We have work to do."

She felt her hackles rise like an angry cat. "It wasn't the sun. And you don't have to watch me."

"What was it then?" He swiped the cloth hat off her head.

"Hey!"

"Getting overheated isn't going to help." He picked up her water bottle. "If it wasn't claustrophobia, what was it?"

She looked away, silent for a moment, watching the vultures sail on invisible air currents. *How to describe it?* She had tried to explain it to people before, but never with much success.

She was eleven or twelve when she first felt these sensations. She had tried to talk to her parents about it, but it just angered her father and scared her mother. Apparently the 'gift' had skipped a generation. Grandma had called it 'their little secret', and she began to understand why.

As she got older, the episodes didn't happen often but when they did, the feelings were stronger. The worst times, like this one, were a sort of possession. Fierce, like a warning, they scared her with visions of trouble to come. Tight, enclosed spaces didn't help.

"I'm okay. I must have been overheated."

She was glad to see Rocky's eyes were on Manuel, who was leading their group across the field without them.

Rocky stood up. "We're getting behind. Are you ready to go?"

He poured water from her bottle into her hat and before she could object, slapped it, dripping, back onto her head. She shrieked as the cold water ran down the neck of her shirt, but the shock worked wonders to clear her head.

She pulled her soggy hat down more securely, happy to let the subject drop. "Sure, let's go."

Putting one hand on the top of the wall, she struggled to her feet, then felt a sudden chill of cold reptilian eyes upon her. Slowly, she turned her head, only to find herself eye to eye with the largest lizard she'd ever seen, at least three feet long, with a row of spikes running from the top of its head to the tip of its tail. It's knobby fingers gripped the stone, its dry scaly skin camouflaged against the dusty rock wall.

She opened her mouth, but no sound emerged. The creature bobbed up and down on short stocky legs, as if winding itself up, then darted toward her faster than she would have believed possible. Pulling her hand away, she jumped back, right into Rocky.

The monster ran right past her along the wall. Closing her eyes, she put up a hand to still her pounding heart. How much more could her poor heart take?

For the second time in minutes, Rocky steadied her with a hand on her arm, but this time he was grinning broadly. "Iguana. They're usually harmless."

Biting her lip, Bernadette looked at the now motionless lizard who was back to sunning himself on the wall, a few feet away. She had to get a grip. If this kept up, Rocky would ditch her first chance he got. Even now, he was striding away, across the field, after the others.

Reaching up to hold onto her hat, she jogged to catch up. "Where are they going?" she asked, as much to change the subject as anything else.

"To the ballcourt."

"How do you know?"

"I did my homework." She felt the criticism in his tone. "That's how you stay one step ahead, Mallow. Too late to bone up now. No wifi in Ox B'alam." He picked up his pace, making a bee-line across the open field for the tall stone walls.

Once again, he was infuriatingly right. It was a ballcourt, but nothing like the one at Ox B'alam. Bernadette walked to the middle of the open field and turned around slowly, taking it in. The wide, flat playing field was almost twice the size of a football field, in both directions. Carved reliefs richly decorated the towering parallel walls that ran the length of each side. So much bigger than the jungle court at Ox B'alam, it was scarcely recognizable as the same type of playing field. Only the stone rings in the middle of the walls near the top gave it away.

Maybe it was its position on the open plain under the direct sun rather than deep in the jungle, but for whatever reason, even though these games must have come to the same grisly end, she didn't feel any of the uncomfortable vibrations she'd felt at the ballcourt at Ox B'alam.

The tour continued for hours with Manuel guiding them among the ruins, weaving around other tour groups on the dirt road that ran from the 'old' town to the 'new'. Now that she was aware of the iguanas, Bernadette saw they were everywhere, regally posing on the hot rocks.

And it was hot. Her head began to swim under the brutal sun. She used a small splash of her precious water to wet her hat again, this time sighing with relief as the cool liquid trickled down her back.

Manuel had a steady supply of stories, often with enigmatic endings that only pumped up the Mayan mystery. Fascinating carvings of skulls and jaguars stared out at her at every turn. Images of the rain god Chaac decorated the eaves of many of the buildings, the roofs engineered so that when it rained, water poured out of his mouth, a gift from the rain god himself. The tour ended at the Magician's Well, a rocky hole in the ground with steep sides and a murky pool of water at the bottom.

Bernadette perched on a rock and listened to Manuel. "These cenotes are common all over the Yucatán. The exposed pools were previously underground and were the source of water for the Maya, who thought they were entrances to the underworld. Priests performed religious ceremonies at this cenote for centuries, burying the dead and throwing in precious articles, including human sacrifices, to appease the gods."

Bernadette pictured Caruthers' body in the lagoon and a pall dropped like a theater curtain on the day. There was no escape—not even here, miles away in the sunshine.

Tipping back her water bottle, the last drops trickled tantalizingly down her throat. Rocky stood back, trying to get her in his shot.

"Get some good pictures?" she asked, determined to mend bridges.

"Yes, I did. We could do a piece on Chichén Itzá alone for another magazine I have in mind. I hope you got some good stuff."

She tried not to be huffy. Professional. That was the key. "Yes, I did. Atmosphere and quotes. Manuel's stories. I can research the details later."

"Just so long as you get them right. I'm putting my reputation on the line with you here."

As he never tired of telling her.

"Time for lunch," Manuel called to his straggling flock, waving his hands and pointing toward the exit. Once back at the van, he handed out bottled water from a cooler and explained, "These are simple people. As visitors to their land, it is courteous to try to learn their customs. We will eat at a nearby restaurant where they serve local dishes. Try them. You might be surprised by how delicious they are." He looked seriously into the faces around him. "Iguana tail. Monkey legs. Snake."

Then he grinned and climbed into the bus.

Chapter 16

"I was really looking forward to trying the snake," Hank grumbled good-naturedly as he poured the last drop of cerveza out of a pitcher and into his mug.

"I had snake in China," Rocky said. "Tastes like chicken."

"They say everything tastes like chicken," Hank replied. "I'd still like to try it."

Instead of exotic, lunch had been bland and unextraordinary, even by Bernadette's standards; chicken and rice or beef fajitas, all tempered for the busloads of tourists who visited the ruins.

The restaurant itself, though, was an anthropologist's dream. Over the centuries, the Mexican people created their own form of Catholicism by combining the religion of the Spaniards with their own ancient stories, and the evidence was clearly visible in the shrines tucked comfortably into every corner of the restaurant. Although Christmas was three months gone, twinkling lights twined over laughing Santas and backlit crosses. A large plastic Virgin Mary glowed, lit from within, beside traditional bowls of fruit left on a makeshift altar as gifts to the Mayan gods.

After eating, the group languished in the close heat of the restaurant veranda and Bernadette fought her eyes drifting shut.

She turned to Manuel and said with a sleepy smile, "Time for a siesta."

He stood up. "A swim in a cenote will restore your energy. I know one nearby that is on private land."

That woke her up. The only cenote they had only seen so far was the Magician's Well at Chichén Itzá. She wouldn't have swum there if you paid her, what with the ritual sacrifices and all, and of course the lagoons were out of the question. This stop was on their itinerary, though, so she'd come prepared.

One by one the members of the group straggled out of the restaurant past the requisite display of local handcrafts by the till. One of the last to go, she spotted a hardcover book sitting on a chair at their table and picked it up. She read the title on the spine aloud. "*Incidents of Travel in the Yucatán, 1842*. Whose book is this?"

"Arthur's," Annie said. "He carries it everywhere."

Arthur had already gone back to the bus, so Bernadette flipped through pages, heavily scattered with glossy black and white photographs and fine copperplate prints. The bookmarked pages were of Chichén Itzá, and although the photographs were dated the nineteenth century, the buildings were still clearly recognizable as the ones they'd seen today.

Annie looked over her shoulder. "I've read that book. The author discovered many of the ruins in the Yucatán jungle, then spent the rest of his life exploring them. They had been abandoned centuries earlier, although no one knows why. The local people knew where many of the ruins were, but apparently, they didn't show much interest in them. Stephens published the book to raise money to finance his expeditions. Since then some of the ruins, like Chicken Itzá, have had real money poured into them, but hundreds of others are still out there, undiscovered and continuing to deteriorate. Devoured by the jungle. You saw what happened at Ox B'alam."

Bernadette stopped at one particularly haunting black and white image. An elaborate carving peeked out of a tangle of tree roots and vines, much larger but not unlike the jaguar carving she had discovered near the ballcourt at Ox B'alam.

"Imagine coming upon something like that in the

jungle," Annie said, looking over her shoulder.

Bernadette caught up with Arthur boarding the van and returned the book to him. He thanked her profusely, treating her to one of his rare smiles.

"Is Ox B'alam in the book?" Bernadette asked, thinking if it was, she could possibly glean a few interesting tidbits for the article.

"No, Stevens never made it to Ox B'alam," Arthur said. "He heard about it, but there were no roads at that point and the village and the ruins were too remote."

They drove for a few minutes, then the bus turned off the highway and followed a narrow dirt road through scrubby jungle for a few hundred yards before breaking out into an open cornfield. A house with a grass roof sat high on a rise in the middle of the field. A man came to the open door and raised a hand. Manuel waved out the open window in a return salute as he drove by.

The road plunged back into the forest for another mile before ending abruptly. Manuel turned to them with a smile. "We walk from here."

In single file, they followed a narrow trail through dry, sparse jungle, blissfully empty after the crowds of Chichén Itzá. Birds hooted and called from their hidden perches, but the only wildlife they saw was a furry tarantula, the size of a child's hand, making its stately way across the path. Everyone clustered around at a respectful distance, watching as it disappeared under a rock.

The trail ended at a sheltered clearing with a big rocky hole in the ground. All that was left of the limestone cap that had once covered the subterranean pool was the jagged rim of the cenote. A movie-worthy jungle pool, vines hung from the rim over the pale rock that glowed in the afternoon sun.

Fifteen feet below ground level, the surface of the water reflected the vegetation that ringed the rim and the ferns that grew out of cracks in the stone walls. On the bottom of the pool, massive chunks of limestone from the collapsed roof were visible through the clear water.

Rocky lifted his tripod off his shoulder and unleashed his camera, quickly capturing the pristine beauty of the scene before the group disturbed the pool's limpid surface.

"It is at least thirty feet deep," Manuel said as he offered life preservers from a roughly built shed on the edge of the forest. "Much deeper than it looks."

Always comfortable in the water, Bernadette declined a preserver. Stripping down to the bathing suit she'd worn under her clothes, she followed Celeste and Eloise, already in their bikinis, along the path that wound down to a level rock at the water's edge. Meredith and Annie followed, with Hank bringing up the rear.

"It is cold," Manuel warned.

Bernadette squatted on the rock, felt the water and laughed. "It's nowhere near as cold as the lakes in the mountains back home."

Rocky raised his camera and aimed it in her direction. The last thing she wanted was a picture of her in a bathing suit in the magazine, so she pinched her nose and plunged feet first into the cool silky water. The cenote looked about five feet deep but when she stretched her legs, she couldn't touch the rocks on the bottom. She took a deep breath and dove down until her breath was exhausted, but she still hadn't reached the bottom.

When she surfaced, Manuel was talking to Rocky and the Morrises, who waited on the shore. "Underground rivers link the cenotes. With a snorkel or tanks, you could swim for miles. Many animals use these routes: fish and snakes, even crocodiles and jaguars."

Bernadette gasped, swallowing a mouthful of water. Coughing and sputtering, she swam for shore. The other women must have heard him too because when she got to the edge, they were all there, struggling for a foothold on the slippery surface.

Above them on the shore, Rocky doubled over with laughter and wiped the tears from his eyes. Bernadette got an elbow in the face, lost her hold on the rock and went under. When she came up sputtering, he reached down and pulled her onto the rocky ledge. Then, one by one, he helped the other women out.

"What do you mean, snakes?" Annie asked Manuel, clearly horrified.

"I've heard, sometimes, boa constrictors."

"What?" Annie shrieked.

"Not here. I have never seen one here," Manuel hastened to reassure her, but she grabbed her towel and stalked off down the path towards the bus in a huff.

Bernadette couldn't believe her ears. "Boa constrictors?"

"You rarely see them," Manuel protested. "I myself have never seen one."

"But you yourself don't swim in the cenotes," Rocky said.

"I never learned to swim," Manuel admitted. "Living in Ox B'alam with only the crocodile lagoons, children do not learn to swim."

At this rate, Bernadette wouldn't be doing much more swimming on this trip, either.

She dozed most of the way back to Ox B'alam. It was almost dark when they turned into the hacienda driveway, just a tinge of orange highlighting the horizon. Her stomach growled loudly, and she fixed her eyes on the window.

Rocky grinned. "Was that you?"

She laughed. "I hope dinner's ready. I could eat an iguana."

Hank stuck his head between them from the seat

behind. "I hope we don't have to. I'd go for a big bloody steak myself."

"I'll be happy to get out of this wet bathing suit and have dinner and a glass of wine," Bernadette said. But at the sight of Pacho's SUV parked in front of the hacienda, *Policia* written on the side in red, her appetite disappeared.

Chapter 17

Pacho's SUV was a grim reminder of the police questioning the previous afternoon. Bernadette hoped he had news of Caruthers' death so, callous as it sounded, they could close the book on this horrible incident get on with the trip. And the job. As it was, when she was at the hacienda and should be working on her notes, she felt paralyzed by the oppressive atmosphere.

The members of the Cultural Tour all trooped wordlessly up the marble staircase to their rooms. Bernadette showered, changed and went back downstairs for dinner. Even though she no longer felt hungry, she fell into line with the others at the buffet, then sat down and picked at her food, one eye on the lobby, waiting for Chief Pacho to appear.

The dining room was grimly silent for most of the meal. Faint music drifted into the room. Somewhere nearby, a Mariachi band was playing, a macabre soundtrack to the current drama.

Across the table, Rocky had retreated behind the shield of his mirrored glasses. He inclined his head a quarter of an inch toward the terrace, such a small movement that Bernadette wasn't sure it was a signal. Then he rose and went out through the arched opening.

She looked quickly away, feeling foolish for the subterfuge. Why couldn't he communicate like regular people? They were supposed to be partners. It wouldn't be unusual for them to get together and talk.

A few minutes later she wiped her lips with her napkin, folded it carefully by her plate and followed him outside.

He was perched on a barstool at the empty terrace

bar, tapping his fingers on the counter. He'd raised his shades and had his eyes fixed on the dining room doorway. When he saw her, he blew out an impatient breath and jumped to his feet.

"Let's go," he said and, taking her hand, started walking towards the pool.

She dug in her heels. "Didn't Pacho say we should stay?"

Insistently, he pulled her along . "Let's get out of here before he makes us."

He led her around the blue-lit pool onto a path that led into the dark garden. Her protests were mostly on principle because getting away did sound like a good idea. The faint Mariachi music carried a promise of margaritas and a change of atmosphere she desperately needed.

She stopped resisting and he dropped her hand. They followed the path deep into the garden where lights hidden in the shrub borders cast mysterious leafy shadows at their feet. Although the stifling heat of the afternoon had lifted, the darkness was warm and still. The scent of night-blooming flowers hung in the air.

"I've wanted to come out and see the garden," she said. "But I was nervous to come alone."

"You're right to be careful. There's a murderer loose." He radiated tension—did he never relax? "If I were you, I wouldn't go anywhere alone until they get more information."

He took her arm, but protectively this time, and she had to admit it felt good.

They took a sharp left onto an intersecting path, the music increasing in volume with every step. Finally they emerged from the shrubbery at the back of the adjoining hotel. Empty lounge chairs surrounded a darkened pool twice the size of the one at Ek B'alam. At the bar on the far side of the pool, loud bar-side chatter competed with the boppy rhythm of a five-piece Mariachi band.

Bernadette's spirits rose, buoyed by the color and laughter, so different from the melancholy atmosphere just a couple of hundred feet behind them. Caruthers had been a member of the Cultural Tour so while she assumed the police were asking questions here, too, they seemed to be focusing their investigation on the hacienda.

Rocky's shoulders began to relax as he surveyed the scene. "Let's get a drink."

"I didn't bring any money. You didn't give me a chance."

"It's okay. I'll buy."

He took her hand and led her around the pool, but she noticed he was scoping out the crowd as they threaded their way through the tables to the bar, instincts he must have developed from years on the road.

The Brits from the zip line greeted them from one table. A young couple from the hacienda sat at another. They weren't part of the Cultural Tour, but probably were trying to escape the tension, too.

They ordered margaritas and Rocky leaned casually against the bar, chatting to the friendly bartender while continuing to assess each group of people. When they finally got their drinks, Bernadette led him to the last empty table in a dark corner near the band, so close that the trumpet blasted right in her ear, but at least it had a good view of the room.

The band wasn't bad, for Mariachi. Gold buttons and tattered braid embellished brightly colored jackets and pants that had obviously seen better days and had possibly served several bands before. Many of the uniforms did not fit quite right, too short in the leg or rolled up at the wrists. The musician's sombreros reminded Bernadette that she still hadn't done her souvenir shopping. Maybe tomorrow on their trip to

Tulum.

Sitting back, she sipped her margarita and began to relax. This was the kind of holiday they hadn't had so far, and she was eager to grab a few minutes of pleasure.

The name of the bar glowed in neon script from the wall. *El Diablo*. Lurid masks with ghastly expressions lined the walls.

"I saw masks like that at Chichén Itzá," she said.

"Shaman's masks," Rocky said. Their gazes held for a minute. At least she thought they did. It was hard to tell through his mirrored glasses.

She smiled across the table at him. "Take off those glasses. What are you hiding from?" She'd thought it was from Pacho—but could it be from her?

He didn't return her smile, but he did take off his shades and slipped them into the pocket of his cream-colored shirt. His dark eyes reflected the light of the tiny hurricane lamp in the center of the table, holding Bernadette's gaze until the smile faded from her lips. Then his mouth quirked in a bit of a smile, just a tug at one corner, and he went back to surveying the crowd.

She never had any idea what that man was thinking.

As the evening wound on and the alcohol flowed, people began to dance. Bernadette loved to dance, but for the moment she was happy to just watch from the sidelines.

They ordered another drink. Along with the wine she'd had at dinner, the drinks were adding up. Her head started to spin. *Oh, my.* It was more alcohol than she'd had in years.

The band was wailing now, pulling old Herb Alpert chestnuts out of their repertoire.

Rocky was staring into the crowd and Bernadette followed his gaze to a table in the corner on the other side of the stage where two Mexican men had their heads close together, talking and gesturing vehemently. The man facing them was tall and angular, his greasy black hair swept back from his face. He looked familiar, but she couldn't identify him in the dim light.

The other man, with his back to them, had a ball cap. He emphasised whatever he was saying by waving his hands sharply. With the band playing right beside them, she couldn't hear what the men were saying, but she could tell from their body language that the discussion had escalated into a full-blown argument.

The man facing her slammed his fist on the table and glared as the man in the cap responded, jabbing a finger in his face. Then the first man stood up, threw down one last retort and shouldered his way toward them through the dancers on the floor. As he passed by, the flashing red light of the *El Diablo* sign highlighted the pulsing vein in his temple and the jagged scar on his neck. It was Ricardo Gonzales, one of the vendors from the Ox B'alam ruins.

But who was the other man? Bernadette looked back to the table, but all she could see was the back of his head. He held up his hand for another drink and then hunkered down in his chair, pulling the brim of his ball cap down to shield his face in a way that said he wasn't going anywhere. Between them, couples swirled on the dance floor.

Rocky said something she didn't quite catch, then he grabbed her hand and led her onto the floor. The music was slow and dreamy, and his arms hung loosely around her waist, belying the tension she could feel in every muscle of his body. Clearly, they weren't here to dance.

The band was too loud for talk, so she drew back and gave him a questioning look.

He smiled reassuringly and pulled her closer. Relaxing slightly, she put her arms on his shoulders and clasped her hands lightly around his neck. He manoeuvred them through the dancers and across the floor to a spot where they could see the profile of the man in the ball cap who had been arguing with Ricardo. Just as they got into position to get a good look, the man looked away, at the band. He looked Mexican, but that was all she could tell.

Suddenly the music changed. Maracas hissed and the tempo took off like a galloping pony. Rocky's eyes flashed to hers and a look of panic crossed his face.

She gave him a slow smile. So, Mr. Falconi didn't dance. Stepping back, she started to move to the beat.

He stood still for a moment, just watching her dance, then he began to follow her moves. As he swayed with the wave of dancers around them, she held his gaze, letting her shoulders accentuate the beat in counterpoint to the rhythm of her hips.

Lost in the music, she felt loose and free. The margaritas might have helped, but she had always loved to dance. Raising her arms above her head, she held his eye as she slowly brought them down, holding her hands out to him, never losing the beat with her hips.

His pupils flared. She grinned and twirled away.

Looking back at him over her shoulder, she laughed as he came after her through the crowd. When he caught her, she put her hands on his shoulders, pulsing back and forth. He responded by putting his hands on her hips, moving more easily than he had before in time to the music. As the band beat out the salsa mix, Bernadette channelled the rhythm through her hips, into his hands, and together they did who-knows-what steps around the floor.

When the music stopped, they fell together laughing. He led her back to the table and as she slipped into her seat, she wished she'd taken the chair beside him. Instead, as the band started another song, a traditional Mexican piece that wailed with emotion, she took a long drink of her now-watery cocktail.

"Shit," Rocky said vehemently.

She looked at him in surprise. Then her eyes flashed to the corner table. The man in the ball cap was gone.

Chapter 18

The boss pulled the ball cap down on his forehead, lit another cigarette and stepped back into the shadows of the courtyard. He had to think. Somewhere in the darkness a howler monkey screamed, but with so many worries, he barely noticed.

Diablo! The police had found Caruthers. The crocodiles didn't finish the job. His own fault. He should have taken the body farther from town.

He felt no remorse. Caruthers deserved it. He was just like all the other greedy tourists.

But the police were looking for the murderer and it was just a matter of time before Pacho stumbled on his record. He had to leave Ox B'alam. And quickly.

But first, he needed some money. He could sell the other statue, but not to the tourists at the hacienda. Too much like the one he sold Caruthers. It would bring in a bit of cash, but not enough.

No, he needed one last, big job. This time the price must be higher. The job must be slick, no room for error. This time it must be the real thing, not a clumsy imitation.

And he knew just where to get a piece like that. A jaguar statue, sleek and black with hypnotic jade eyes— any collector would drool when he saw it. He had gotten other artifacts out of the temple; he could do the same with the statue. But this time he would not share the take with anyone.

Then, once the money was in his pocket, he would vanish, like the jaguar, silently into the night.

Tuesday, Day 3

"I cannot imagine a picture more horribly exciting than that of the Indian Priest, his white dress and long hair clotted with gore, performing his murderous sacrifices at this lofty height, in full view of the people ..."

J.L. Stephens, <u>Incidents of Travel in Yucatán, 1842</u>

<u>Chapter 19</u>

The next morning, Bernadette danced across her hotel room floor as she headed for the shower, humming the mariachi tune from the evening before. Last night at *El Diablo* she'd felt young and sexy, flirting with Rocky when they danced. She shook her head and blushed. Must have been the margaritas.

She felt some guilt about sneaking away and enjoying herself with a murder investigation going on right here at the hotel, but sometimes a girl just needed a break.

After her shower, her mood continued to soar when she checked the itinerary and saw it was Tuesday, Day 3, and that meant another field trip. This time it was to Tulum, the ruins on the Caribbean coast, sixty miles away in the opposite direction from Chichén Itzá. She crossed her fingers, hoping the knock on the door meant they were still going because, ever since the discovery of the body, they'd had to take their plans day by day.

The body. It had ceased to be a person to her anymore. *Mr. Caruthers.* She tried to fix his features in her mind, but she had barely known him and now could hardly summon up a picture of his face.

She was glad they were leaving town again. Ox B'alam, the jungle, the lagoon, the crocodiles—it was all becoming increasingly oppressive. She longed for open skies and the fresh breeze off the ocean that Tulum's seaside location promised.

Her editor Jen's words, "not a surf and sand vacation," came back to her with new meaning. So far, she'd been dead right, but today Bernadette was looking forward to exactly that—some surf and sand. She'd read that Tulum boasted one of the nicest little beaches in the Yucatán and she planned to enjoy it. After pulling on her clothes over her bathing suit, she loaded her daypack with supplies.

Apparently, Tulum was a real town, and the itinerary showed they were going out for lunch and would have time to shop in the afternoon. She planned to ask Arthur to show her that antiquities shop he had mentioned. She still wanted to find a nice memento of the trip. Perhaps it was extravagant with her bank account so depleted these days, but she wanted something a little nicer than what she had seen at the vendors' booths at Old Ox B'alam. She'd been particularly drawn to the jaguar sculptures, the Night Sun God carved in shiny black obsidian, but the ones Ricardo sold had sharp edges and poor proportions that didn't do the sleek jungle cats justice.

Right now, just after dawn, the air was still fresh and clear, but she had been in Mexico long enough to savor the moderation. By mid-morning, the steamy heat would rise, and she knew she'd be hot and sticky again.

She made an entry in her notebook:

The rainy season has started, and enough rain had fallen in the weeks preceding our arrival that the low Guano Palms, whose leaves the Maya use for their traditional roofing, are losing their winter brown and shooting up fresh, green leaves.

When the sun beats down at mid-day, steam rises from the damp ground. We have been lucky, the rain god Chaac has looked down favorably on us and the weather is clear again today.

Locking her hotel room door, she crossed the hall and hurried down the stairs to the lobby, trying to ignore the red police tape that still barred Caruthers' door. In the dining room, everyone seemed on edge and conversation faltered as they waited for the bus.

When they finally pulled away from the hacienda, all heads turned toward the water. It was like passing an accident scene on the highway—you didn't really want to see, but it was impossible not to look.

They drove in silence around the forbidding lagoon. Ragged grasses lined the muddy banks and the dark backs of crocodiles floated offshore. One rickety listing dock, partly submerged, had a hand painted sign warning, 'Keep Out'.

On the distant shore, she could pick out a spot of red in the reeds. More police tape?

"I wonder if that was where they found Caruthers?" Rocky said softly in her ear.

"I don't know. And I don't think I really want to know."

Then the bus turned the corner and headed down the highway toward the outside world.

* * *

Bernadette stood on the edge of the cliff at Tulum, holding onto her hat and enjoying the stiff breeze. After the gloom of the jungle, the bright sun and open spaces made her spirits fly, and the fact that there was not a crocodile in sight made her positively giddy. The commanding presence of the pyramid, hanging right on the edge of the cliff against the azure backdrop of the Caribbean Sea, made up for the archeological site's relatively small size.

As she stood at the base of the *Castillo* steps, Annie breathed a reverent sigh beside her. "Imagine how Stephens must have felt when he discovered this pyramid."

Having seen the black and white plates in Arthur's book, Bernadette could easily imagine how awe inspiring it must have been for the Conquistadors to gaze up from the deck of the Spanish galleons and see the town riding high on a bluff over the ocean. Twentieth century reconstruction had pushed back the jungle, replacing it with an open park laced with paths and dotted with trees, but the buildings had not changed much since Stephens's time.

"Tulum was a much more recent city than Ox B'alam. Newer even than Chichén Itzá," Annie said. "It grew after 1000 A.D., centuries after cities like Ox B'alam and Tikal had died."

Bernadette thought Annie was probably right. The buildings were in much better condition than the piles of rubble at Ox B'alam.

"Tulum was still inhabited when Cortez sailed up this coast," Manuel said. "These buildings on the cliff were painted blood red, a spectacular and probably terrifying sight. The Conquistadors compared it to Seville, which at the time was the grandest city in Spain. It took the Spanish seventy years to destroy Tulum, but by 1600 it was deserted. Some blame the Spanish, but some blame the pirates that followed the explorers.

"The temple at the top of the pyramid was used for blood sacrifices to satisfy the gods," Manuel continued. "One can only imagine how, as the terror of the conquistadors grew, so did the number of beheadings."

A while later, Bernadette found a large rock in the breezy shade of tall swaying trees and sat down to make some notes.

I have become increasingly blasé about beheadings. These buildings are not as spectacular as Chichén Itzá, but I find sitting here in the shade at Tulum, with the ocean breeze and just a sprinkling of tourists, to be a more pleasant experience.

Ox B'alam is at the other end of the spectrum. Deep in the jungle, the oldest and least developed of the three sites, the overgrown buildings there are by far the most inspiring.

Each site had its own unique ambiance and she was glad she had seen all three so she could compare and contrast them in her article.

The original wall still surrounded this site and as the morning wore on, tourists streamed in through an arched opening. Manuel had made sure they were there early again and by eleven o'clock, even with the wind off the water, the heat was building. The members of the Cultural Tour straggled down the wooden staircase to the white sandy beach. With turquoise breakers rolling in and the Castillo perched high on the cliff above, it was another Caribbean postcard moment. The surf and sand opportunity she'd been waiting for.

Throwing her pack down on the sand, she stood with her face to the sun, her eyes closed, and breathed in the tangy salt air. This might be the only chance she had this trip to swim in the ocean and she wanted to experience it with all of her senses.

As she began to unbutton her blouse, Annie ran past her and plunged into the surf. The Aussies threw off their skimpy clothing, exposing even skimpier bikinis beneath. Rocky had his camera up but, even with the Aussies posing nearly naked nearby, he was watching her.

Bernadette stopped with her fingers on a button of her blouse, hoping he didn't want to take her picture again. She wasn't camera shy, but this was beginning to feel like too many pictures of her.

She undid another button and his gaze dropped to her hand. The wind blew his long black hair off his face and the gold earring glinted in the sun. Framed by the palm trees behind him, he looked like he'd stepped out of one of Manuel's stories: a dangerous pirate, or a Spanish explorer just off the ship. His eyes came back to Bernadette's and held. Her breath hitched. Then he lifted his camera and turned to the sea. She shook her head, trying to chase away the vision he conjured.

She didn't really know anything about him.

Her blouse sloughed off onto the sand.

She didn't think he was married. No ring.

Her shorts slipped down her legs and joined the blouse.

A girlfriend? Not one he'd ever mentioned, but then, they hadn't talked very much. He did seem to be getting friendlier, though. Maybe it was time they got to know each other better.

She'd invite him for a drink. Tonight.

Dropping her hat onto her pile of clothes, she raced down the beach and plunged into the breaking surf.

Chapter 20

An hour later, Bernadette shook the sand off her clothes and pulled them on over her damp bathing suit, hoping it would keep her cool. It was bound to be steamy in town as the sun crept past noon.

Tulum Pueblo was five miles from the ruins. A backpacker's paradise for many years, only the adventurous had discovered its pristine beaches. Now though, with the new road, it was an easy two-hour drive south from Cancun and some of the rustic beachside hotels had gone upscale. On the main street, Avenida Tulum, the sidewalks had sprouted curbs, and parking spaces lined a central island planted with baby palm trees. Still only four-feet-high, they illustrated just how recent this transformation was.

The five blocks of Avenida Tulum that made up the town center were still a ragged combination of thatched roof hotels and restaurants, bike rentals, souvenir stalls and internet cafes. Scattered among them were food stores and *farmacias* that catered to Mexican locals. Most of the tourists on the street were still hard-core trekkers in cargo shorts, hats and backpacks, not the resort folk that poured off the tour buses at the ruins in flip-flops and tube-tops.

Manuel herded the group under a drooping thatched roof into a restaurant called *Charlie's* and they settled at two wooden tables that stood side-by-side on the covered, street-side patio. Although the ocean was blocks away, a stirring offshore breeze kept the restaurant cool under the grass roof, even in the mid-day heat.

"Looks promising," Rocky said, pointing to a giant red chili pepper painted on their tabletop.

The table rocked on the rough stone floor like a ship on a stormy sea. Eloise handed Bernadette a matchbook with *El Diablo* stamped on the front to pass on to Hank. He folded the matchbook in half and getting down on his hands and knees, slipped it under one leg to steady the table. When he sat back up in his chair, Meredith turned to him with adoring eyes. You would have thought he'd built the table with own his bare hands. Annie didn't miss the exchange either and turned to Bernadette with eyebrows raised.

Manuel said *Charlie's* served food plain enough to suit the Morrises and Bernadette, but also made traditional Mexican food spicy enough for Rocky and Hank. Bernadette hated being placed in the same wimpy category as the Morrises, and ordered fish tacos, hoping they wouldn't embarrass her again in front of Rocky.

Thankfully, the tacos were delicious. They finished eating and were drinking their coffee when Rocky pulled out his camera and began taking shots of the group, with the lively main street in the background.

At the next table, Eloise and Celeste stuck out their chests to pose for the camera, framed by the conch shells lining the wall behind them. They were outrageous, but Bernadette got a charge out of their *joie de vivre*.

She called across to the other table. "Arthur, where is that dealer you told us about?"

He pointed out into the glaring sun. "Right across the road. I found it when Manuel brought us here for lunch the last time I took the tour."

Seeing Annie's scowling face, Bernadette added, "Did you say he has reproductions of relics?"

"Yes, reproductions and old journals, original art, all kinds of things. Some of it is junk, but some is worth looking at."

Rocky turned his camera on the chaotic street, where colorful signs sailed over the stores.

"I'd like to go," Bernadette announced, peering into the blindingly bright street beyond the shaggy roof, trying to pick out the store across the wide boulevard. She looked for Eloise, but she and Celeste were already walking into the souvenir shop next door, so Annie and Rocky volunteered to go with her instead.

"Go ahead dear," Meredith told Annie. "I'll just take a walk and meet you later at the van."

Bernadette wasn't surprised to see Meredith head out with Hank. A little romance? Too bad they hardly had any time left to get to know each other with the tour almost half over.

Happy to help in the cause of romance, Bernadette stood up and smiled at Annie. "Let's go, kiddo."

They crossed the road, Annie her usual chatty self. Bernadette suspected she was half-hoping to sniff out an illegal antiquities dealer. They all needed a break from the tension surrounding Caruthers' death and seemed to have managed to leave it behind for the day. Hopefully some of the horror would have faded by the time they got back to Ox B'alam.

The window of the antiquities shop looked like something out of a fifties B movie. A dusty painting of a bloody beheading on top of the *Castillo* dominated the back wall, blood dripping luridly down the white stone steps. Three priests stood at the top. The one on the left, in feathered ceremonial garb, held the victim's head triumphantly aloft. Another, on the right, raised what looked like the victim's heart, cradled in the palms of his hands.

The high priest stood in the center, draped in the skin of a jaguar, a black obsidian dagger raised high above his head. Behind them, the sun rose over an unnaturally blue Caribbean Ocean, the sky aflame with yellows and reds that lit the carmine walls of the temple.

"Very colorful," Rocky said in her ear. "It would look

lovely over the sofa."

Bernadette laughed. "Maybe *your* sofa."

A layer of whitish powder from decades of limestone road dust had sifted over a jumble of objects that made up the rest of the window display. A collection of broad, red clay bowls lined the back wall. Statues of people and animals carved out of shiny black stone littered the floor and, in the center, in an attempt at order, obsidian knives were laid out in a circle, blades pointing in. The black volcanic stone from the Sierra Madres was smooth and shiny when polished, sharp and deadly enough to make into knives and scalpels when split into blades.

Painted on the window in a circular motif were the words, "F. Akam, Dealer in Mayan Treasures." Bernadette reached out to touch the window as she walked by, her hand trembling as a low vibration rumbled through her. She frowned, but the tinkle of a bell distracted her as Rocky, a playful grin on his face, held open the door for her and Annie.

She shook off the uneasy feeling. She loved poking through a jumble shop like this, where you had to dig to find the treasures and, taking Annie's arm, she stepped into the gloomy interior.

Dust hung in the air, along with the faint musty smell of age and eucalyptus. Two tall shelves divided the space, making it impossible to see everything at once. Some items, broken pottery and tattered pieces of woven grass mats, looked like leftovers from a Meso-American garage sale. But who knew? There could be rare archeological finds hidden in the clutter, too.

The shelves held modern pieces as well, worn household items and even a sombrero. Remembering her promise to her son, she picked it up, but the crown was broken, so she set it gently back on the crowded shelf, careful not to start an avalanche for which she might ultimately have to pay. Surely Colin would prefer a bright new sombrero like the ones she had seen at the vendor's stall at the ruins in Ox B'alam.

Guilt settled on her shoulders. She hadn't called her son again. But really, what could she say? *Guess what? We've got a dead guy here and a murderer on the loose?* The last thing she wanted was for him to worry.

Rocky stood in front of a deadly display of armaments. Knives and spears with black obsidian blades marched across the wall like the weapons of a fallen army.

"Wicked," he said as she approached. "I wouldn't want to come up against one of these babies." He indicated a broad-faced club studded along the edges with prismatic obsidian blades.

"Whoa," she exclaimed.

"It's a *macuahuitl*," said a soft voice behind her.

She spun around, coming face to face with a short swarthy man with a twisted Salvador Dali moustache.

"They were used for rituals in the Late Classical period," he said. "That one is a reproduction. They are popular with tourists. Perhaps that is what you are looking for?"

"No!" She stepped back abruptly, and then smiled. "I mean, I don't think they'd let me take it on the plane."

The man bowed his head. "I am Fernando Akam, the owner of this shop. What can I find for you today?" With a wave of his hand, he indicated the packed shelves.

"I am looking for a sculpture. A reproduction," she hastened to add as Annie came around the end of the nearest shelf. "Maybe obsidian. I was hoping for a jaguar. Something with more finesse than the ones sold at souvenir stalls."

Mr. Akam's eyes widened. "You are in luck." He beckoned for her to follow him into the dim recess at the back of the store.

Mangy, taxidermied animals paraded across cabinets

on the rear wall. She recognized an armadillo, a monkey and a moth-eaten ocelot. Akam shuffled through the mess of books and papers piled on the long counter and pulled out a parcel, loosely wrapped in newspaper. He carefully unwrapped it and stood the stone carving on the counter.

Bernadette drew a sharp breath. It was exactly what she was looking for; twelve inches long, a black jaguar on the prowl. You could almost see him slink, muscles sliding under his loose skin. Her hand reached out and stroked his sleek back, a cool shiver of delight running through her. His pale green eyes seemed to glow from within. She didn't care whether the statue was old or new, she just knew she wanted it. At any price.

"The Night Sun God. Ek B'alam. It came in today. The Day Sun God is usually carved from golden onyx, but this black obsidian is used for the Night God.

"Strange," he continued, almost to himself. "I saw another obsidian piece very much like this one just last week. A man brought it in to have it authenticated. I had to tell him the piece was not old. A good copy, yes, but just a reproduction. "

A voice at her shoulder said, "That's what she wants, a reproduction." Bernadette turned to find Annie glaring at Mr. Akam. His eyes narrowed.

"And that is what I sell," he replied smoothly. "Reproductions." He turned back to Bernadette, the congenial salesperson once again. "This just came in. I have not had a chance to price it yet, but for you, nice lady, a good price. I think sixty American dollars." He smiled, showing a mouthful of yellow teeth.

"Ridiculous," Rocky said, at her other shoulder. Bernadette pursed her lips and shot him a look, but that didn't stop him. "She'll give you three hundred pesos."

"But—" She didn't have three hundred pesos.

"Impossible," Akam said, eyeing Bernadette. He put

his hand on the jaguar and she had to fight the impulse to reach out and snatch it back.

"Fine, then." Rocky took her arm and started for the door. She tried to pull away—she wanted that cat! —but his grip was firm.

"All right," Akam called. Rocky stopped and waited. "Three hundred and fifty pesos."

Rocky smiled.

"How much is that?" Bernadette whispered. "I only have ten pesos left."

"Thirty dollars," he said softly as they spun around and walked back to the counter. "Thank you, Señor. Three hundred and fifty pesos will be fine." He pulled out his wallet and counted it out. "You can pay me back later," he said to Bernadette.

Señor Akam pocketed the money swiftly. He carefully re-wrapped the sculpture in the newsprint and placed it gently in a plastic bag. Not trusting the heavy parcel to the plastic handles, she cradled it to her chest. "May I please have a receipt?"

Akam growled a response in Spanish. It didn't sound good.

"I'll need it for customs," she pressed.

Clearly unhappy, he brought out a yellowed pad and scrawled something across a page. There was no store name at the top, but the price and description were correct so she supposed it would have to do. Tucking the receipt into her shoulder bag, she picked up her precious parcel and together with Rocky, made her way toward the halo of light by the front door.

"Hey, guys," Annie called from deep in the store. They turned back into the gloom, towards the sound of her voice.

She was on the far side of a shelf crammed with piles of paper and rows of books, fighting to open a tightly rolled scroll. With Rocky's help, she managed to unroll it. Although not terribly old, the map appeared well used, the paper smudged and wrinkled. Looking over Annie's shoulder, Bernadette recognized the layout of the grounds of Ox B'alam.

"This is an archeologist's map," Annie said, clearly excited.

Bernadette looked at Rocky. "How many pesos do you have left?"

He grinned. "Enough." Together they walked back to the counter.

Bernadette stepped outside to wait. Heat rose in waves from the pavement. With her jaguar clutched to her chest, she leaned against the glass under the sign, 'Mayan Treasures', but this time she didn't feel any vibrations through the glass. It could have been her imagination the first time. Her mind playing tricks in the heat.

By the time Annie and Rocky emerged from the store, Annie triumphantly waving a cardboard tube containing her treasure, Bernadette was wilting from the heat. The bus was waiting not far down the street and they headed eagerly toward it. It was beginning to feel like home, a caravan for their group of gypsy travelers.

"It will take about an hour to get back to the hacienda," Manuel told them as they boarded the bus. "So, you can relax."

The bus pulled away from the curb and Bernadette sat back and stared out the windows, exhausted by the early morning, the hours of sun, swimming, shopping and lunch in town.

She'd never understood why people gave up the freedom of independent travel for a bus tour before, but now she got it. In Manuel's capable hands, she could truly relax. She felt pampered. There was nothing she had to do, nothing she had to think about. No one to pick up after or answer to. No plans to make, no bills to pay.

The only uneasiness was caused by the death at the hotel. It hovered on the periphery of her consciousness and really, she couldn't do anything about that, either.

They soon left the suburbs of Tulum behind. No shanty stores lined this road, just a green blur of jungle foliage that blocked any long-range views. Her eyes grew heavy and she sank back into the soft seat, feeling like a tired child after a school fieldtrip. Visions of ancient Mayan grandeur flickered through her brain as her eyelids drifted shut.

She was back at Tulum. The tourists were gone, and the crumbling ruins were whole and glorious, blood red against the startlingly blue sea, the limestone steps shining white in the sunlight.

She was scaling the pyramid, step by step. Her limbs were powerful and the climb was effortless. Moving strongly on all fours, her hands and feet ate up the distance, her limbs growing stronger with every step. Beside her, a man kept pace. A loincloth draped around his hips and a feathered breastplate covered his chest. More feathers, brilliant and exotic, decorated his headdress. As they continued their ascent, the stone steps turned pink, reflecting the setting sun.

At the top of the pyramid, the temple was gone. She was faintly surprised, but not afraid. They stepped up onto the platform, then turned to each other. The man looked familiar; his long black hair curled around his face, the setting sun glanced off his powerful shoulders. A smile curled his lips and as they turned to face the sunset, a cheer went up from people below.

Bernadette opened her mouth. A primitive and powerful cry uncoiled from her belly and she roared.

Her eyes flew open. She was on the bus.

Rocky looked at her quizzically, a sly smile quirking one side of his mouth. "Did you just snort?"

Her ears burned in embarrassment. "No, I did not. If you must know, it was a roar."

His eyebrows rose as he pulled his stupid sun glasses down on his nose with one finger and looked at her smugly over the lenses.

"Yes, a roar." She turned her face to the window and mumbled into the glass. "I was a jaguar."

It was Rocky's turn to snort.

Okay then. She certainly wouldn't tell him that he was the high priest.

Chapter 21

Back at the hacienda, Bernadette went up to her room, took off her sticky bathing suit and showered. Tonight, she felt like dressing up. She told herself there was no reason, but as she remembered dancing with Rocky the night before, a blush crept across her cheeks.

How high school. A crush on my partner.

She pulled on her dress and put on the silver earrings she'd bought from Ricardo. Looking in the mirror, she was glad to see her Vancouver winter pallor had disappeared. The dreaded freckles were popping out across her nose, but at least she had some color in her cheeks. A touch of mascara and she was ready to go.

Dinner was a quiet affair. Only two other couples shared the dining room with the members of the Cultural Tour. Everyone spoke quietly to their immediate neighbors, uncomfortably aware of the shadow of murder that lurked in the corners of the room.

After dinner, feeling oddly deflated, Bernadette returned to her room to work on her notes on the visits to Chichén Itzá and Tulum while the experience was still fresh in her mind. Pulling out her laptop, she settled in the chair in the corner. When she looked up again, an hour had passed. Satisfied with her effort, she set the laptop aside and wandered out onto the balcony.

The moon had not yet risen, and the lagoon loomed like a black hole in the darkened landscape. The only visible lights in the distant murk were the few dim bulbs at the restaurant at the main crossroad, off to the right across the lake. Crocodiles barked their ominous mating call back and forth in the distance and despite the oppressive heat, the thought of what might have gone on two nights before in the deadly lagoon sent a chill down her spine. The uneasy feeling forced her back inside, but restlessness propelled her to pick up the bag containing the jaguar statue and head downstairs, hoping to find someone at the bar.

Arthur was there, sitting with Hank. A strange pairing, but then, Hank seemed to get along with everyone. She settled onto the stool beside him and Salvador appeared to take her order.

"White wine, please," she said, out of habit. When the drink arrived, it looked pale and uninteresting and she said to Hank, "I have to try something more tropical next time. Any suggestions?"

A laugh rumbled out of his chest. "I'm not the one to ask. I always drink bourbon." He nudged the plastic bag. "What have you there?"

"A statue I bought today. I thought Arthur might be interested to see it." That finally got Arthur's attention and he watched as she carefully removed the mummy-like wrapping. "I bought it from the dealer you recommended."

While she worked on the wrapping, Rocky slid onto the seat next to her. He held up a finger and Salvador immediately got to work on his cerveza with lime.

A moment later, the black jaguar stood unfettered on the bar.

"Oh," Arthur breathed. "May I?" He reached out a hand for the sculpture.

Bernadette pushed the statue toward him down the smooth marble surface just as Salvador placed Rocky's beer on the bar. The glass caught the lip of the counter and plunged to the ground, smashing into a thousand pieces on the stone floor at Rocky's feet, icy cold beer splashing onto Bernadette's legs.

Salvador's eyes flashed from her face to Rocky's. "I'm sorry."

The sound of the breaking glass brought Luis rushing out of the kitchen. When he saw the mess on the floor, he disappeared back through the door, returning seconds later with a mop and pail. Salvador went down the bar to get Rocky another beer.

Celeste and Eloise arrived and crowded around Arthur, oohing and aahing over the statue. His shoulders shrank, as if to avoid the unwanted contact. As soon as Salvador delivered their fancy drinks, the two women moved to a nearby table, eyeing the spot at the end of the bar next to Rocky where Luis was cleaning up the mess of broken glass.

Bernadette eyed their tall, colorful glasses. The Aussies were obviously the ones to ask about tropical drinks.

Annie and Meredith appeared next, taking the stools next to Arthur.

He stroked the jaguar and murmured, "It's beautiful. So powerful. Are you sure it's a reproduction?"

"Of course it is," Annie snapped. "Bernadette wouldn't buy an illegal artifact."

Arthur looked at her, his eyes hardened, then he dismissively turned his back to her and faced Bernadette.

"I'm quite sure it's a reproduction," she said. "If it had been a real antique, I wouldn't have got it for thirty dollars. But I think the workmanship is lovely. You can really see him slinking through the jungle."

At that moment, Manuel walked into the bar with Chief Pacho. Silence descended over the group as if the specter of Caruthers had followed the pair into the room. Luis and Salvador turned their backs to the customers and busied themselves polishing the back counter.

The Chief stopped dead when he saw the jaguar on the bar. His eyes fixed on the statue, he walked over to Arthur who still had his hand on the cat's back.

"Is this yours?" Pacho asked quietly.

"No," Arthur squeaked, pushing the statue back down the bar towards Bernadette.

To save everyone trouble, she spoke up. "It's mine."

Pacho swung toward her. "Where did you get the statue?"

"I bought it today. In Tulum."

His face was unreadable, but from his overly restrained tone of voice, she knew it was bad news. Eyes back on the statue, Pacho waved a hand to summon his deputy who was waiting by the door. The young man hurried over.

"Wrap the statue in the newspaper," the Chief ordered. "Then take it into the office. Carefully. Do not touch the stone."

Even Bernadette knew what that meant. Fingerprints. And hers were all over it.

Of course they are, she reasoned, trying to calm her racing pulse. She had just admitted to owning the piece.

Admitted? It all sounded horribly accusatory.

She struggled to control her hysterical thoughts. All she had admitted to was buying the statue. Thankfully, she had the receipt tucked in her purse upstairs. She was glad she had pushed Akam for it.

"Please follow me," Chief Pacho said to her and headed for the lobby. As she slipped off her stool to follow, Rocky reached out and gripped her hand.

She looked at him in surprise but couldn't read the expression on his face. Was it anger or frustration? She felt he would jump to her defense if she asked, but surely she didn't need that. She hadn't done anything wrong. This turn of events obviously upset him though, and once again she realized how little she knew about Rocky Falconi.

Then she remembered her previous thoughts on the matter: perhaps he had been in trouble with the police.

She softened, feeling strangely protective.

"I'll be all right," she murmured. Then gently pulled her hand from his and followed Chief Pacho out of the room.

Chapter 22

The boss took a deep breath. He must remain calm. Appearances were everything.

His plans were going horribly wrong. The investigation was grinding on relentlessly and soon Pacho would stumble onto his background.

Remain calm, yes, but time to make his move.

Amazing how quickly the crowd at the bar dissolved into thin air when Pacho appeared. The one person left was, by his calculation, his best bet for one last lucrative sale before he disappeared.

Now was the time.

With a smile on his face, he stepped up to the bar.

Chapter 23

Her stomach in knots, Bernadette walked into the hotel office. Her bravado in front of Rocky was a sham. She was scared.

The deputy set a straight-backed wooden chair in the center of the room.

"Please sit down," Chief Pacho said, taking a seat behind Señor Ferrara's desk. "Now tell me about the statue."

He pulled a pad of yellow paper in front of him on the desk and raised a pencil, ready to take notes. The deputy stood by the door, as if she might try to escape.

Bernadette sat as instructed. Her hands were shaking so she clutched them together in her lap. She was in a foreign country—*Mexico!*—facing small town cops. She would have to answer Pacho's questions carefully.

And where did that come from? She had nothing to hide.

Taking a deep breath, she began. "I wanted to buy a memento, and although I liked the jaguar sculptures in the souvenir stands, I wanted something of a little better quality. So today at lunch, when we were in Tulum, I noticed a store across the road and a couple of us went over to see what they had."

"What store was that?"

She thought back. "Something like, 'Mayan Treasures'. Across the road from *Charlie's*."

She waited while Chief Pacho made a note. "Is that where you bought the statue?"

"Yes. I asked for a jaguar statue and the owner said he had one. We bargained a bit, and in the end, I bought it."

Pacho's eyes narrowed. "Why did you ask for a jaguar statue?"

"They caught my eye at the booths in the ruins parking lot here in Ox B'alam, but I didn't like the ones they had on display."

Chief Pacho made a note on the pad, then he looked up at her. "Why did you go to that particular store?"

She tried to keep her face expressionless while she considered how to answer this. Surely Arthur didn't need protecting. Anyway, wasn't the truth always the best policy? "Arthur, one of the members of the group, had been there before –"

"Mr. Bickenbaum," the Chief interjected.

Of course he knew Arthur. He had interviewed them all just two days before. "Yes, Mr. Bickenbaum had mentioned that the place had interesting souvenirs and pointed it out to me at lunch."

"How did Mr. Bickenbaum know about the store?" the Chief asked.

She paused. She had always had a strange feeling about Arthur. It was probably better not to try to explain his actions. No, he was on his own in this. She shook her head. "I'm afraid you will have to ask him that."

"Did you go to the shop alone?"

"No, Rocky and Annie went with me."

"Did you buy anything else?"

"No."

Chief Pacho stared at her for what seemed like an eternity. Her cheeks burned but she held his gaze firmly, reminding herself she had nothing to fear. She had done nothing wrong.

Finally, he sighed and said, "You may go. For now."

She stood up, released from the uncomfortable wooden chair. She reached for the sculpture but Pacho said sharply, "Don't touch that. We will keep it for now, as evidence."

"But why?" It was *her* jaguar.

"It is evidence in the homicide investigation," he said

impatiently.

She dug in her heels. "How could it be? I just bought it today."

Chief Pacho was silent for a moment. Elbows on the desk, he regarded her intently over pudgy steepled fingers. "It is the identical to the statue we found in Caruthers' room."

Bernadette's eyes flared in horror. Now she really was scared. She had bought the same statue to Caruthers', and Caruthers was dead. Murdered. This hit way too close to home.

She turned abruptly and left the office. As she walked through the empty dining room and onto the terrace, her knees shook as if an earthquake rumbled beneath the stone floor. Salvador was alone behind the bar. He frowned solicitously.

"Everything okay?"

"Yes," she said, then sighed and slumped down on a stool with her elbows on the cool marble counter. Exhaustion rolled over her. She rested her forehead on her fingertips and closed her eyes. "No, everything is not okay."

She raised her head as her indignation roared back. "Pacho kept my jaguar. I need something strong and colorful, Sal. And put one of those little umbrellas on top."

Salvador smiled. "You got it."

He went to work and soon a tall glass layered with colorful liqueurs stood in front of her. The pink umbrella on top raised her spirits considerably.

"What's it called?" she asked, turning the drink around to admire its elaborate construction.

He flashed her one of his electric smiles. "Mayan Rainbow. My own invention."

She took a tentative sip. Although it looked day-glow scary, it was icy and sweet and slid down incredibly easily. "This is fantastic."

Salvador smiled and nodded humbly. Maybe he wasn't such a bad guy after all, when he turned off the macho come-ons.

Taking the little umbrella off the top, she twirled it between her fingers. No wonder people liked these drinks.

He asked where they had gone that day and she told him about the trip to Tulum. She ended her story with the purchase of her jaguar and that reminded her of her interview with Pacho. She reached for her glass which, surprisingly, was empty. One glass of wine usually lasted her all evening. Disconsolate, she dropped her head onto her arms on the counter.

When Rocky arrived, Bernadette was alone at the bar. To be accurate, her head was *on* the bar. He wondered what Pacho could have said.

"He kept my jaguar," she moaned into the marble counter.

"Who kept your jaguar?"

Bernadette raised her head. "Pacho," she said, spitting out the word. She was obviously feeling no pain.

Salvador set a drink on the counter in front of her. Layered with toxic colored liqueurs, it looked strong enough to fell a horse.

"My God," Rocky said. "What's that?"

"Mayan Rainbow," Bernadette replied carefully. She sipped and then smiled wanly at the bartender. "Perfect, Sal."

She was already loaded, and probably wouldn't last much longer. If he wanted information, Rocky knew he'd better get it now.

"How did it go?" he asked, holding up a finger to Sal for a beer.

"What go?" She swiveled her head toward him

without removing her lips from the straw.

"What did Pacho want?" He didn't trust that guy and didn't like the way he seemed to be singling out Bernadette.

"He just wondered where I got the statue."

She took another sip of her drink. "You are a talented man, Salvador," she said, then added petulantly, into her drink, "He kept my jaguar."

"Why?" Rocky asked.

"He said it was evidence. A cloo-ue." Her eyes narrowed in what would have been a knowing look if her eyes hadn't crossed in the effort.

She took another sip. "This drink is great," she said, removing the green umbrella and twirling it between her fingers. "Apparently Caruthers had one too."

"An umbrella?"

"No. A statue."

Rocky looked at her sharply. "The same?"

"I-dentical."

Rocky rubbed his chin thoughtfully. "I guess he could have bought it at the same place."

"No doubt they will try to find that out," she answered, enunciating each word precisely. She tipped the glass back to get the last drop and then carefully set the empty glass on the bar.

When she started to slide off her stool, Rocky put out a hand to catch her. He grinned at Salvador. "Those things ought to come with a warning."

"I can take care of myself," she said and tried to wrench her arm away, only to knock her funny bone hard against the marble counter. "Ow," she said, gingerly rubbing her elbow.

Rocky put his arm across her back, under her arms, to hold her up. "Let me escort you to your room." For once, she didn't resist. In fact, she lay her head on his shoulder. "It's been a long day and tomorrow will be here in no time."

He steered her across the dining room and she leaned on him heavily as they climbed the stone stairs. He glanced at Caruthers' room as they passed. The police tape was still up but through the open door he could see Pacho's deputy inside. The man was wearing latex gloves and bagging a statue that looked just like Bernadette's.

"I want my jaguar," she whimpered.

"I wouldn't hold my breath." Rocky spun her around to her own door and held out his hand for her key.

She fumbled in her pocket and pulled out a used tissue, a pink umbrella and then a green one. Holding one umbrella in each hand, she asked, "How many did I have?"

"Enough." Rocky suppressed a grin and dipped his hand into her pocket, retrieving the key.

"Hey. Don't try anything funny," she said, struggling to stand straighter.

He opened the door. "Don't worry Mallow, I wouldn't think of it."

"Why not?" She crumpled against him again. "Don't you think I'm pretty? Nobody thinks I'm pretty. You know, I haven't had a date in three years."

"Really?" That answered his question of if she was married. Who then was the person she called 'sweetheart' on the phone? While he thought she would tell him anything right about now, it probably wasn't fair to ask.

He manoeuvred her into her room and sat her on the bed. She immediately fell backwards, arms akimbo. Long and slim, she lay with her eyes closed and a faint smile on her lips. He had a sudden desire to run his hands through her sun-streaked hair that spread out in waves on the embroidered coverlet, down her bare arms and her long legs. The sun had pulled faint freckles out on her nose. She looked young and desirable. And drunk.

Maybe he should help her undress.

He huffed out a laugh. Sure. That wasn't looking for trouble. Better to get out, now.

He reached for her hands and pulled her to her feet until she stood with her nose a few inches from his. She closed her eyes and canted forward until their noses touched. Her eyes flew open.

"You're cute," she said.

He laughed. "You're loaded."

He reached one arm around behind her and pulled down the zipper on her dress. "Get yourself undressed and into bed. They're getting us up early tomorrow morning and you're going to feel bad enough as it is."

Once he was sure she could stand on her own, he set her key on the nightstand and went to the door. She was right behind him. He put both hands on her shoulders and said, "Wait here."

Weaving slightly, she put a finger to her lips.

He stepped out into the hall and closed the door behind him, then turned to consider Caruthers' door. The deputy was gone but the red tape remained. He crossed the hall, pulled his shirt sleeve down over his hand and reached across the police tape for the doorknob. It turned in his hand and the door swung open.

Dammit. Now he had to go in.

He glanced down the staircase beside Caruthers' door. The coast was clear. As he stepped over the tape, Bernadette's door opened behind him and he turned just in time to catch her as she careened across the hall after him, zipper down, dress gaping open at the back.

"You're snooping," she said loudly, her eyes wide.

"Go back to your room, Mallow," he said softly, but she had already slung one leg over the tape. Suppressing a sigh, he took her elbow and helped her over.

"I don't think you're supposed to go in there," she

whispered.

He pulled her inside and quickly shut the door. Propping her back against the door, he said, "For God's sake be quiet and don't touch anything."

"Fingerprints," she said, nodding sagely. Crossing her arms on her chest, she pinned her hands in her armpits. He lowered his brows, trying to impress on her the seriousness of the situation, then slowly began to prowl the room.

A moment later he felt her creep up behind him. He glanced back. At least she still had her hands under her arms.

He followed her lead and put his hands in his own pockets. All he needed now was to have his fingerprints found in Caruthers' room.

Suitcase. Clothes piled neatly on the bed.

Everything was neat, nothing noticeably out of place. Caruthers hadn't been there long enough to unpack. Of course, the murder had probably not happened here, and there was no telling what the police had already bagged as evidence. Besides the jaguar.

He walked over to the bathroom and stopped in the doorway. He could feel Bernadette right behind him, peering over his shoulder. He tried to keep his mind on track, a neat trick with the heat of her body pressed against his back.

Toiletry case in the bathroom. Toothbrush. Blood pressure pills.

The cops hadn't said how Caruthers was killed.

Rocky turned around and Bernadette was right there. He put his hands on her upper arms and firmly moved her to the side. She wavered slightly when he let go, but when he was sure she could stand on her own, he crossed the room and looked in the garbage can.

Their heads cracked together as she bent to look with him.

"I told you to stay by the door," he hissed, rubbing

his forehead.

"Shhhh," she said.

Chocolate box. Folded piece of paper.

She reached down to pull it out.

"Don't touch it."

Her hand jerked back as if burned by a flame.

Taking a tissue from a box by the bed, he used it to cover his fingers as he picked the piece of paper out of the trash and spread it open on the desk. A sales receipt, the type you could buy in any office-supply store, handwritten for three hundred pesos. Someone had stamped, *Gonzales Souvenirs*, at the top. He had seen that stamp before.

Bernadette whispered, "Ricardo."

"Bingo. Let's get out of here." Carefully using the tissue to crumple the receipt back up, he dropped it into the garbage can.

With his hand on the distractingly bare, small of her back, he ushered her to the door. Then he used the tissue to turn the handle, wiping both doorknobs as he shut the door behind them.

They stepped over the tape and, taking Bernadette's hand, Rocky pulled her behind him across the hall and into her room, closing the door behind them.

His brow contracted in a thoughtful frown. "Three hundred pesos. That's almost what you paid for your jaguar in Tulum. I don't remember Ricardo having anything that good in his stall."

Bernadette shook her head forcefully, then stopped and put a hand to her forehead. A moment later she looked up, fairly clear-eyed. "There was nothing like that jaguar in Ricardo's stall. He wanted one hundred pesos for his cheap copies."

She walked over to the bed and stood beside it, dress gaping open at the back revealing the strap of her bra and a hint of white panties. She looked tentatively over her shoulder at him.

It was a struggle, but he stayed by the door. *Not tonight.*

"Get yourself undressed Mallow and get into bed," he said softly. He opened the door again and fiddled with the lock to make sure it would catch after him. Then turned back for one last look.

Her back was to him when her dress hit the floor. He grinned as she fell, face first, onto the bed, then he stepped into the hall and shut the door behind him.

Wednesday, Day 4

"...we entered a gloomy forest, [that with its] deep green foliage and mysterious buildings around, presented an image of a grove sacred to Druidical worship."

J.L. Stephens, Incidents of Travel in Yucatán, 1842

Chapter 24

When the knock sounded on her door the following morning, Bernadette's head throbbed like a jungle drum and all she could do was groan.

Struggling to drag herself out of bed, she got as far as sitting on the edge, head held in her hands. Someone was throwing daggers at her skull and hitting more times than they missed.

They were climbing the pyramid at Ox B'alam this morning. The sunrise from the top had better be worth it.

Her memory of the previous night was foggy. She vaguely remembered that the police were here and—that's right—they questioned her again.

And Pacho kept her statue.

She straightened abruptly at the thought, wincing as lightning bolts struck her skull. Squinting into the darkness, she remembered Rocky and Salvador were at the bar.

Her gaze fell on the two tiny umbrellas, one green and one pink, on the nightstand beside the bed and she groaned, "Oh, no," as she remembered the Mayan Rainbow.

Then she saw her dress lying on the floor and sucked in a sharp breath. She didn't quite remember that part of the evening. Luckily Rocky had acted like a gentleman—she thought—because she'd been in no shape to be in charge. She vaguely remembered some distinctly steamy thoughts on her part, although the order of events was cloudy.

Hoisting herself up from the bed, she was glad to see she was wearing underwear. She staggered to the shower. No doubt she would hear all about it at breakfast.

She emerged much clearer headed and the memories started to trickle back. She stopped with her shorts halfway up her legs and her jaw dropped when she remembered Rocky opening Caruthers' door. *Please, no.* But she couldn't remember any more than that.

She tugged on the shorts, then thought better of it, took them off and pulled on jeans. You never knew what might be lurking in the jungle at night, waiting to bite your ankles. And it was still definitely night.

Despite the headache that beat at her temples, she was determined to climb the pyramid this time. It might be easier without the brilliant sunshine. She'd take her lightweight travel flashlight and ditch her shoulder bag. It would be too much trouble while climbing in the dark. One of those headband flashlights would have been great. She'd make a note to get one for the next trip.

If there was a next trip. Things had been going dreadfully wrong and even though none of it was her fault, she hoped she could pull it together in the end and get a good story to Jen. She had to try to keep the emphasis on the cultural tour and not turn the article into a murder mystery. Headings like *Tourist Slain—Eaten by Crocodiles* didn't conjure up a traveler's dream vacation.

Cautiously, she looked in the mirror. Still not good. Dark circles ringed her eyes, the curse of a fair complexion. She peered at her reflection more closely. One good day in the sun and the dreaded freckles had popped out all over her nose. Her hair hung wet to her shoulders. Not too curly yet, but it would be when it dried. She twisted it up on top of her head and slapped on her hat to hide the damage.

When she stepped out into the hall, the red crime scene tape on Caruthers' door brought more memories flooding back. Her eyes widened as she remembered stepping over the tape and into the room. *What were we thinking?*

She had obviously *not* been thinking. Pacho had better not find out they went into Caruthers' room. She averted her eyes and, determined not to let the murder investigation spoil yet another day, headed down the stairs to the dining room.

Glancing quickly around, she was relieved to see there was no sign of Rocky. Annie—who was way too perky for the middle of the night—informed her that Rocky had already been down and had gone back up to his room to get his gear.

Thank God.

Her head was still pounding, and she wanted at least three cups of coffee before she heard the details of what had happened last night.

As it turned out, she only had time for one cup before Manuel arrived and hurried them out to the van. He looked annoyingly crisp in his white cotton suit. "You are lucky to be on the full moon tour. It is the only time it is safe to climb the pyramids before dawn to see the sun rise from the summit. It will be worth it."

She tried to believe him as she took her regular seat in the van. A few minutes later, Rocky jumped in and sat down beside her. He was full of energy. She could almost see his mind working, but then, he was used to these pre-dawn excursions. He'd told her he got his best shots either very early or very late in the day. It had something to do with the quality of the light.

She, on the other hand, was never good this early. She leaned her head against the cool glass of the van window and looked out at the full moon. Still high in the sky, it gave a faint glow to the water as they drove around the lagoon. Scanning the shallows, silhouettes of reeds stood out against the silvery water, but it was too dark to see if any predators lurked within the cover.

Where do crocodiles sleep? she wondered. Do they hunt at night? She vaguely recalled from her son's school report, that crocodiles have hardly changed since dinosaur times. Essentially the same as their prehistoric ancestors, the thought of their primitive, cold-blooded brain gave her the creeps.

Moonlight lit the white gravel parking lot at the ruins. Everyone tumbled out of the van and gathered their gear. Manuel supplied flashlights, but Bernadette stuck with her own, new, lightweight travel model.

The group assembled at the gate and funneled in, one at a time. The archeological site was not fenced in, as Manuel had warned on their first visit. The entranceway was just for show, a simple gate made of poles adjoining a fence that resembled a flimsy midway stockade and petered out forty feet on either side.

The jungle canopy quickly snuffed out the faint light of the parking lot and all but a few stray beams of moonlight. Flashlights clicked on around her and she cursed her thin pencil beam, wishing she'd accepted the weight of a more substantial light. She shone her flashlight left and right. Although not enough light to see by, it reflected hundreds of tiny insect eyes glinting evilly back at her from the thickets.

Rocky, as usual, was in the lead, his white shirt glowing faintly in the dark. She jogged around the pack of bouncing lights to catch up with him and fell in step beside him, reassured by his bulk and confidence.

The jungle seemed unnaturally quiet, the crunch of their footsteps on the path the only sound as they marched the coral trail through the darkness. A blood curdling shriek pierced the night and she jumped, her heart hammering in her throat. Rocky chuckled and she realized that she'd grabbed his arm.

"You are annoyingly calm," she said, stepping quickly away.

"That's because there's nothing out there to worry about. Except maybe a jaguar hunting for his breakfast."

She could hear the teasing note in his voice.

"Or a tarantula," Hank said, right behind her.

"Dawn is a great time for wildlife shots. Maybe we'll see a pit viper," Rocky added.

As he and Hank proceeded to amuse themselves, Bernadette dropped back a few paces and tuned them out. Instead, she listened to the first quiet twitter of birds as the jungle awoke.

The exotic predawn atmosphere heightened her senses. A buzz ran just under her skin. She felt ready for anything,

The trees thinned and moonlight paved the ground. A faint glimmer ahead lit the way to the clearing. In the center, the pyramid glowed, white stone steps shining under the full moon.

Rocky already had his tri-pod on the ground and was attaching his camera on top. He stood at the edge of the trees, far enough back to frame the entire structure in the shot and snapped the glowing monolith in the moment it took for the group to stop and catch their breath before they swarmed up the steps.

Bernadette took out her recorder and spoke into it softly. "My heart pounded in awe when we emerged from the dark jungle into the dusty plaza of the kings. Moonlight shone like a spotlight on the pyramid in the center of the clearing and I could feel the power of the ancient Mayan Kingdom—the glowing pyramid reaching majestically up to the sky, the full moon and the gods."

As the team surged up the face of the monument, Rocky continued taking shots from the edge of the clearing, now focusing on the climbers.

She shouldn't wait for him. He always walked faster than she did and even with the burden of his gear, he would be up the pyramid in half the time it would take her to get to the top.

As she turned to go, a shadow moved in the jungle, separating itself from the black columns of tree trunks.

Beside her, in the darkness, Rocky's head came up and he scanned the forest. He'd seen it too.

"Wildlife," he whispered and snapped the tripod closed, turning to follow the shadow. She watched him move stealthily into the blackness, his flashlight beam low, raking the undergrowth.

"What is it?" she whispered, following him into the trees. Snapping on her light, she swept the narrow beam across the dense foliage. As she waited for her eyes to adjust to the darkness, gravel crackled and ten feet ahead a large shape split in two.

Her mind grappled with the illusion, finally realizing a person had stepped out from behind a tree to Rocky's right. Before she could warn him, a dark hand snaked out from behind the tree next to her and covered her mouth. A strong arm encircled her waist, pulling her roughly back, tight against a man's sinewy body.

She struggled, her elbow hitting a tree trunk sending a hot bolt of pain up her arm to her shoulder. Her flashlight flew out of her hand.

"Quiet, lady," a man whispered in her ear in a low, heavily accented voice. "Be quiet and you be all right."

She stiffened. He held her tightly from behind. She

couldn't see his face and couldn't have moved if she tried. His hand was clamped roughly over her mouth, heavy rings cutting into her lips. A smoky, resinous odor filled her nostrils, combined with an acrid scent of fear that she was sure was her own.

He swung her around. The crunch of breaking plastic sounded loud and unnatural as she stepped on her flashlight, crushing out its fragile beam. She'd lost sight of Rocky, but she could hear him grappling with another man in the darkness.

Arms pinned to her sides, her assailant jerked her along with him as he dragged her further into the jungle. Lurching through the undergrowth, she faked a stumble to slow him down, but he yanked her roughly to her feet.

His large sweaty hand covered her nose and her every breath was a struggle. She tried to bite his palm, but her teeth couldn't get a grip on his taut flesh. Fear darkened the edges of her mind as a lack of oxygen caused her vision to grow dim. Her eyes drifted closed. Somewhere in the far reaches of her brain, she remembered a scene from a movie. Sandra Bullock, dressed in a ridiculous folk costume, demonstrated self defence moves as her partner grabbed her from behind. Bernadette couldn't remember the anacronym, but the actions were clear in her mind and her brain took over.

She stamped on the man's foot with her heel and his arms loosened enough for her to elbow him in the soft spot just under his ribs. He grunted and his hand released her mouth. She sucked in a painful, jagged breath and her eyes widened as a tri-pod came at her in the dark. She ducked as it smashed into her assailant's head.

The man gave her a shove and she fell to the ground, coral-sharp gravel grinding into her palms and knees.

Another strong arm circled her waist and hoisted her to her feet. Before she could struggle, Rocky yelled,

"Run!"

Chapter 25

Rocky released Bernadette and she took off at a run. He grabbed her hand and jerked her back in the opposite direction and together they crashed through the bush, glancing off trees and stumbling over piles of cut stone that littered the ground like a pre-Columbian obstacle course.

Rocky's bare arm hit a tree and she heard him curse. He dropped her hand and she ran full out behind him, following blindly, hoping he knew where he was going—praying they weren't heading deeper into the jungle.

Branches and razor-sharp palm leaves slapped her arms. One hit her in the face and whacked the hat off her head, but she kept on running.

It seemed to be getting lighter. Either the jungle was thinning or the sun was rising. Either way, it meant she could run even faster.

They raced down a narrow trail, making so much noise she couldn't tell if their assailants were still following. Then, from behind, she heard a shout. The chase was still on. Adrenalin shot to her heart and legs.

They seemed to have a good lead, but her lungs were burning and her knees screaming. She couldn't keep up the pace much longer. How long did adrenaline keep pumping? Did it suddenly run out and you collapsed on the ground? If so, lost in the jungle, they'd be easy prey for whoever was chasing them.

Rocky skidded to a stop and she ran into his heaving back. She doubled over, hands on her thighs, trying to catch her breath.

They were surrounded by a group of poles, each the diameter of her leg. A staircase arose in the center. *The zip-line tower.* She straightened, still breathing hard. That meant the park entrance, the parking lot and the van should be just to their right.

She concentrated on trying to hear their attackers over the rush of blood in her ears. In the darkness, distant voices called out in Spanish. The voices came from the right, getting closer by the second. The van was out of the question.

She leaned against a post, breathing in spasms. Her eyes met Rocky's.

"Up," he ordered.

Her jaw dropped as he bolted to the tower stairs. Surely not. They'd be trapped like rats up there.

But the sound of snapping underbrush and the voices that were getting louder by the second propelled her up the stairs after him like a stone from a slingshot. Their footsteps echoed on the flimsy wooden treads. There was no turning back now.

Hearing a bang above her, she looked up. A square of dim light had appeared over their heads. There was a trap door at the top of the stairs, and Rocky disappeared through it. Seconds later his arm, writhing with dark tattoos, emerged from the opening. She reached up to grab it. His strong hand wrapped around her forearm and hauled her up through the opening, dropping her onto the wooden floor.

"Shhh!" they both hissed.

Looking down through the opening to the clearing below, Bernadette saw movement in the growing light. Freeing the trap door, she swung it closed as quietly as she could, but couldn't suppress the final thud. She threw the bolt and they were safe—for the moment. If safe is being trapped in a tower with the enemy below and no way out.

Taking a steadying breath, she turned around. Rocky had slung his camera and tri-pod onto his back and was strapping himself into the zip-line harness.

"NO," she cried.

"Yes," he said firmly as he hooked the last clasp. Reaching over his head to where the harness connected to the line, he gave a sharp tug.

What choice did she have? Zip-line over the crocs in the lagoon or deal with whoever had chased them to the tower. She didn't have time to compare and contrast. The zipline was the only way out.

But there was only one harness and Rocky had commandeered it. Surely he wouldn't leave her trapped in the tower?

Sharp footsteps echoed on the tower stairs as the men began to climb.

She looked desperately into Rocky's eyes.

"It held Hank," he said, daring her with a lopsided grin.

Her eyes flared. He had to be kidding. She looked down at the trap door. The sounds below were louder now; each footstep rang out on the stairs like a gunshot.

She closed her eyes, resigning herself to her fate. Then she opened them to meet his. "How?"

He reached out and tugged the corner of her shirt, pulling her toward him. The grin on his face widened to a real smile.

Her jaw dropped. He was loving this.

His smile pulled her like a magnet until they were eye to eye. He wrapped both arms around her waist pulling her into a tight embrace. Her hands moved to his shoulders and his lowered to cup her bottom.

"Jump," he whispered, and she did. He pulled her in even tighter and she wrapped her legs around his waist, tightening her arms around his neck.

She stared into his eyes for a moment, but a sharp bang on the door under their feet snapped them back to reality.

"Hold on," he said, and ran toward the end of the

platform.

They leapt into oblivion. Air whooshed past her ears as they flew out of the tower. There was one moment of weightlessness, then a sharp jolt as the harness took hold. Rocky's hands squeezed her tighter.

Inches below the soles of her feet, the upper branches of the trees whisked by. A family of monkeys in a treetop froze, eyes wide. A baby monkey clung to its mother's neck, much like she clung to Rocky.

Frantically she tried to figure out their combined weight and compare it to Hank's. Spots flashed in front of her eyes and she realized she was holding her breath. Pushing all the air out of her lungs, she sucked in a fresh gulp.

They soared out beyond the trees and across the road towards the lagoon. They were flying free. Looking over Rocky's shoulder, she saw two men break into the tower room—too late.

Time stopped, and they clung together, her legs clamped tightly around him, his strong arms holding her close as they flew over the water. She could feel their hearts hammering together in overdrive and she pressed her cheek to his, the stubble of his morning beard rough against her skin. As the sky began to fill with gold, a grin spread across her face.

Her gaze drifted down from the brightening sky to the trees on the far shore and finally to the dark water below. She was flying backwards, but she could feel the water advancing by the second as they whizzed in low, barely skimming the sparkling surface. As they flew over black mounds of crocodile backs floating near the shoreline, she suddenly remembered she wasn't belted in. Ice ran through her veins and she clutched Rocky's neck even tighter. But strangely, as they neared the shore, she felt a twinge that might have been regret.

Rocky's feet hit the landing platform and he threw his

hands out in front of him. She clamped her legs tighter around him as momentum carried them across the hut.

Her back hit the hay bale with an impact that forced all the breath from her lungs. The platform spun. She closed her eyes and leaned back into the prickly hay.

Rocky's hands slid under her again, taking up her weight. She opened her eyes and saw his, inches away, hot and unfocused. Then his mouth closed hungrily on hers.

She met his lips with equal force and his sharp, quick heat shook her to the core. Adrenalin pumping, her hands clutched his head, fingers twining in his hair, as she'd wanted to do for days.

Then he pulled away, the grin still on his face. "Can you stand on your own now? You're no feather weight you know."

She wasn't sure she could, but she unlocked her legs and put her hands back on his shoulders as he set her gently on the platform. The weightlessness was still in her limbs and she sank slowly to the floor.

Rocky unclipped the harness and rubbed his shoulders where the straps must have dug in. Her extra weight probably hadn't helped.

"You almost strangled me back there," he said.

She shook her head, trying to clear it. Visions of the race through the jungle rushed back with a jolt. She sat up straighter. Her eyes dropped to a pair of crocodiles, watching them with interest from the shore.

Dragging her gaze up from the crocs to meet his eyes, they held the look for a long moment. *What just happened?* Her cheek burned from the scrape of his beard as they'd soared across the lagoon and her heart kicked again as she replayed their passionate kiss. Was it adrenalin? He was humming with it too, she could tell. And she wanted to do it again. All of it.

Her tongue darted out on its own volition, to taste

him on her skin. His eyes dropped to her lips and she quickly came back from wherever she'd been.

"Sorry I grabbed you," she said, "I suddenly remembered the crocs."

He glanced at the shore, the smile leaving his face. "They gave me a moment too, at one point." Then he laughed, a freer, more honest sound than she'd heard from him yet. "But my God—wasn't it fantastic?"

She put her head back and laughed, with exhilaration and relief. She could see how adrenalin could be addicting.

He reached into his back pocket for his cell phone and punched in a number, then frowned at the welts rising rapidly on his forearm. "These beggars are really starting to hurt. I wonder what I ran into?"

He sank down beside her, as if the adrenalin had suddenly drained from his muscles. A moment later Manuel answered his cell. From where they sat hip-to-hip on the floor, she could hear Manuel's frantic tone.

"She's with me," Rocky said. "We're okay. Ran into some trouble but we're back near the hotel now, at the zip-line dock. Keep the group together and get back here as quick as you can."

He snapped his phone shut and rubbed a hand over his face. "Think that'll make a good story?"

She wrenched her eyes off the croc that was staring at them from the shallows twenty feet away and looked back to the tower across the lagoon. "What was it all about? Who were they? What did they want?"

Rocky rubbed his neck. "I think they wanted my camera. My guy almost tore my head off trying to get it."

"But why?"

"I don't know."

They continued to sit, legs straight out, backs against the itchy hay bales. Soon, headlights turned out of the parking lot across the water and the van made its way around the lagoon in the misty morning light.

"If they wanted your camera enough to attack us and chase us through the jungle, I guess the fact that they didn't get it isn't reassuring."

"No. Probably not."

"Why would anyone want your camera? This wasn't just a snatch and grab. They followed us right up into the tower. Who knows how far they would have gone if they'd caught us?"

Shrillness had crept into her voice as the possibilities became clear. "We could have ended up two more tourists, floating in the lagoon." They looked at the crocs, which had lost interest in them and were creeping into the shallows.

She felt Rocky shudder. "I hate those crocs," he said softly. "I wonder if Caruthers was dead when he hit the water."

She groaned. "Thank you for that. I've been trying not to think about it."

"Pacho isn't saying."

"No. He's certainly keeping his cards close to his vest."

"I have to wonder if it's just good police work, you know, suppressing the facts, hoping someone will say something they aren't supposed to know, or if it is part of a cover up."

"Very comforting, Falconi."

"I don't trust cops. They can be as dirty as anyone else." He muttered the last bit mostly to himself as Manuel's van pulled up on the road beside them in a cloud of dust.

Chapter 26

Bernadette had never been as glad to get back to the hacienda as she was that morning. Luis immediately brought a pot of strong coffee into the dining room and after two cups, her nerves began to settle.

"Tequila would be even better," Rocky said.

He was only half joking, and if it wasn't still shy of ten in the morning, she might have agreed.

Hard to believe it was still morning. Most of the others had gone to their rooms to change into clothing more suitable for the rising heat, but Hank and Manuel joined her and Rocky in the dining room.

Her adrenalin must have stopped pumping because her knees and palms hurt like she'd been stung by a hundred bees from her fall on the coral path. When she tried to pick out the tiny pieces of white gravel embedded in her palm, Manuel saw her and leapt into action, pouring disinfectant on her hands and knees. It burned like acid.

She squealed. "Ow."

"Suck it up," Rocky said. "It's easy to get infected in the tropics."

"We must report this attack to the police," Manuel said.

Bernadette's heart sank. "Do we have to?"

Two interviews in two days with Chief Pacho had been more than enough. She had been a little excited about the first one, never having been interviewed by the police before, but although she was not the least bit involved in the case, even that had turned out to be surprisingly uncomfortable.

Then, last night, her jaguar interrogation. She didn't want to go through that again. Actually, she would prefer not to speak to Pacho at all until he found the murderer. She had a sickening feeling the Chief was beginning to think that she was involved.

And she could see by the set of Rocky's jaw that he was opposed to reporting the attack, too. But then, he never seemed to want to talk to the police. She suspected he had something to hide, maybe didn't want Pacho to run his name through the system. Possibly had a previous arrest or had even done jail time.

She glanced at him sideways. That would explain the tattoos.

Not that she thought he was connected to Caruthers' murder. Hoped not anyway, because she had to admit, the guy was growing on her.

"It's okay," Rocky said to Manuel, his tone deceptively mild. "We weren't hurt, and they didn't get anything. These things happen when you're on vacation."

These things happen? She turned to him, her eyebrows so high they nudged her hair line. Being attacked, chased through the jungle and then having to escape on a zip-line? *Excuse me*. These things did not happen to her, vacation or not. She squinted and bit her lower lip, trying to figure out what he was up to, but came up blank.

"They don't happen here," Manuel said indignantly. "This is not Cancun. We are proud of the safety of our guests. And of our own people. No one here wants thieves."

He shook his head sadly. "Things have changed in recent days. Something is very wrong. First Mr. Caruthers, now this. And both incidents to members of our tour. What is happening to my village?"

He hoisted himself out of the chair like a tired old man and slowly walked out of the dining room.

Silence descended. Finally, Hank said, "So, what do you think is going on?"

Rocky shook his head, his lips pressed firmly together. "I don't know, but whatever it is, I don't like it."

* * *

After lunch, Manuel gathered the group in the lobby, trying to get the tour back on track. Bernadette's heart went out to him as he struggled to keep his head above water while his schedule disintegrated around him.

"We will go to Ox B'alam village," he announced. "We can do nothing more here. My friend Maria is expecting us and will be disappointed if again we do not come."

"I don't think we'll go," Mrs. Morris said, taking a step back.

Bernadette had to admit she felt awkward too, like a rich gringo voyeur going to look in strangers' houses.

"That is up to you," Manuel said seriously. "But my friends will be hurt if you do not go." He looked around the lobby at the rest of the group. "They will think, 'these foreigners think my house is not nice enough to visit.'"

Mrs. Morris looked chastened. "Well then, all right. I wouldn't want that."

Bernadette hid a smile. Manuel was good. He'd managed to ease her own mind about the visit, too. In the end, everyone climbed into the van and they retraced their regular route along the shoreline, past the zip-line hut and the sinking dock. Near the restaurant on the corner, two skinny dogs, tails between their legs, were pulling garbage from the bins. She had meant to get down to the restaurant to try some authentic local food, but between day trips and police sequestering, they had been too busy to fit in a meal under the colorful plastic streamers on the restaurant patio.

This time, as they passed the restaurant, they drove

right past the road to the coast that they usually took and continued around the lagoon.

Since they'd found Caruthers' body, her reaction to the lagoon had been downgraded from 'tropical and exotic' to 'bleak and menacing'. There was something discomforting about the undefined shoreline. Anything could be hiding in the reeds.

She still clung to the hope that the authorities would discover that Caruthers' killing had been a random attack, a robbery gone wrong, and would tell them that the murderer had left the vicinity.

But what about their assault in the jungle this morning? Were the two attacks related? It was hard to believe otherwise. Last night she had been worried because she had bought a twin of the statue the dead man had in his possession, but now she didn't even have the statue anymore and yet she felt sure someone had targeted them in the jungle that morning.

She was scared, and decided that from now on she would stay closer to the group, or in the hotel. There had to be safety in numbers.

A quarter of a mile past the restaurant, the van turned away from the lagoon onto an unpaved road. She wrenched her eyes away from the water and her mind from thoughts of its primordial residents, and concentrated instead on the brightly colored, concrete block buildings that lined the road and the village square, which was dominated by a large two-story building with arched verandas that was painted bright royal blue.

Once past the square, the scene changed. Here most of the houses were small, grass roofed structures. Whitewashed, loose-stone fences ran the length of the street, keeping small children and livestock corralled in the yards.

"There. Maria is waiting," Manuel said, pointing to a petite Maya woman standing patiently by her gate, hands folded in front of her, a pleasant smile on her face. Her long dark hair was pulled back into a smooth bun and she wore a white cotton dress with three inches of heavy, colorful embroidery on the hem and yoke. When she saw the van, her smile broadened, dispelling any qualms Bernadette may have had about intruding.

Manuel went alone to speak to Maria first and, as if a cloud had passed over the sun, the smile left her face. They spoke in low voices for a minute, no doubt about the murder, and Bernadette couldn't help thinking how devastating it must be for everyone in the community.

When Manuel and Maria turned to address the tour group, however, the smiles were back on their faces. The tour was business, and they wouldn't want to spoil the tourist experience.

Manuel explained that Maria spoke only Mayan and he would translate everything she said.

Rocky was already exploring the yard, photographing a fat little pig that rooted at the base of a fruit tree in a garden where vegetables grew exuberantly, in no apparent order. Although Bernadette wanted to join him, she followed Manuel over to the house instead. He was speaking as he walked, so she pulled out her recorder and hurried to catch up.

The house was constructed of vertical saplings lashed together to form walls atop a whitewashed stone foundation. A thick grass roof overhung the top of the walls making the doorway so low that Bernadette had to duck when she followed Maria and Manuel inside.

The house was composed of one large room with the front and back doors lined up to catch the breeze. Bernadette made notes, her gaze darting around the room. Half of the building was devoted to the kitchen; a counter and dry sink tucked under open shelving, with a two-burner stove and miniature refrigerator. The other half of the house was filled with woven sleeping hammocks, hung like fishing nets from wall to wall. Exposed electrical wires ran from a light bulb in the ceiling, around the interior perimeter of the roof, then out to the pole in the yard where black electrician's tape spliced it to the main power line in a tangle of wires that looked like a fire ready to happen.

An old Singer treadle sewing machine stood in a prime spot under a splash of light from the front door. Maria sat down and began working on an intricate, half-finished piece of embroidery, her feet efficiently working the treadle. There was no zig-zag stitch on the machine, but she expertly manoeuvred the white cotton fabric back and forth making colorful flowers bloom under the needle, just like the ones on her dress.

Bernadette bent down and ran her hand over the familiar black ironwork of the antique machine, a trademark spider in a web worked into the casting of the stand. "I learned to sew on a machine just like this one," she told Manuel. "It belonged to my grandmother."

When he relayed the message to Maria, her face lit up. Rocky squeezed into the doorway beside Bernadette just in time to shoot the pleased look on Maria's broad face without a flash, using the shaft of natural light.

Warmth spread through Bernadette's chest and she stood a little straighter. Finally, they were working as a team.

Always with a smile on her face, Maria led the group into the backyard where kitchen implements lay on tables and benches under the trees. Amidst scrubby plants and free-range chickens, a kinkajou, the family pet, was sleeping, chained outside his cage, in the shade of a broad-leaved avocado tree.

The rich, sweet fragrance of orange and grapefruit blossoms filled the yard. Bernadette scribbled madly, trying to capture the mood through details in her notes.

The village children, well dressed, bare foot but clean,

converged on the backyard. The tour group's visit was obviously a village event. A gang of boys grinned and pushed each other around, shy but eager to meet the guests, all wanting to be in Rocky's pictures.

Bernadette watched from across the yard as Rocky knelt to show the boys his tattoos, flexing his biceps, making the pictures move. The boys, laughing and squealing in delight, turned to Manuel, talking and gesturing the way little boys do. Not so different from her own son and his friends back home.

Manuel laughed and said to Rocky, "They think you are a superhero."

Rocky seemed genuinely pleased and once again Bernadette was struck by how little she knew about the man.

The children crowded around Manuel and he led them as they proudly counted together in English.

"They learn English in school," he said. "It is important if they want to work in the coastal resorts when they are older. Or, like Maria's son Luis, at our own hacienda."

The tour moved on, down the road to another house that boasted a small TV in a room full of hammocks. Outside, women were weaving more hammocks to sell at the local co-operative store.

While the others watched the weavers, Bernadette followed Manuel around to the back of the house, making notes as she walked.

"Where are the men?" she asked.

"Working at the resorts, or in the city. If they are lucky, they come home once a week."

In the back yard, in the shade of blooming fruit trees, an old woman sat on a white plastic chair, her deft fingers sorting skeins of colored yarn that hung on the wooden, ladder-back chair in front of her. When she saw Manuel, her craggy face lit up. Stiffly, she rose from the chair and came forward to greet him, taking his hand in both of her own as she spoke.

He kissed her softly on one wrinkled cheek.

"This is Mama Rosa, my great aunt and a wise woman of the village."

He introduced Bernadette to her in Mayan. Mama Rosa spoke softly and smiled. The old woman dropped Manuel's hand and took Bernadette's face in her small gnarled hands. Her gaze was hypnotic, and Bernadette felt a wave of calm washed over her. She couldn't look away. Didn't want to. This was the safest, most relaxed she'd felt since she had arrived in Ox B'alam.

Mama Rosa spoke in Mayan and Manuel translated. "She says, she can see in your eyes that you, too, have the sight. She says, times will get darker but you will find the way."

"What does she mean, 'darker'?"

Manuel asked the old woman, but she just cackled warmly, as if at a child who asked foolish questions. Then she dropped her hands, releasing Bernadette from the spell.

"She says, you will know."

Mama Rosa waddled back to her chair and sat down. Still smiling, she picked up her rainbow-colored yarns and went back to her task.

Manuel seemed to accept this prophecy as completely normal. Without batting an eye, he turned to talk to the rest of the group who, Bernadette suddenly realized, had congregated behind them.

"This is the end of our formal village tour. Feel free to continue to explore the village if you wish and make your own way back to the hacienda. A pleasant walk. For those who wish to go straight back, we will go now in the van."

Still dazed, shaking off Mama Rosa's spell, Bernadette turned and found Rocky's eyes burning into

her.
   Rats.

Chapter 27

From the questioning look in Rocky's eyes, Bernadette could see he had heard what Mama Rosa had said, and Bernadette wasn't ready for the fallout.

"I'll walk back to the hacienda," she said quickly.

"Me too," Rocky countered, not taking his eyes off her.

Thankfully, Annie, Meredith and Hank decided to walk back with them as well. They set off down the dusty road and were soon out of the village and on the road at the edge of the lagoon. Rocky stuck to Bernadette like a burr on a dog.

"You don't have to follow me," she hissed, trying not to attract the others' attention.

"I think I do. Who knows what you'll do next? Maybe pass out in the lagoon."

She shot him a narrow-eyed look meant to stop him in his tracks, but he just grinned. She vowed to work on her 'drop-dead' look.

"So, tell me what she meant about the sight," Rocky asked.

"She's just a foolish old woman," she replied, trying to brush off the incident. The woman's words had left her shaken, though. Dark times? That couldn't be good. But Rocky finding out about her sight wouldn't be helpful either.

She looked at him boldly. "Surely you don't believe any of that."

As they passed the restaurant at the main corner, the other three turned toward the hotel, but Rocky took her arm and pulled her up onto the restaurant's wide, ramshackle veranda.

"You must be hot," he said. "Let me buy you a beer."

She protested weakly, but when he raised an eyebrow in challenge, she decided to play dumb and change the subject as soon as possible.

"Fine. Thank you," she said, showing her teeth in what she hoped would pass as a smile. Choosing the cleanest plastic lawn chair on the veranda, she plunked herself down.

"*Dos cervezas*," Rocky said to the waiter with the charming smile he seemed to reserve for everyone but her. When he turned back to her, his eyes narrowed. "Now spill it."

"I don't know what you're talking about. Whatever Mama Rosa thought—"

"I don't believe you. You were buying it."

He flashed a smile at the young waiter as he set the cold glasses of beer on the table in front of them and left. Then Rocky was back on her like a dog on a bone.

"It's true, isn't it?" He snapped his fingers and pointed at her. "You weren't passing out at the ruins. You have the sight."

"Don't be ridiculous—"

"You can't fool me, I'm Italian."

Bernadette rolled her eyes. "Okay, it might be something like that. Something I inherited from my grandmother. Just a fey thing that happens every once in a while." She tried to dismiss the idea with a wave of her hand and casually took a sip of her beer.

"Do I need my amulet to protect me?" he asked.

"Amulet?" She squinted at him skeptically, and he pulled a colorful glass medallion out from inside his shirt and held it out between them like a cross to a vampire.

She frowned. "What on earth is that?"

"A gift from my *nonna*, to ward off the evil eye."

"Oh, put it away." She batted at the medallion in his hand. "You don't believe in that evil eye crap, do you? And who exactly is your *nonna*?"

"My grandmother. She lives with my parents back home in San Francisco. She gave me this medallion when I first took the job, to protect me on my travels. They were common where she grew up in Italy. She believes and she's no fool. She's seen a lot."

Bernadette considered what he said as she drank her beer. She held the cool bottle up to her heated cheeks and the condensation dripped onto the skin in the open neckline of her blouse. Rocky's eyes followed the trail of droplets that trickled into her cleavage. She quickly set the bottle back on the table.

"Okay," she said. His gaze snapped back to her eyes. "Sometimes I see things, or more accurately, feel things. It sort of feels like a dream, sometimes they *are* dreams."

"Like the jaguar dream, in the van," Rocky cut in.

"Maybe," she answered slowly. "I'm not very skilled at interpreting the…episodes. I don't even know what to call them. Often, I don't know what one means until later, when all the pieces fall into place. The jaguar dream could just have been a reaction to Manuel's stories." *And you*. She looked at him, sitting across the table, looking so dark and intense and so darn attractive. Rocky had been the priest in the dream.

"And in the temple at Chichén Itzá?"

"Well, yes, the temple." She paused, peeling the label off her empty bottle. How could she explain it? "That felt more like a warning. Caruthers' murder, my jaguar, and camo-man, who grabbed me at Old Ox B'alam…"

"You think it's all related?"

Bernadette looked him in the eye and shook her head. "Maybe. I don't really know."

* * *

When they got back to the hacienda, Bernadette took her tape recorder, notebook and laptop out to the terrace to work on her story. The buzz of conversation around the bar made it difficult to concentrate, so gathering up her gear, she checked the map in the lobby, looking for the patio by the small lagoon, really more of a pond, that she had seen from Rocky's window.

She took the path past the swimming pool, through a lovely garden where hibiscus bushes towered overhead. A bougainvillea-covered pergola by the tiny back lagoon sheltered the small patio from the sun. It was much quieter here than at the bar and she settled into a chair to work.

Her plan was to write up her notes for the article, but even here she had trouble focusing on the job. Since they'd arrived at the hacienda four days before, events had happened quickly, one right after another, carrying her along like a leaf in a whirlpool, spiraling down to a dark and sinister place.

She hadn't signed on for murder. It was difficult to concentrate on the story Jen wanted—so pale by comparison to what was really going on. Ox B'alam without the crocodiles? Without the atmosphere of death that hung over the hacienda? And not just death, but murder.

No wonder she was having trouble concentrating on the Cultural Tour.

She hadn't made it to the top of the pyramid to see dawn break but *had* seen it from the zip-line over the lagoon, and she had no idea how to write *that* without including the chase that preceded it.

The pyramid at dawn would have been a great angle, but now she wouldn't go back into the ruins in the dark even if Manuel did offer to take her.

This small lagoon was scarcely larger than the swimming pool back by the hacienda. More like a regular cenote, in the bright sunlight, it was not as scary as the big, marshy lagoon on the other side of the road. There was movement in the branches of the trees in the jungle across the lagoon where birds, or maybe monkeys, fed on ripe dragon fruit.

Something had been waiting for them in the jungle that morning and it wasn't wildlife. Someone had targeted her and Rocky, and whoever it was hadn't gotten what they wanted.

Her neck tensed as a prickle of unease skittered along her arms. Nervously, she scanned the bushes across the water. Were they out there now, whoever they were, watching her from the underbrush?

She tried to envision the surrounding territory, placing the hacienda, the lagoons, the ruins and the village on a mental map, but she couldn't picture how far it was as the crow flies through the jungle from the hacienda to the ruins. She'd have to look at Annie's map.

There must be something in the jungle, or on Rocky's camera, or both, that someone didn't want them to see. She thought back to Mama Rosa's prophecy—if you could call it that—and tried to get a peek of what was to come. She focused, or rather unfocused, her mind, the way you unfocus your eyes when you daydream. But her sight wasn't a gift she could conjure at will and after a few minutes of staring blankly, she gave up.

With a frustrated sigh she sank back into the soft chair, tapping her pen on the pad. She wrote 'Tulum' at the top of the page and tried to think of a title for that segment. *And Heads Will Roll*. Probably not a good title for a tourist piece.

Tulum meant "wall" in Mayan, but its original name was *Zama*, or Dawn, since it faced the east. A much more dramatic name. She could certainly spin a story about the location, how the Conquistadors discovered the blood red fortress above the azure sea.

Lunch in Tulum Pueblo had been delicious, and she checked back in her notes for the name of the place.

Charlie's. That could provide story material. She wished she'd had more time to look around in town. Maybe they could go back. If not, Rocky had taken all those photographs of the group in the restaurant. Looking at them might stir some ideas.

The visit to the antiquities dealer had been fun at the time, although buying a statue just like the one they found in Caruthers' room was a disturbing coincidence.

Soft footsteps crunched on gravel behind the pergola. Despite the hot, sultry air, a chill crept up her spine on spider's legs. The high shrub border provided a convenient screen for anyone who wanted to get her alone.

And she was very much alone.

In her mind, the expanse of garden between the pergola and the hacienda telescoped to a risky distance. What happened to her pledge to stay with the group?

Her heart pounded fiercely as whoever-it-was crept closer. Struggling to get enough air to her lungs, she leapt to her feet and spun around.

The intruder's outline was faintly visible through the loose wall of foliage. She held out her pad of paper like a shield and sucked in a breath, ready to scream.

Chapter 28

Bernadette's scream came out as more of a yelp when Luis stepped out from behind the screen of bushes. She blew out a huge sigh of relief and put a hand to her chest.

"I didn't mean to frighten you," he said in alarm.

"You just startled me." Although embarrassed by her overactive imagination, she was glad for his company.

He seemed agitated, not the same calm, gentle man who had served them dinner their first night. Bad as the murder was for the members of the Cultural Tour, it must be much worse for the locals, wondering which of your friends or neighbors—or which of the tourists—might be the murderer.

"I wondered if you wanted anything. A drink perhaps?"

"No, thank you, nothing to drink. I think I'll walk back to the hacienda with you, though."

Quickly, she gathered up her things and they started back through the garden. "I met your mother in the village today. She's a lovely lady."

Luis smiled broadly. "I'm fortunate to be able to live close by the village. I see my Mother often and can take care of my family when my Father is away working."

Bernadette smiled. "When you see her, thank her from all of us for her hospitality."

The late afternoon air was heavy and still as they walked the narrow path through the lush foliage and even that short walk broke beads of sweat out on her forehead.

"The events this week must be hard on the community," she ventured.

"Everyone is worried," Luis said, his words spilling out. "I am sorry to hear that you, too, had trouble in the forest this morning." His face was a misery of concern. "That is not normal here. We do not know who is responsible."

Bernadette had done a brief stint as a chamber maid in college and knew that the staff were always the first to know what was really going on. "Has there been any word on what happened to Caruthers? How he was killed?"

Luis looked around uneasily as they entered the terrace and circled the pool. He lowered his voice. "They say it was a knife. Very sharp. Perhaps obsidian, like the ancient ceremonial blades." He glanced over his shoulder. "I must go now." Then he darted through the kitchen door, leaving her standing alone by the bar, deep in thought.

Salvador startled her out of her contemplation. "A drink, pretty lady?"

He was leaning quietly against the back counter of the bar, polishing a glass with a linen towel, his gaze heavy upon her. When he smiled, his gold tooth glinted in the low sun that slanted in under the terrace roof.

Once again, Bernadette felt like he was hitting on her. He was very attractive, if you liked that type, but he made her uncomfortable when he focussed his attention on her. The Aussie women seemed to like him and flirted right back, but then, anyone in pants seemed to be fair game for them.

Maybe it was just harmless flirting. It could just be a cultural misunderstanding, or it could be nothing at all. Bernadette had never been very good at flirting, but she smiled pleasantly back at him and slipped up onto a stool. "White wine, please."

He went down to the other end of the bar to pour a glass.

A voice murmured in her ear. "Isn't it time you tried something a little more local?"

Rocky slid onto the adjoining stool.

She laughed. "I don't think so. Not after what happened last night. Those Mayan Rainbows are deadly."

Salvador returned with her wine and a look of understanding flashed between the two men. She pretended not to notice but groaned inwardly. *How bad had it been?*

"I was thinking of something more traditional," Rocky said. "Tequila, please, Sal."

Salvador set a small glass and the necessary accoutrements in front of Rocky and then said to Bernadette, "We have ways with tequila here. Often, we flavor it with fruit or coffee. It makes a very nice drink."

"The wine's fine, thank you very much."

She turned to Rocky and lowered her voice. "I heard something very interesting via the grape vine."

Rocky's eyebrows rose questioningly as he licked the salt off his hand, so she continued. "Word is, Caruthers was killed with a knife."

Although Salvador had his back turned to them, out of the corner of her eye she noticed his shoulders stiffen. Maybe she had discovered this before some of the staff.

"A knife usually indicates a crime of passion by a violent individual, rather than a premeditated strike," Rocky said. He tossed back the tequila and then grimaced.

She gave him a skeptical look. "Good?"

He grinned as he squirted lime into his mouth. "The best."

She tried to look serious. "They think it might have been an obsidian knife. Maybe one of the tourist copies."

Rocky's eyes narrowed as he thought. Or it could have been because of the lime. "Those blades are razor sharp. Make a clean cut. A cut like that might not bleed very much, depending on how it was done."

Bernadette remembered their visit to Akam's shop in Tulum. There had been a lot of those blades for sale there. Visions of decapitations made her stomach roll. She didn't want to know how Caruthers had died.

"Could have been anyone," Salvador said coming over to wipe down the bar. "Those blades are very common here. Even the old ones show up pretty regularly in the ruins."

Jose came in through the door to the dining room and with a nod of his head, relieved Salvador for his break.

"Jose," Rocky said. "I'm a bit of an amateur archaeologist."

Bernadette's eyebrows shot up. *Since when?*

"I've heard you can find those old obsidian blades out in the ruins if you go poking around."

Jose came over, as always, eager to chat. "The area has been well gone over. Not much turns up anymore. Unless you really know where to look."

Rocky leaned in closer and lowered his voice. "I heard Caruthers was murdered by one of those blades."

Jose frowned and murmured. "The temple."

"What temple?" Rocky asked. Bernadette wouldn't actually say he pounced, but he was having a hard time concealing his excitement.

A stricken look crossed Jose's face. He looked uneasily over his shoulder and mumbled something about *Black Jaguars* as he put Rocky's beer on the bar.

Rocky smiled encouragingly and laid a generous tip beside his drink.

"It's not really a temple anymore," Jose said, and then, with a look that was supposed to be a smile but failed dismally, he scooped up the money and scuttled into the kitchen.

"Great," Rocky muttered. "Now he's spooked."

"Can you blame him?" Bernadette asked.

"He seemed happy enough to talk until I asked about the temple. I don't think he meant to let that slip. And who are the Black Jaguars?"

"What do you have to do to get a drink around here?" Eloise asked loudly, taking the seat next to Rocky. He sent Bernadette a warning look.

"Euww, that looks good," Eloise said, indicating his empty tequila glass. "I'll have one of those." She winked at Salvador, who was back from his break. He grinned at her and she thrust out her ample chest. The man would have to be blind not to get the message.

Well, at least she wasn't aiming that pair at Rocky any more. Bernadette took a sip of her wine. Not that she cared.

That evening, dinner was a desultory affair. Humidity hung heavy and the air crackled with the electricity that often foreshadows a storm. When they finished their meal, conversation lagged, and Bernadette went up to her room. She looked over her notes and the empty page with "Tulum" written at the top, but she couldn't concentrate. Didn't want to think. She stepped out on the balcony to clear her head, but the oppressive air was far from fresh.

Marimba music played softly in the distance and the memory of dancing with Rocky at *El Diablo* raised one corner of her mouth into a half-hearted grin. That evening had been the most fun she'd had so far. Almost the only fun.

At first, she could tell he didn't want to dance, was only getting out on the dance floor to get a better look at the man who was arguing with Ricardo in the corner. But then he got into it, put his hands on her hips and let the rhythm flow right through her and into him.

And now, today, he had kissed her. They'd kissed each other.

Slow down, she reminded herself. It was the heat of the

moment.

But she couldn't deny he was getting under her skin, like an irritating rash, and that was bad. Sure, he was attractive, in a swashbuckling kind of way, but she had to maintain a professional distance. Concentrate on the job. Better to become good partners than—whatever the alternative was.

Chapter 29

Rocky sat alone at the bar, nursing a beer. He looked around the empty room. *So, this is Ox B'alam on a weeknight.* The only movement was the fan, turning slowly overhead. Even Sal was nowhere in sight.

Canned marimba music played quietly in the distance. He couldn't believe he'd danced with Bernadette at *El Diablo*. He didn't dance. A faint grin played over his face. But last night, watching her sway to the music, he'd been mesmerized. When he put his hands on her hips, the rhythm flow from her right into him and before he knew it, he was moving to the beat. He'd wanted to pull her closer and experience firsthand the damage those hips could do, but even then, he'd known it was a bad idea. Unprofessional. And, of course, there was Samantha. But he had certainly seen another side of Miss Good-and-Proper last night, waving her hands over her head as she danced. No wonder he lost sight of his quarry. His eyes narrowed as he considered to whom Ricardo might have been talking.

Sometimes, like now, he missed his old partner. It wasn't like they'd had a lot in common. Shuster didn't read and wasn't interested in sports. In fact, now that he thought about it, Rocky didn't really know what he was interested in. They only met sporadically in exotic locations and spent their time together either working or talking over the events of the day, the thrust of the story, at the hotel bar. But if nothing else, he was someone Rocky could bounce ideas off.

On this trip, without his old partner, he felt like a middle-aged guy alone in a hotel. He looked around the empty terrace. And right now, he felt like a middle-aged guy alone in a hotel bar.

Picking up his drink, he moved to a table by the wall. He took the cell phone out of his pocket, stared at it for a minute, then punched in a number.

He usually called Samantha a couple of times a week when he was on the road. So far this time, he hadn't. It was almost a week since he'd talked to her. Leaving it any longer was probably a big mistake. But she'd been so mad, storming out of his place the night before he left for this trip, that he didn't know what kind of reception his call would receive.

He was tired of the scenes she pulled every time he went away. It was his job, for heaven sake. Couldn't she see that?

They'd been down this road before and she had always come around. But this time, he wasn't so sure. And he wasn't even sure he cared.

The phone rang twice. She picked it up.

"Hi," he said.

"Oh, hi. It's you." She sounded disappointed.

"Who were you expecting?"

"No one. You, maybe." She sounded defensive, but it could have been disinterested. Lately, he'd been wondering what she did, who she saw, when he went out of town.

"How's the trip?" she asked.

"Fine. Quiet. We're in a small hotel in the middle of the jungle."

"Mosquitoes?"

"A few. Not too bad."

Empty silence hung on the line. Finally he asked, "What have you been doing?"

"Nothing much."

Ha. Samantha always had a hundred things on the go, was always bugging him to go somewhere with her when he just wanted to stay at home.

"How is the new writer working out?" she asked.

"Are you bonding?"

Samantha was always jealous—another problem—so Rocky let more irritation than he actually felt seep into his voice. "She's a total novice. I have to walk her through every step of the trip."

"She? I didn't know it was a woman ... Is she pretty?"

Sam would have a fit if she knew how pretty Bernadette was.

"Pretty? No. She's a writer for God's sake."

A noise behind him caught his attention and he turned in time to see Bernadette's back disappearing into the ladies' room.

Crap. He dropped his forehead onto his free hand. He'd had no idea she was there.

"You don't have to worry," he said with a sigh. "She's hardly even talking to me."

And that, he thought as he ended the call, *is probably the truth.*

* * *

Bernadette had gone down to the bar looking for a little company but when she heard Rocky's comment, had ended up making a hasty retreat to the ladies' room. She put her hands on the cold porcelain lip of the sink and let her weight drain down into her arms. *So, that's how he feels.*

It was one thing to say she was a novice—her chin came up and she looked herself in the eye in the mirror—that was true. But he was not walking her through the trip. She was carrying her own weight.

She'd hoped they had bonded, at least a little, after their adventure this morning. She had pushed the scary feelings aside and decided to call it that, an adventure, picturing herself in fatigues—or camo—her hat on her head like Indiana Jones.

Except that she'd lost her hat in the jungle this morning. And apparently, they hadn't bonded. Not one bit.

She turned on the faucet full bore, aware of how ridiculous that sounded. They only worked together, and not all that closely. She could do her job without him, could damn well work completely on her own.

She splashed cold water on her face, took a couple of deep breaths and, shoulders back, walked out of the washroom.

And there he was, leaning against the wall in the narrow hallway not ten feet away, waiting for her.

"Excuse me," she said as she pushed past him.

He took her arm. "Hey, wait a minute."

She stopped and looked coldly at his hand. "You have a bad habit of doing that."

He dropped her arm and she turned to go.

"No, please. Just wait a minute."

She stopped, but only turned her head in his direction. "What."

"I guess you heard me on the phone."

Now she did turn to face him, chin up, struggling to keep her humiliation from burning in her cheeks.

"I was talking to my girlfriend. She's the jealous type. I didn't mean it. Any of it," he finished lamely with a little-boy-caught-in-the-cookie-jar look that infuriated her even more.

"That's too bad," she said crisply, and headed towards the lobby stairs.

"Look, could I buy you a drink?"

She shot him a look. "No thanks, I don't think so. I have work to do. See you tomorrow." She swept through the lobby and up the stairs with her head held high.

At the top of the stairs, the red police tape across Caruthers' door hit her like a slap in the face. Her shoulders fell, and she slunk across the hall to her room.

The door closed with a final *thud*, and once inside, she leaned her back against the door, suddenly wishing she had stayed for that drink. She didn't want to be up here alone.

Maybe she had overreacted. Her story was going nowhere. It might help to talk it over. A lot was riding on pulling together a good piece for the magazine. If Jen published the story, it could mean more assignments. And the tear sheets, copies of her article torn out of the issue, would be her pass to more work with other magazines.

She crossed the darkened room, slid open the glass doors and stepped out onto the dark balcony, wishing there was somewhere else to go. Even though it had cooled off significantly since mid-day, the air still felt muggy and warm.

Jen was the only one who had any faith in her ability to hand in an article fit to print. Even her mother had called the trip, "a nice little vacation in the sun." But she owed her mum. If it wasn't for her, Bernadette didn't know how she would have survived as a single mother. Colin's father lived on grants and couldn't send much child support, and her little nest egg, most of which she'd inherited from her grandmother, had almost disappeared.

Rocky had made it clear from the start that he had no faith in her writing ability and, for some reason, that stung. She wanted his respect, maybe because it was so hard to win. She wanted to be colleagues. Partners. The events of the past few days hadn't helped and even though she was really getting a feel for Mayan culture, both ancient and modern, it was increasingly difficult to concentrate on the article she wanted to write.

With her hands braced on the balcony railing, she leaned out, searching for that sweet fragrance of flowering trees she had noticed the first night. But the musky scent of the lagoon overpowered everything else, conjuring images of crocodiles converging on Caruthers' body as it floated in the murky water.

Why were the police taking so long? They seemed to be making no headway at all in finding the murderer.

She stepped back inside and closed the sliding door. The room seemed dim and smaller than when she'd first arrived. She couldn't stay up here alone tonight. She'd go down and see who was at the bar. Maybe there would be someone to talk to. Meredith or Hank.

Or even Rocky.

She heaved a heavy sigh. Maybe he did have a jealous girlfriend. She didn't know anything about him and had not really tried to be friends.

Except for the other night at *El Diablo*.

A blush rose from her neck to her cheeks. She still didn't know what had come over her. She had flirted shamelessly with him on the dance floor and, although he'd played along, it hadn't led to anything. Now she knew why. He had a girlfriend.

That was okay because it wouldn't help their working relationship to become...involved. Anyway, he was not her type. Too dark, and there was something dangerous about him.

Although, now that she had seen his playful side, that only made him more intriguing.

Thank goodness he'd been a gentleman last night, when she had been—indisposed. At least she thought he had been. She frowned at the spot on the floor where her dress had lay, but still didn't remember how it ended up there. She squeezed her eyes shut and tried to think back.

Nothing.

Okay. They would start again. She would swallow her pride and go down and buy him a drink.

She marched to the door and as she reached for the

knob, a sharp knock sounded from the other side. Her heart thumping wildly, she leaned her hand on the wooden frame and put her ear to the door.

No sound. Not a clue as to who stood on the other side.

Taking a deep breath, she called softly, "Who's there?"

Chapter 30

"It's me," Rocky said softly through the door. "Come on. Open up."

Bernadette's lungs deflated with a whoosh. Of course it was Rocky. Who else would it be? She opened the door and leaned against the jam with her arms crossed over her chest. He cradled a bowl of chips in one arm and swung two frosty beer bottles by their necks between his fingers.

"Come to my room," he whispered. Her heart lurched unexpectedly. "We'll go over my pictures."

His face was inches from hers. She searched it for an alternate meaning to his words and decided, with just a smidge of disappointment, that he was all business.

"Okay," she whispered back, not entirely sure why they were whispering. Stepping into the hall, she locked her door behind her, then turned to find him contemplating the red tape across the hall. For one terrible moment, she thought he would suggest they search Caruthers' room again.

"Real party spoiler, isn't it?" he said, then led the way to his room, next door to the crime scene.

As he settled on the bed with his laptop, she walked over to the window and looked out at the view of the hotel swimming pool. Beyond it, the hacienda gardens twinkled in the dusk and in the distance, she glimpsed the small lagoon where she had sat that afternoon. Beyond that, a thick mat of impenetrable vegetation stretched to the horizon.

"You're lucky you don't have the view of the lagoon," she said. "It's depressing to see it every time you look out the window. Knowing what happened there.

"Every morning I wake up and there it is. Then I

open the door and the police tape reminds me, in case the lagoon hadn't, that someone has been murdered. If this was a real vacation, if there hadn't been a murder this week, I would love to go for a walk along those paths again, now, in the evening when it's cool and the flowers smell so sweet. Go and sit by the little lagoon at the back, like I did this afternoon, and listen to the sound of the jungle at night." She sighed and turned away from the window to find Rocky glaring at her from the bed.

"You went back there alone? Are you crazy? You shouldn't go walking around alone. If you want to go anywhere, come and get me."

She usually didn't like him telling her what to do, but in this case he was probably right.

He sat on the bed in the dim light of the bedside lamp, his bare legs stretched out in front of him, and she bit her tongue at the sight of his dusty sneakers on the embroidered bedspread. A long A/V cord ran from his laptop across the room to the small television in the corner. The bowl of potato chips sat beside him on the bed, the two open beer bottles leaving sweat rings on the small bedside table.

"Come and sit," he said, patting the spot beside him on the bed. "Beer?"

She was surprised and sort of touched that he had snagged one for her. Maybe they could be buddies after all.

His fingers flew over the keyboard, his eyes intent on the TV screen. She pulled the heavy armchair up beside the bed and took the beer.

"Where did you get those?" she asked, indicating the chips.

He glanced up with a grin. "One of the girls in the kitchen slipped me a bowl."

Of course she did.

"What are you doing?" she asked as computer menus

popped up on the TV screen.

"I thought we could go over my photographs and see if anything clicks. See if we can figure out what's going on. I figure the guys who chased us this morning thought there was something they wanted on my camera. Hell, I have pictures of everyone—everyone on the tour, the other guests, all the staff. Even the people in the village. You never know what people will object to you photographing in these remote areas. Maybe someone saw me taking pictures of something they didn't want us to see and decided to get the camera and the photographs."

"That's what I thought," Bernadette said, settling in to watch.

"Of course," he said absently, "I don't leave anything on my camera. I empty the memory card at least every night and sometimes once during the day. The photographs are all right here, on my laptop. Then I back them up on a hard drive.

"This is my first shot yesterday morning." The first picture popped up on the screen, the pyramid at Tulum silhouetted against the low morning sun.

"Something's going on here," he said, "and somehow, one of us is involved. If they are after a photo, it has to be a recent one—one they thought was still in the camera. We'll start with yesterday. If we go through them, we might see a pattern. Maybe we'll see something or someone who looks out of place. We're not looking for the good shots for the story right now, just sort of free associating."

"I can do that," she said.

Rocky looked at her thoughtfully. "You might be very good at it, what with your...gift."

Bernadette blushed and turned her face to the screen. The pictures changed every few seconds in a slideshow format. Rocky's hands relaxed on the keys and he leaned back against the headboard of the bed as the photographs moved slowly through the events of the previous day.

It had been a nice day. At least to begin with.

The pyramid at Tulum, facing the turquoise sea, overlooking the white sandy beach. The steps where heads had rolled. The little house where the heads were kept.

Grizzly, really. But it hadn't felt that way at the time with the sun shining and the breeze blowing in off the water.

White stone walls with lazing iguanas. Bernadette on the beach in her bathing suit, ankle deep in the water. Celeste and Eloise, looking like bikini babes playing in the water. Back to Bernadette, looking demure, almost prudish by comparison in her one piece. Then back to the Aussies.

She laughed in mild embarrassment. "Okay, I get the picture."

"Hey." Rocky grinned sheepishly, then took a hit of his beer. "Those are the shots that pay the bills. But those two are sort of scary when they gang up on you."

She swiveled her eyes toward him and raised her brows inquiringly.

"No way," he exclaimed. "Not here. I mean at the bar. I'm not crazy enough to hook up with those two. Or even with one of them."

He was actually flustered. She snorted with laughter.

He pulled his brows together in an attempt at serious. "You know what I mean. Here we are in Tulum Pueblo," he said, attempting to direct her attention back to the slide show.

Plates of food. Annie and Meredith eating with the bright street in the background.

A prickly sensation ran down the back of her neck.

The street. The antiquities dealer's window.

An icy finger moved across her shoulders.

Annie and her, peering in the window.

The chill raced down her arms. "Can you go back a bit?"

"Sure. Did you see something?" Rocky backed the pictures up to the first shot of the antiquities dealer's store.

"I don't know. Can you go back even farther?"

He wound back through chaotic street scenes to the restaurant and they both watched without speaking as the pictures rolled by. She felt it again, somewhere between lunch and visiting Akam's shop, a creepy sensation that she couldn't name.

She was missing something. But what?

Suddenly someone rapped on the door and they both started guiltily.

Rocky laughed. "It's okay. What else would we be doing?" He called out, "Come in."

The door opened and Hank popped his head in. When he saw Bernadette, he said, "Sorry to interrupt," and quickly started to back away.

"Come on in," Rocky said. "Have a seat."

Since Bernadette was sitting in the only chair in the room, she scooted onto the bed to give Hank the chair, rather than make him sit on the bed beside Rocky.

Hank was not his normal jovial self and she was surprised to see him looking so serious.

"I've been thinking about what happened this morning," he said to Rocky, glancing meaningfully at Bernadette.

"It's okay," Rocky said, stopping the slideshow at a shot of her in her bathing suit, sitting on a rock above the cenote. "We were just talking about the same thing. We're going over the photographs of the trip so far, looking for a clue to what's going on. Want a chip?"

He offered the bowl to Hank, who took a handful in his big paw. "Looking for what?"

"Anything," Bernadette said. "Considering suspects."

"Suspects?" Hank laughed. "Could I be a suspect?" When they didn't respond, the smile faded from his face. He looked from her to Rocky. "Well, could I?"

"You could be," Rocky said with a half-smile. "We all could be. We all met Caruthers and we were here when he was murdered. Do you have an alibi? Do any of us? However, maybe more importantly, do any of us have a motive?"

"I don't see how anyone on the tour could have a motive. We all barely met the guy," Hank said.

"Unless someone had a prior connection to Caruthers," Bernadette said. "Being on the same tour does indicate a conjoining of interests. Maybe. I don't know. If this were a movie there'd be a relic with supernatural powers—something worth millions on the black market and everyone on the tour would be scrambling to find it."

"Maybe a hot-headed history student killed Caruthers in a rage because he stole the artefact," Rocky said.

"Or maybe one of the staff felt slighted—or just wanted his money and passport," Hank said with a sigh. "But murder?"

Rocky shrugged. "It's been done for less."

"I guess it could be anyone," Hank agreed sadly.

They all fell silent, then Rocky rubbed his hand over his face. "Is anyone acting suspiciously? We still don't know why Caruthers was killed. I'm worried that if they don't find the killer, he could strike again."

Bernadette wanted to cry, *for God's sake, don't say it out loud,* but managed to keep silent. The guys would only laugh at her superstitions.

"The victim was a tourist from Manuel's tour, just like us," Rocky continued. "Two days after his tour ends, he's found dead in the lagoon. Crocodile dinner. Nobody seems to have any idea who did it, so that means the perp is probably still out there."

She shot him a grin. "The perp?"

He gave her an inscrutable look, then turned back to Hank. "I just want to make sure none of us, or no one on the next tour, ends up in the lagoon. So, taking your question one step further, mightn't you be approached next? You're outgoing and free with cash here in the village. Has anyone approached you about anything illegal?"

"Not that I remember," Hank said, taking another handful of chips.

Rocky started the slideshow again, this time going back even further. They were in the parking lot at Old Ox B'alam and everyone was climbing out of the bus. Bernadette saw now why Rocky always sat in the seat by the door. That way, he could jump out and photograph the rest of them disembarking. In this shot, the open-front stalls that circled the parking lot formed a colorful backdrop with their displays of blankets, hammocks and sombreros.

The photo seemed to trigger something for Hank. "One thing I do remember—Ricardo, at the souvenir stand, was pretty persistent the other day about showing me some of the better pieces that he keeps in the back. What he called 'the real thing'."

"Did you look at them?" Rocky asked.

"I did. They were better than most of the stuff he had out front but weren't real artifacts. And not worth the price he was asking."

"How much did he want?"

"A couple of hundred dollars apiece for the ones I saw. I'm no expert, but I'd say they were worth one tenth of that."

"What was he selling?" Bernadette asked.

"Obsidian carvings, like out front, but more finished and maybe carved from better stone. As a matter of fact, they were a lot like the piece you bought in Tulum."

"Interesting," Rocky murmured, his eyes following the images on the screen.

They watched the montage in silence for a few more minutes, then after another handful of chips that pretty well cleaned out the bowl, Hank hoisted himself out of the chair. "I'll leave you to it," he said, then let himself out, closing the door behind him.

Rocky and Bernadette continued to sit on the bed, legs stretched out in front of them, watching the week in slow review.

The airport. Arriving at the hacienda. Dinner the first night.

Rocky stopped the slideshow there and slowly went through the photos one by one until he came to one of Hank, gesturing with his wineglass with Caruthers in the background. Caruthers' eyes were focused on something across the room. The look on his face wasn't pretty.

"Not in a very sociable mood that night," Rocky murmured. "I'd love to know what was on his mind."

The rhythmic flow of pictures was hypnotic but when they had gone through all the photos and started back at the airport again, Rocky stopped the slideshow, shut his laptop and they sat in silence, staring at the blank TV screen, processing what they'd seen.

The minutes ticked by and Bernadette began to feel awkward, sitting beside him on the bed with the memory of their kiss that morning still fresh in her mind. The kiss hadn't lasted long, but it was intense, not just a casual brush of the lips. There was definite chemistry there.

She tried not to let her thoughts show but her cheeks warmed and her eyes were wide and dry as she stared at the blank screen.

The kiss was probably just a reaction to the adrenalin they both had pumping after the zip-line. Probably no reason to mention it again. Rocky obviously didn't think it was important enough to talk about or, heaven help them, repeat.

Theirs wasn't that kind of relationship, and that wasn't the kind of relationship she wanted to foster with Rocky. What they were doing tonight was better, a step toward developing a solid working partnership. She hoped he was beginning to trust her. To develop a bit of respect.

That was probably why he had invited her to this screening of his pictures. That, and to make up for what he'd said to his girlfriend on the phone. Anything else would just get in the way, and of course, he had a girlfriend back home.

Clearing her throat, she said, "Some great shots there. The magazine will be happy."

"Yeah, I think so," he said, his mind obviously elsewhere.

She slid off the bed. "I didn't see anything out of the ordinary though. Nothing I can put my finger on, anyway."

"No. I didn't either." He stared at the blank TV screen.

"Seeing them will help me with my article though." She edged towards the door. "I guess I'll go then. Thanks for the beer. See you tomorrow."

She looked back as she let herself out the door. Rocky had opened his laptop again and his eyes were focussed on the shifting images on the screen.

Chapter 31

The boss ground his cigarette angrily under his heel and fingered the knife in his pocket as he waited for his partner to return.

He is loco if he thinks he's getting half of the money this time. I found the mark. I found the relic. He did nothing on this job. The last job, yes, and he was paid for that. Although he was no help when the American returned.

He had not been this angry since that night in Cancun when his last partner had double-crossed him. This new man would see what happened when he demanded too much.

Everything was different now. All deals were off.

He was ready when his partner came back into the room. In a fistfight, the two would be equally matched, but he'd make sure this was not a fair fight.

The knife flashed in the lantern light, deadly as the flick of a serpent's tongue.

Thursday, Day 5

"The whole long façade was ornamented with sculptured stone. At the left end of the principal building, in the angle of the corner are the huge open jaws of an alligator, or some other hideous animal, enclosing a human head."

J.L. Stephens, Incidents of Travel in Yucatán, 1842

Chapter 32

Rocky greeted Bernadette at breakfast the next morning with a silent nod. In fact, everyone was quiet except for the occasional request to pass the butter or salt, murmured in a low voice.

When they had finished eating, Manuel announced, "Today is a free day. It has been a..." He groped for the right word, then smiled wanly when it came to him. "An exciting week. Today you can go back to the ruins at Old Ox B'alam on your own, or visit the souvenir stands. The local taxi will take you into Tulum or wherever you want to go. But perhaps you just want to take a real vacation and relax by the pool."

Sitting by the pool sounded great to Bernadette. Every night she was too exhausted to read, and she had only finished the first chapter of the book she'd brought along. Today the air was heavy with clouds piled in the eastern sky. If the weather turned, this might be her last chance to sit in the sun.

Jen's words echoed in her head. *This is not a surf and*

sand vacation.

She pulled out her itinerary. It was already Thursday and they were leaving on Saturday morning. She hoped. Ox B'alam was beginning to feel like a prison and she couldn't wait to get away. The problem was, Pacho had not given the okay yet for them to leave.

But she, for one, had to get home. Colin had called again the previous evening after she left Rocky's room and she had detected a note of 'mom-sick' in his voice.

She could use the day to write up her notes and fill in any blanks on the off-chance they could leave as planned on Saturday. Maybe she could take another look at Rocky's pictures. Sitting with him last night had been comforting, in a weird sort of way. Made her feel like she wasn't in this alone.

She looked across the breakfast table at him now. He sat in his usual casual sprawl, sunglasses on, coolly surveying the room like a cowboy in a spaghetti western. She was about to ask him about his plans, when Arthur rose from his seat and walked stiffly across the room to Manuel.

"How does one get in touch with the taxi?" he asked.

"Where do you want to go?"

Arthur lowered his voice. "Tulum."

"So do we," Eloise shrilled. "I want to do some real souvenir shopping. We didn't get half way down the strip the other day. We could share a cab."

Arthur stiffened even more. Now he had no alternative but to go with the Aussies. Bernadette bit her top lip to hide a smile. She had never seen anyone more uncomfortable around women than Arthur. What she wouldn't give to be a fly on the windscreen of that cab.

"Well, I want to go back to the ruins," Annie said.

"I guess we could go for a while," Meredith said, looking wistfully at the empty loungers around the pool.

"I'll go with her," Hank offered. "Then maybe you

and I could go for a walk after lunch."

Meredith smiled. "Thank you. I'd love that."

"I want to go to the site too," Rocky said to Annie. "Could we look at your map first?"

Thrilled to be asked, Annie ran up to her room, returning moments later with the dusty tube. Bernadette flinched when Annie unrolled it on the white linen tablecloth, but Rocky and Hank didn't notice, just gathered up saltshakers to weigh down the corners.

Hank looked closely at the map. "Definitely Ox B'alam."

"I know," Annie said. "I looked at it last night, and here you can see the main trail, the road we walked in on both times. It goes right past the ballcourt to the pyramid."

She traced the route with her finger. "This map calls them 'roads", which was what they were in the beginning. The Maya built long paved roads between villages. Sometimes up to fifty miles long."

"Kind of strange for a culture with no wheels," Bernadette said.

Hank looked up in surprise. "No wheels? I thought they were so sophisticated."

"In many ways they were," Annie said. "But with no large domesticated animals to pull the carts, I guess it just never happened."

"It may have been a way to keep control of the people," Bernadette added thoughtfully. "Make them the beasts of burden."

The map looked a lot like an architect's drawing with the roads and buildings marked in blue pen, then hand labeled in block letters.

"What are these?" she asked, pointing to the smaller numbers printed in blue, scattered across the map.

Luis, who was serving coffee at a table behind them, looked over her shoulder at the map. "Those are stelas, the stone markers."

The buildings were named and numbered, and she started reading the names aloud, beginning with number one, the Pyramid. The ballcourt was number two. The numbers went up to sixty-two, so it was evident that many of the buildings on the map were still covered by the jungle.

Everyone chimed in, trying to identify the buildings they had seen when they toured the site with Manuel. Together they managed to remember all of the first ten, except for one.

"Luis," Bernadette asked. "What is this building? None of us remember it. It's labeled number eight." She squinted at the blurred letters. "Temple *of* –something. Maybe *Temple of the Jaguar*."

Luis's eyes darted around the room. "I don't know," he said, backing away. "So many buildings on that map have not been restored." He hurried into the kitchen.

"I'd love to play poker with him," Rocky murmured.

He traced his finger along another 'road' that ran from the pyramid past the far end of the ballcourt and swooped back almost to the parking lot. Bernadette's eyes flared and she caught her breath when she recognized it as the route of their escape path the morning of the attack. Her gaze flew to Rocky's face, but he didn't look up from the map.

Another path crossed the main trail at right angles, ran through the ballcourt and crossed their escape path, forming the cross bar of an H. Then it kept on going, straight to the Jaguar Temple and beyond.

The spot where she had seen camo-man was surprisingly close to their escape path. She'd had no idea where they were in the dark. She tried subtly to get Rocky's attention, but he was still intently searching the map. Not wanting to speak in front of Hank and Annie, she pulled out her notebook and pencil and made a rough drawing, showing the position of the Jaguar Temple in relation to the paths and other buildings they knew. Then she stood up. "Let's go. Before it gets hot."

Rocky looked up briefly but didn't reply, so she said distinctly, "Rocky. Meet you in the lobby in ten minutes?"

Getting a grunt that she took as a yes, she went up to her room to get ready. She laid out her gear on her bed. Since losing her hat the previous day, she felt less like Ms. Intrepid Travel Reporter and more like an average tourist. Piling on the sunscreen in front of the mirror, she reaffirmed her decision to stick close to Rocky and Hank today. In a group in broad daylight, what else could happen?

Ten minutes later, she stood in the lobby, waiting for Rocky.

Ten minutes turned into fifteen and she was just about to go up and knock on Rocky's door when he raced down the stairs, his eyes wild.

"Someone has stolen my camera."

Chapter 33

"They what?" She'd heard him, she just couldn't believe it.

"Stole my camera," Rocky repeated, enunciating every syllable in frustration.

"Who did?"

"I don't know."

"Are you sure?"

"Of course I'm sure. I tore my room apart. Before breakfast I piled everything on the bed, ready to go, and everything is still there, except the camera."

"Were any pictures on it?"

"No. Nothing. I emptied the camera last night, as usual. Shit!" He pounded his fist on the wall, obviously forgetting it was solid stone. It could have been humorous, if he hadn't been so upset.

Manuel heard the commotion and hurried out of the office. "What is the matter?"

Rocky turned on him vehemently. "Someone stole my camera."

Manuel's shoulders slumped. "Are you sure?"

"Of course I'm sure. Christ. Would everyone quit asking me that?" By this time, a small crowd had gathered.

"Are you insured?" Hank asked.

"Yes, but that's not the point."

"Are you sure the door was locked?" Manuel asked.

"Yes. I'm sure," Rocky said impatiently. "I have so much equipment, I always keep the room locked."

Bernadette believed him. He was very methodical about the security of his cameras. She had seen the way he inventoried his equipment several times each day.

"It couldn't have been one of the maids," Manuel

said. "They are just arriving and haven't picked up the keys yet."

"The door wasn't locked when I got up there. Someone must have picked the lock. They aren't exactly state of the art. If whoever it was had a key, they would have locked the door when they left."

Bernadette was glad to see he was starting to calm down and think logically.

"Do you have another camera for today?" she asked.

"Yes." He sighed, or more like deflated, the expulsion of air signaling his acceptance of the inevitable.

"I will question everyone on the staff," Manuel said briskly, but Bernadette was pretty sure nothing would come of it. Rocky hadn't reported their previous attack to Pacho and she doubted he would report this one, either.

She put her hand on his arm. "Let's go to the site anyway. You have the photographs that were in the camera on your computer. You have another camera. I don't think there's anything we can do here. No use wasting the day."

Jaw working, he closed his eyes briefly in resignation.

"Why don't you go up and get your other camera?"

He nodded and trudged back up the stairs.

Thank God. Anything was better than hanging around the hacienda.

He came back down a few minutes later looking more like his old self. His shades were in place and another camera hung over his shoulder. "Let's get out of here," he said, marching right past her and out the door.

Yup. That was more like the old Rocky.

She ran to catch up with him and soon they were striding through the hacienda gates. Chief Pacho's beat-up four-by-four was parked in front of the two staff bungalows that sat against the outer wall in a small grove of trees.

"I guess you don't want to tell Pacho," she said.

"No," he answered shortly.

"He's keeping a pretty low profile for a murder investigation."

"Nothing's going to come of it," Rocky growled. "This is Mexico, remember."

She was afraid he was right. It was a tricky investigation, what with the victim and so many the people on the scene being foreign nationals. It would probably be easier for the local police to let them all go home and give up the search.

They headed down the road that skirted the lagoon, towards the ruins. Annie and Hank were far ahead, a colorful smudge on the soft grey road. With no hint of a breeze, the rank scent of the lagoon hung in the air. It didn't matter where she went, Bernadette couldn't seem to escape reminders of the murder.

"Did you see anything important in the photographs last night after I left?" she asked.

"No, but I think you were right. There's something in the ones of our lunch at Tulum. I just haven't been able to put my finger on it."

"I won't be sorry when this trip is over," Bernadette said. "I'm sorry it ended up like this, but don't worry, I'll hand in a good story." She tried to muster a smile. "How's your arm?"

"Not too bad." He held up his arm and pulled back his sleeve to show her the red, blistered rash that ran like road burn across his forearm and up past his elbow.

"Makes the eagle look particularly snarly," she said. "What do you think caused it?"

"Lucinda, the cook, said it was the sap of the poisonwood tree. Apparently, you just have to brush up against it to get a nasty reaction. She makes a clear lotion from the bark of another local tree and put that on it. It helped a lot, but the sap had been sitting on my skin for quite a while before we got back to the hacienda. She said it wouldn't have been nearly as bad if we'd grabbed some leaves off the antidote tree right away. Too bad we didn't know, although we hardly had time anyway," he said with a lopsided grimace.

They walked in companionable silence for a minute, then Bernadette said, "I lost my hat."

He looked at her sharply. "We should go back and find it."

"No." She shook her head vehemently. Even now in broad daylight, thinking about that deer path—or jaguar path— gave her the creeps. Rocky, however, seemed to take it as a challenge.

"We'll be fine. We were only a few feet from the main trail the whole time."

"You knew where we were? I had no idea."

He grinned. "So I noticed when you bolted off in the wrong direction."

A white car with a U.S. Embassy logo on the side sped past, stirring up a cloud of dust and forcing them to step off the road.

"I wondered when they'd show up," Rocky said. "They took their time, but I guess there wasn't much they could do once Caruthers was dead. I just hope they don't start questioning us, too."

"Chief Pacho was not very friendly the night he took my jaguar."

"When is that bastard ever friendly?"

"I want it back. I want to take it home. He can't keep it, can he?"

"I don't know. I guess he could keep it as evidence."

She sighed. "Well anyway, I still have to buy some gifts for my mom and Colin."

"Your husband?"

She shook her head. "No husband. Colin is my son. My mom is taking care of him this week."

"How old is he?" Rocky asked.

Proud as she was of Colin, she'd never been one to flash pictures of him to just anyone. She decided, however, that she had to open up if she wanted to get to know Rocky better. Digging around in her shoulder bag, she pulled out a picture of Colin in his soccer team uniform, one foot up on a ball, a big smile on his face.

"He's ten," she said, passing the photo to Rocky.

He stopped in the middle of the road and took a good long look. "I used to play soccer."

"Do you have kids?" she asked, surprised he would give the photo more than a cursory glance.

He passed back the picture and continued walking. "Haven't had time."

"I noticed you're good with kids," she ventured. "Do you want some?"

He glanced at her, then back at the road. "Maybe someday."

When they turned into the parking lot at the ruins, the vendors' booths stood open for business.

"Colin asked for a sombrero," Bernadette said, pausing at the first booth. "I'm not looking forward to taking it home on the plane, though."

Rocky picked a particularly garish one, the brim a yard wide, off the wall and placed it on her head.

"These are the ones you see on ten-year-olds in the airport," he said with grin.

Laughing, she took off the hat and hung it back on the wall, fending off the vendor with a wave of her hand. "I don't think so. My mom has been great to help this week, so I want to get her something too. Something *small* and easy to carry."

Glancing across the parking lot, the tin front of Ricardo's booth was still padlocked shut.

"I was hoping he'd be open," she said, pointing out the booth to Rocky. "I saw a pair of earrings in there the other day that would be perfect for my mom."

Rocky frowned. "Weird he's still closed." He thought for a moment. "There was a receipt from *Gonzales Souvenirs* in Caruthers' room."

She squinted, trying to remember. "Was there?" She gave a half laugh. "Was *I* there? The Mayan Sunsets seemed to have left a permanent fog on my brain."

"We were only in there once."

"Was the police tape across the door?"

He nodded. "We stepped over it."

She winced. She couldn't believe they'd ignored the tape.

At the entrance to the archeological site, the gatekeeper recognized them from the tour and amiably waved them in. The wide trail ran straight into the tunnel of trees, but Rocky immediately veered off onto a smaller path that skirted the back of the zip-line tower.

At the tower, Rocky turned left onto another, smaller path. Bernadette stopped when she recognized it as the one they had raced down the previous morning.

"Oh, no. I'm not going down there."

He kept walking. "Come on, don't you want to find your hat? Besides, I want to look for Temple Number Eight."

Chapter 34

Bernadette had no choice but to catch up with Rocky. She planned to stick to him like glue today. No way was she going to be left behind in the ruins. "I wanted to talk to you about the path to the temple. I think that was where I saw camo-man."

"Who's camo-man?"

"The man who grabbed me near the ballcourts that first day. He was dressed in camouflage with black stripes on his face."

Rocky stopped for a moment and she could see the gears turning in his head. "That could have been the beginning of it," he said, then started back down the path.

Oh, really? Nice to finally be taken seriously. "From what I saw on Annie's map, the spot is near the turnoff to Temple Number Eight. Maybe he was trying to protect the Jaguar Temple."

"Maybe."

As they walked along the narrow path, she caught glimpses of Hank's bright print shirt on the main trail off to their left. Rocky was right, their path did run parallel to the main trail, but it was far enough removed from the tourist traffic that birds she'd never seen on the main tourist trail flew between the trees above their heads.

She watched them flit from branch to branch as she walked. She had heard the morning squawks and jungle chatter but had seen disappointingly little wildlife so far. Except for the iguanas that posed on every warm stone wall and the vultures that soared on heat currents high overhead.

Although it was early, the air was still and the heat

already oppressive, so close that it plastered her light tank top to her skin. Humidity glistened on every leaf. She mopped her face with a handkerchief, pretty sure she was glistening too.

They startled a flock of parrots that soared over their heads, across a small clearing and into the trees. Camouflaged by their emerald green feathers when still, their wings flashed sparks of red and electric blue when they flew, like heat lightening in the heavy air. Her eyes on the birds, Bernadette walked right into Rocky's back. He grinned at her over his shoulder, reached down and pulled her hat out from beneath the leaves of a Guano Palm. He hit it against his thigh a couple of times, then held it out to her, none the worse for wear.

Her spirits soared like the parrots. Finally, a good omen. Slapping the hat on her head, she was ready to go. She pulled out her sketch of Annie's map, tracing the path through the middle of the ballcourt with her finger. "The path to the ballcourt should cross this one pretty soon."

Rocky looked over her shoulder at the map. "The trails on Annie's map radiated out from the pyramid like the spokes of a wheel."

"I didn't draw them all. I just wanted to be able to find building number eight."

"Well, the only trails we've crossed so far were deer tracks," Rocky said.

A few yards farther along, they came to a wider path leading off to the left. On the corner of the jungle intersection, vines trailed across a stone wall creating a matted web. In the dappled shade, down the path to the left, she recognized the spot where she'd seen the jaguar carving and met camo-man.

"This is it," she cried, darting down the trail. "This is where he grabbed me by the arm."

"What were you doing here?"

"The ballcourt is just over here," she said in her defense, pointing down the path toward it. "I walked over to look at this plaque."

Rocky followed and watched as she pulled aside the hanging ferns, exposing the jaguar plaque on the side of the crumbling wall.

"Great. Hold it just like that," he said, and photographed her holding the leaves away from the carving.

"Camo-man told me to stay away."

"From what?" Rocky asked, his voice muffled behind his camera.

"I don't know. He pointed for me to go back to the ballcourt." Bernadette pulled out her map. "We are here, so Temple Number Eight should be that way." She pointed in the opposite direction.

They looked toward the court, then walked back the way they had come and stopped at the corner again. The trail from the ballcourt ended abruptly in blank wall of foliage at their escape route path. She looked at her map in confusion. "My map says this trail crosses the other one, but it looks like it stops here."

Rocky crouched down and examined the soft dusty ground. "Footprints. Lots of people have been this way, but they've been careful to cover their tracks." He pulled back the branches and they peered through.

Bernadette was surprised to see that the path continued, and consulted her map again. "The temple should be on the left, although I'm not sure how far along."

He held back the screen of foliage and they slipped through. "The building must be in pretty good shape to make the top ten on Annie's map. Maybe the carving on the wall back there was like a road sign, pointing the way to the Temple of the Jaguar."

They walked another hundred yards and, just to be

certain, investigated every overgrown pile of stones on both sides of the trail. None of them looked like a temple, but then, Bernadette wasn't sure what they were looking for.

The thin, wispy clouds that had closed in overhead created a layer that obscured the sun but did nothing to lower the temperature. Bernadette felt like she was walking through water, the dense air almost dripping with humidity.

One pile of rocks had steps rising from the forest floor to a platform, five feet off the ground. Trees grew out of the top and the roots of strangler figs threatened to tear apart what was left of the upper structure. She examined a chilling ring of skulls that stared out at eye level from a frieze around the platform while Rocky searched the base. He walked completely around it, scouring the underbrush, but came up blank.

Thank God. She didn't want to explore a structure decorated with skulls. Heaven only knew what they'd find inside. She was better with pot shards than with human remains.

The air was still. The flat, dead light lent an ominous tension, and a hush had fallen over the forest. Bernadette took a drink from her water bottle. In this heat, she was sweating it away as quickly as she drank. Luckily, she'd come prepared with two full bottles.

Their current path became even narrower than their escape route had been, and they were forced to walk in single file. Rocky led the way, pushing through branches. One snapped back and slapped her square in the face and after that Bernadette reached out for each one as he let it go.

"One path on the map led close to the small lagoon behind the hacienda," Rocky said. "This might be it. It heads in the right direction. It shouldn't be too far now."

Bernadette didn't have a clue what direction they

were going. A large root looped out of the ground and catching it with her foot, she pitched forward, putting out her hands to avoid falling on top of Rocky who had stopped in the middle of the path. She peered over his shoulder.

A large vertical stone stood sentinel in front of them. It seemed unnaturally rectangular, but of course, at one time, all the stones in the archeological site had been cut into blocks. This one was at least thirty inches wide and four feet tall with an eroded design carved on the face.

She couldn't keep the excitement out of her voice. "It's a stela, like the marker Manuel showed us." She consulted her map. "There's a stela outside the Jaguar Temple."

About ten feet away through the trees, a vine-covered structure rose eight feet in height from the ground. They walked toward it through the open forest and climbed the broad steps to a platform where remnants of walls and broken columns rose from the floor. The ruins of a structure that had been significant in its day, now ferns and saplings grew out of cracks in the stone.

"It might have been a temple at one time," she said. "But I don't think anyone has met here for hundreds of years."

She plucked at the front of her tank top, pulling it away from her sticky chest, but felt no relief. Dryness clawed at her throat. Sitting on the steps, she took out her water bottle, wishing she had enough left to pour some over her head. Instead, she took a carefully measured sip.

Rocky went back down to ground level and worked his way around the foundation, patting down the wall and pulling away handfuls of vegetation.

A few minutes later he called out from the far side of the structure. "I found something."

With a sinking heart, Bernadette followed the sound

of his voice and found him crouched in front of an opening roughly the size of the stela, in the foundation.

"Is it a door?" *Please say no.* She didn't want to crawl under the temple. Anything could, and probably did, live in there. Critters with more than two legs, or worse, critters with none.

"Could be a door." She could hear the excitement in Rocky's voice. "When the Spanish arrived, most of the Maya were only four feet tall. Even in later days they remained very short."

Like the tiny crone who had tried to sell Bernadette a souvenir at Chichén Itzá.

"Hold this open," Rocky said, parting the foliage screen like curtains. Bernadette tentatively held back the vines, praying that nothing in the vegetation with teeth or a stinger would take offense at the intrusion.

Rocky bent over, almost crawling on the ground through the opening in the wall. Bernadette waited a few seconds, then called, "See anything?"

He poked is head back out, giving her a start. "This is probably it," he said cheerfully, coming out and stretching his back as he stood.

Then he held back the vines for her. "Go check it out."

Chapter 35

The last thing Bernadette wanted to do was check out a hole in the ground. Okay, not quite in the ground, but close enough. Maybe she *was* claustrophobic and had just never had a chance to find out before. She couldn't wimp out now though, not with Rocky watching. Taking the flashlight from his hand, she stooped and crept through the opening as he held the vines apart.

To her relief, the tunnel was only a few feet deep. At the end, a plank door, about five feet high with a wrought iron handle, was set into a wooden framework attached to the stone. She swung the beam of light over it and discerned from its battered condition that it had probably been there for a very long time. Possibly hundreds of years.

A padlock the size of her fist secured a heavy chain to the door frame. Sticking the flashlight under her arm, she took the handle in both hands and pulled. The door didn't budge. She dug in her heels, put her weight behind it and pushed. Nothing.

Thank God.

Rocky was still holding the vines apart when she scrambled back out a moment later.

"Nope, we won't be getting in there," she said, brushing the dirt off her palms.

He grinned. She didn't care if he heard the relief in her voice, but the locked door did mean they'd come all this way for nothing.

"Let's keep going," he said. "I think this trail will eventually lead back to the hacienda."

Bernadette looked nervously over her shoulder, back the way they had come. "Remember what Manuel said about getting lost."

Rocky laughed. "I think he was talking more to you than to me. The hacienda must be straight ahead. Anyway, this is a strong trail. If it peters out, we can just retrace our steps. It's a long way back to the main trail and then we'd have to backtrack all the way along the road."

He was right, they'd come a long way and hadn't seen anyone for an hour or more, not since they lost sight of Annie and Hank. And she certainly wasn't going back alone.

The atmosphere was oppressive and it was increasingly hard to breathe. Rocky took a drink, but from the angle of his bottle she could see he was out of water. The jungle was unnaturally still, except for the irritating whine of mosquitoes. She slapped a big one and scratched the bite.

A scream split the air. Her heart jumped into her throat and she grabbed Rocky's sleeve.

He put a reassuring arm around her shoulders. "It's a Howler Monkey. It would be cool to see one." He scanned the branches overhead. "Haven't you heard them at night?"

"I haven't been so lucky," she said, pulling herself away.

"Maybe not. You're at the front of the building."

An unusual smell drifted on the still air and she realized that was what was catching in the back of her throat. Taking a fresh bottle of water from her pack, Rocky watched as she took the top off the bottle and drank. The water was warm but soothed her parched throat. She held it out to him and he took it gratefully.

"Smoke," he said. handing back the bottle. As soon as he said it, she could see it, hanging low in the trees with no breeze to blow it away. A narrow trail ran off to the right and Rocky started down it.

"No," she cried, grabbing his arm. "You said we

would stay on this trail."

"It's okay," he said over his shoulder as he disappeared down into the underbrush. "I won't go far."

She gave him three seconds, then dashed after him. Catching up easily, she walked inches behind him, pushing the branches aside, not sure anymore there even was a trail. The smoke became noticeably thicker as they crept along.

At the edge of a small clearing, they stopped. An old man in traditional white Mayan clothing stooped to tend a smoky fire that burned between three large rocks on the ground. Four colored stakes marked the four sides of the pit, piles of fruit surrounding each stake. A cross hung on a nearby tree.

The old man saw them, smiled through broken, yellowed teeth, and beckoned for them to enter the clearing. Picking up a metal dish with a long handle, he scooped up some of the smoking coals. Holding the dish in front of him, he offered it to each of the four colored stakes. Then he came over and passed the dish in front of Rocky and Bernadette, letting the choking smoke swirl around them.

"A ceremony," she whispered.

Rocky smiled at the man and motioned with his camera. The man smiled back and nodded. Rocky raised his camera, but only took a few shots before lowering it again.

The old man replaced the coals in the fire. Then he turned back toward them with a cup in his hand. Still smiling, he bowed and offered Bernadette the cup.

Obviously a ritual, but she had no idea what it meant. He seemed friendly though, so she reached for the cup. Rocky was right beside her, snapping that too. As she brought the cup to her lips, the smell of flowers mixed with the resinous smoke in the air. A sweet smoky taste coated the inside of her mouth.

"It's like honey," she said, offering the cup to Rocky.

He drank and then handed the cup back to the man, thanking him in Spanish.

The old man motioned for them to follow as he crossed the clearing to a pile of logs. Bees crawled in and out of holes drilled in rows in the ends of the logs.

"He's a beekeeper," Bernadette said, nodding and smiling at the man who smiled and nodded back. "Gracias," she said, wishing she knew more Spanish.

Rocky asked, "Donde el hacienda?"

The man pointed down a narrow path that exited the clearing opposite the point at which they'd entered. They were on the right trail after all.

Rocky thanked the old man again. Bernadette couldn't wait to get out of the jungle and struck out into the forest on the possum path the old man had indicated, this time with Rocky close behind.

Moments later they emerged from the undergrowth on the far side of the neighboring hotel. Skirting the hotel, they made their way out to the road. Even here in the open beside the lagoon, the heat was stifling. No hint of a breeze ruffled the water.

When they walked in through the front gates of the hacienda, Chief Pacho's police SUV was parked in front of the hotel, along with the white American Embassy car. Rocky grabbed Bernadette's arm and pulled her back out, swinging her around until they stood with their backs to the perimeter wall, facing the road and the lagoon.

"Let's go back to town," he said. "Back to the restaurant. I'll buy you lunch. This might be our last chance to have a meal there."

Bernadette wasn't fooled. Rocky wanted to go to the restaurant so he wouldn't have to talk to the officials. She'd go with him, but decided that over lunch she'd talk to him about the obvious problem he had with the police.

They walked back along the hot dusty road and by the time they reached the restaurant she was ready for the ritual cervezas. They both ordered enchiladas, Rocky indicating to the waiter he wanted his extra *picante* and, to her chagrin, told him not to put any chilies on hers.

The waiter laughed all the way to the kitchen and a moment later she could swear she heard a loud guffaw from the cook.

Her cheeks burned with embarrassment, but she was determined to talk to Rocky about his issue with the police. Chewing her lip, she considered the best approach. How to put it delicately?

The waiter brought their cold beer and left. She took a sip, put down her frosty bottle and began. "Rocky. I've noticed you have a problem relating to Chief Pacho."

"Not really," he said, reaching for his drink.

She felt her cheeks redden again but was determined to stick to her plan. She truly felt it would be better for him to open up.

"Have you," she paused while he took a sip, "been in trouble with the police?"

His face turned the color of red chili salsa and he began to cough convulsively. She jumped up and pounded him on the back. He pushed her away with the sweep of his arm and, reaching for a napkin, wiped the tears from his eyes.

His face was still scarlet, but once his coughing had subsided, she sat down and waited nervously. He took another drink and, setting the bottle down with a *thunk*, stared at the table. Then his eyes came up and he glowered at her. The seconds ticked by. She waited, lips pressed tightly together.

Finally, he said, "What makes you think that?"

His voice was expressionless. She had no idea if he was angry or embarrassed or amused by the question. It had obviously taken him by surprise, though. He must not have realized her keen powers of observation.

"I see you are uneasy around the police." Understatement of the century. But now that the subject was out in the open, she didn't want to spook him.

"Angry, in fact," she continued carefully. "And it occurred to me, there must be a reason."

He continued to stare, and her shoulders crept up to her ears as the silence stretched out. Finally, she started again, just to break the silence. "I only mention it because I think, under the circumstances, I mean with the murders and all, that it might be better to cooperate with the police rather than irritate them."

She gave him a moment to respond, kept her brows high, her face open, receptive, encouraging. He remained silent.

She started again. "Maybe it's not my business—"

"It's not. Keep out of it." He took another drink. "Anyway, I was cleared of the charges."

Her eyes widened. She was right. He had been in trouble. His answer, however, raised more questions than it answered. What charges? Was that how he got shot? She was doomed to wonder since he obviously didn't want to talk. Their food arrived just then, so she decided to let the matter drop. For now.

There was one hilarious moment—at least the waiter seemed to think it was hilarious—when she choked on a forkful of Rocky's extra spicy enchilada that the waiter served to her—by mistake. As she chugged her beer, Rocky exchanged their plates without comment and after that, they ate in silence.

I tried, she thought, watching as he inhaled his fiery lunch.

She was beginning to think that they made a good couple. Team, she corrected. She was beginning to see a future for them as a travel writing *team* and she'd hate to ruin it by being too nosy.

But maybe, when she got back to Vancouver, she'd ask Jen if she knew his secret.

Chapter 36

After they finished their restaurant lunch, Rocky said, "Let's go back one more time and see if Ricardo is at his booth yet."

They'd been out for hours and Bernadette was ready to hit the hotel pool but, happy he didn't seem angry after their little talk, she agreed to go. Anyway, she still wanted to get those earrings and to look at the sombreros again.

Clouds covered the sun, but the white gravel lot continued to radiate heat. With dismay, she saw that Ricardo's booth was still shut and padlocked. If he didn't open soon, she'd have to figure out another gift for her mother.

A teenage boy sold bottled water out of a plastic cooler in the next booth. Rocky bought two bottles and handed one to her, then leaned on the counter in that relaxed, friendly way he had that seemed to put everyone at ease. "Do you speak English?"

The boy nodded shyly. "Little."

Rocky smiled and inclined his head toward the locked booth. "Have you seen Ricardo today?"

The boy glanced furtively at Ricardo's booth. "No. No today. Maybe later."

"Something's not right," Rocky said to Bernadette in a low voice. Then he smiled again at the boy and asked, "Where is the taxi?"

The boy pointed across the dusty parking lot to a beat-up car sitting in a shady spot behind another booth. A bold hand had painted TAXI on its side in acid yellow paint.

"Where are you going?" Bernadette asked, dragging her heels as she followed Rocky across the lot to the taxi, annoyed that, once again, he was making a decision without consulting her.

"Tulum. I want to check out a few things."

She didn't have a problem with going to Tulum—she certainly didn't want to hang around the hacienda—but she would have liked to shower and change first. He was probably right, though, about steering clear of the hacienda. She'd seen those cars in the driveway. They might not get away again if they went inside.

They had both heard Manuel tell Arthur how much a trip to Tulum should cost and Rocky negotiated a fare with the driver for the trip there and back.

The backseat was held together with duct tape, but the air conditioning worked and soon they were flying over the jungle road to Tulum. The car obviously had no shocks and every bump reverberated up Bernadette's spine.

"What do you want to do in town?"

Rocky raised his eyebrows and tipped his head warningly toward the driver. It seemed overly cautious and a tad melodramatic—until she remembered they were investigating a murder. So, when he said, "I want to pick up a few things," she just nodded and fixed her eyes on the scenery for the remainder of the trip.

Regardless of the circumstances, or maybe because of them, she felt energized to be getting out of Ox B'alam. When they arrived in Tulum, the brisk ocean breeze of their first visit was just a memory. Instead, she slipped out of the deliciously cool cab into hot muggy air. Just like back in the jungle.

A dark shelf of cloud was moving in off the Caribbean. A storm was heading their way.

They asked the taxi to wait in front of *Charlie's* restaurant, but instead of going inside, they crossed the road to the Akam's shop. Bernadette brushed her fingers experimentally against the glass as they walked past, but this time felt no discernible vibration.

The bell jangled when Rocky opened the door, announcing their arrival. Inside, the musty smell of age hung in the air. They went straight to the back counter where Mr. Akam was unpacking a variety of wooden artifacts.

His eyes narrowed when he saw them, then he smiled, probably with the expectation of another sale. "My friends, how may I help you today?"

"We have a few questions about the statue the lady bought here the other day," Rocky said, his manner friendly, gesturing to Bernadette as he spoke. "What are the chances of getting another one of those statues?"

The dealer rolled his eyes to the heavens. "I only wish I could get more of them. I could have sold that one more than once."

Rocky smiled and leaned on the counter, ready to talk. "They're popular?"

"It was a nice enough piece, but I am surprised at the interest it caused." Mr. Akam went back to unpacking the crates as he spoke. "First, the man who wanted the appraisal of his statue. Then another man brought in a second one to sell. That was the one you bought Señorita." He gave her his best salesman's smile.

"Who was that? The man who sold you that statue?" she asked. "Maybe we could find him and get another."

"I know nothing about him. I have not seen him before or since that day. He insisted on a cash transaction. All I can tell you is that he was Mexican."

"Too bad," Rocky murmured.

"The police were in asking these same questions yesterday. That poor American. Murdered. I am beginning to think the statues are cursed."

Bernadette drew a sharp breath. Cursed? She hadn't felt anything like that when she held her jaguar. And the way her senses were acting up, if there was a curse, she would probably have felt it.

"And then the other man, just today," Akam continued.

Her ears perked up.

"He described the same statue to me and would have bought it like that." He snapped his fingers in front of her face. Then his shoulders fell. "But I did not have one to sell."

"What did he look like?" Rocky asked. "That might be our friend."

"He was small, American, with round glasses. He was in here before a few weeks ago and bought some nice antique pieces. I was sorry I had nothing for him today. Is this your friend?"

"Sounds like him," Rocky said, glancing at Bernadette.

She nodded. It had to be Arthur. He was desperate to get that jaguar statue.

"Perhaps I could interest you in one of these beautiful carved wooden masks," Akam said hopefully, holding up a brightly painted devil's mask complete with long twisted horns and red-rimmed eyes.

"Not this time," she said, backing away. After what had happened with her jaguar, she wouldn't buy anything from him now.

When they were back on the street, she said, "Arthur. He really wanted my jaguar that night at the bar. If Pacho hadn't interfered, I might have had to wrestle him for it."

"But who was the man who sold the statue to Akam in the first place?" Rocky asked.

"Akam said he was Mexican."

"Well that narrows it down," Rocky said, making no attempt to hide the sarcasm in his voice.

"At least Pacho is following some leads. Maybe he's getting somewhere," Bernadette said.

While Rocky went to find their taxi, she walked down the street to a dry goods shop. Its large, garage-style doors were open to the street, the shelves packed with everything from shovels to teacups. She bought a bottle of water and a flashlight to replace her smashed pen light, this time, a larger one. One thing her run through the jungle had taught her, when you need light, you want it bright.

Back at the restaurant, Rocky had rounded up their taxi. The humidity was tangible, and she felt like a spot of grease as she gratefully climbed into their humble but cool cab.

"I need a swim," she said. "I'm going back to the hacienda."

"Okay," Rocky said. "Just one more stop."

Chapter 37

Rocky was pleased to see Bernadette revive in the air-conditioned taxi. He wanted to check on Ricardo again and by the time they got back to Ox B'alam, she agreed to stop at the ruins. He had a bad feeling about the vendor's disappearance, one that only increased when he saw that Ricardo's booth was still locked.

"Pretty coincidental," Bernadette said.

Rocky huffed a laugh. "You mean that he should disappear hot on the heels of the murder? I'll say. And with that receipt from Ricardo's stall in Caruthers' room? I'm afraid Ricardo is long gone."

"Too bad. There goes my plan to get my mother those earrings. I should have gotten her something in Tulum. Oh, well. Time to face the music—and Pacho. Let's go back to the hacienda and go for a swim."

In silence, they walked back towards the lagoon and the road to the hacienda. Thunder growled low in the distance as the leaden cloud they had seen in Tulum bore down on Ox B'alam. Ozone tainted the air and Rocky glanced uneasily at the sky, expecting flashes of heat lightning.

Just past the restaurant, Bernadette suddenly dropped her bag and left the road, heading off across the rough stretch of grass and weeds toward the water and the rickety dock they had seen many times from the bus.

A tattered, hand-written 'Keep Out' sign hung from a limp rope, cordoning off the listing dock. The only dock on the lagoon, it sat low, almost floating on the water, hemmed in by reeds and rushes. It didn't look like it would hold a person's weight, so he watched in surprise as Bernadette stepped over the rope.

It was totally out of character for Ms. Rule-Follower

to ignore the sign. And besides, the dock looked dangerous. He hurried after her, climbed over the rope and grabbed her by the arm. "Bernadette."

She turned on him with feverish eyes. Startled, he let her go and stepped back. But just a step.

He followed her gaze as it swept the reeds, searching for something he could not see. She started to move out on the floating pier and he followed, close enough to grab her if she faltered on the rotten boards, but not so close that their combined weight would sink the rickety structure. The last thing he wanted was a swim in this crocodile infested water, but he was worried—and fascinated—by Bernadette's actions. What did she see that he didn't?

He followed her out onto the dock, every step washing water over the uneven boards. Spying a broken plank ahead, he reached for her again but stopped as she easily stepped over it, without even looking down.

His pulse raced and his eyes flickered from the uneven dock to Bernadette then out to the water where he scanned for crocs. They were there. They were always there. The thick reeds that hugged the shore provided perfect cover.

At the end of the dock, a small platform floated on the water. Bernadette stopped and swept her eyes from the marshy shore on one side of the dock, out across the water and back to the shore on the other side.

Rocky stopped a foot behind her and ran his eye over the water too. The grasses and reeds were thinner here. In places logs poked up out of the water, looking too much like crocs for his liking. A shiver ran down his back.

He was just about to call her back when he saw something else bobbing in the water. The shape was indecipherable. Not a log, more organic and meaty.

A body—or most of a body—was floating in the

reeds. Whoever it was, he was clearly beyond help.

Rocky heard a low animal groan and turned to see Bernadette collapse in a heap on the dock. Heart pounding, he dropped to his knees at her side. Water washed up over the boards, soaking them both.

Calling her name, he lifted her shoulders out of the water. Her eyelids fluttered but did not open. Reeds shuddered to his left, ten feet out. A croc, coming in to investigate. It wouldn't be the only one, not from what he could see of the floating body.

All he could think of was getting her off the dock. ASAP. She was too close to the water—too vulnerable to the crocs. He'd seen on TV how fast those bastards could attack. One lunge out of the water and she'd be gone in seconds. And he would be helpless to stop it.

He tried to pick her up in his arms, to raise her out of the water, but the frail dock sank deeper under their weight. He set her back down.

"Work with me, Bernadette," he growled, but her head just flopped to one side.

Putting a hand under each of her arms, he walked backwards, one step at a time, dragged her through the slick film of water. Their only hope was to spread their weight over as many boards as possible.

Her feet bumped over every board. He scanned the reeds. They grew too close to the dock. If a croc came for him he wouldn't have a chance.

His foot hit dead air and his heart rammed into his throat. Glancing down he saw the broken plank a split second before his sandal hit the water. His bare leg scraped the rough broken edge of the board as his foot went down, seemingly forever, before finding the soft ooze on the bottom.

He sprang back up, out of the water, shuddering at the thought of what might be lurking in the murk.

Lifting Bernadette higher, he dragged her over the

broken board. He remembered crossing it before. They must be almost at the shore. Her foot caught a raised plank and he lost one of her arms. It splashed down into the muddy water that swirled around his feet.

Surrounded by the wall of reeds, panic rose like an ache in his chest, cutting off his wind and making his head spin. Giving in to the urge, he lifted her into his arms, clear out of the water, and raced the last few feet to shore, water sloshing over his sandals.

He lay her gently on the rough ground and then sank down beside her, flat on his back, his breath coming in painful spurts. With one arm around her, he pulled her close and lay her head on his heaving chest.

Closing his eyes, he said a short, all-purpose Italian prayer. Then he sat up, resting her head on his lap and shook her shoulder gently, calling her name.

Her eyes fluttered open and she stared at the sky. "Vultures," she whispered.

Rocky looked up and saw the birds circling on hot air currents, black against the slate grey sky.

Bernadette moaned. "Oh, no." Briefly, she closed her eyes again. Then they opened, and she focused on him. "I'm sorry. What happened?" Her eyes widened, and he saw she remembered. She struggled to sit up.

He said, "Take it easy." But she pushed him aside. She seemed all right, so he let her go and moved a few inches away. They should move anyway. They were still too vulnerable, this close to the water.

He got to his feet. "Can you stand?" He held out both hands to her. She took them and he pulled her to her feet, and together they stumbled up to collapse on the road.

Rocky took out his phone and punched in Manuel's number.

* * *

Bernadette sat on the edge of the pavement, elbows on her knees and head in her hands, feet dangling over the side of the roadbed where it dropped off to the weedy shoreline. Rocky stood up on the road, waiting for Manuel to arrive.

This was bad. A second murder. How could she explain to Pacho why she was right in the middle of it all again? Her head was clearing but her body still shook. That had been a bad attack. She wasn't used to this. Years went by with hardly any episodes and now she seemed caught in a vortex she couldn't explain. It wasn't as if these spells clarified anything or produced any new and helpful information.

Then her head came up as she remembered the body. *Shit.* Maybe this time it did.

In her mind's eye, she could still see it floating, partially submerged. But something was wrong with the picture. It was the wrong shape. It wasn't all there. Her head began to spin, and she dropped it in her hands again, barely holding onto her lunch as her stomach heaved.

Chief Pacho and his deputy were the first to arrive, raising a cloud of dust as they swung the police SUV around, blocking the road. The Chief got out of the four-by-four and hitched up his pants. A man on a mission. The deputy got out of the passenger side, reached into the back seat and pulled out a shotgun.

Perfect.

Rocky stepped forward and spoke to Pacho. Thank God he was handling it. She wasn't sure she would be coherent if she tried.

He told the Chief they'd had lunch in town and were just walking back to the hacienda when they saw something floating in the water. It could have happened to anybody.

But it hadn't. It had happened to her. At least he was sticking by her.

When Manuel arrived, Pacho left him to guard Rocky and her. She almost laughed. What would he have done if they'd run? And anyway, where could they go?

Pacho and his deputy walked out onto the dock to investigate. Upon sighting the partly devoured bloated corpse, Pacho left the deputy there with his rifle, guarding the body from the crocs, she supposed, until they could get it out of the lagoon.

Chief Pacho splashed back on his own to deal with Bernadette and Rocky.

Chapter 38

The Chief immediately separated Rocky and Bernadette, and moments later she found herself alone, shivering in the back seat of the police car on her way to the hacienda while Rocky went with Manuel.

She watched cop shows too. She knew what the Chief was doing. He didn't want them to talk to each other, to work on their story. Not that there was any story. Just the part she was planning to leave out, the part about her episode, which wouldn't help the investigation anyway. In fact, it would only get in the way.

The stink of lagoon water clung to her wet clothes and her skin, and she desperately hoped the Chief would let her get cleaned up before whatever was going to happen, happened.

He gave her five minutes alone in her room with the heavy-set deputy who'd been guarding Caruthers' room standing guard outside the door. She showered in two minutes flat, then pulled on her dress and clean sandals. Her hair still dripping on her shoulders, she followed the deputy back down the stairs, but at least she felt refreshed and clean.

Rocky, still wet and muddy, stood with another deputy in the lobby and stared silently into her eyes as she walked by. If he was sending her a message, she had no idea what it was. At the office door, she looked back over her shoulder and saw the deputy escorting him up the stairs.

Officer Perez, ushered her into the office and shut the door, leaving her alone. A single wooden chair stood in the middle of the room, just like the last time she met with Pacho.

This time though, she stayed on her feet and waited,

arms crossed over her chest, rather than resume that submissive position.

The door burst open, but instead of Chief Pacho, a tall blond man with a briefcase entered. He held out his hand to shake. "I'm Paul Mathers, from the American Consulate."

Bernadette's spirits soared. The cavalry. Just in time. She took his hand and clung to it. "Mr. Mathers, I am so glad you're here. This has been a terrible week. First Mr. Caruthers, then this body. I don't know who it is. All I could see was his back. I hope it wasn't anyone from the tour."

She was babbling, but it was such a relief to pass off the responsibility. Surely he would work it all out for them now.

"Yes, I understand," he said, extricating his hand from her grip and taking the chair behind the desk. She sank limply onto the uncomfortable chair in the middle of the room.

Mathers opened his briefcase, took out a file and pulled out a form. "I just want to make sure this information is correct. You and Mr. Falconi are the last two I need to speak to.

"Now," he said, consulting the paper. "Your full name on your passport is Bernadette Mallow, no middle name."

It was a statement, not a question. He had her passport, which she had left in the hotel safe. It shook her to realize the hotel staff would release it to him without her permission. He rattled off her information: address, phone number, emergency contact.

"Are you going to help us?" she asked when he finished.

"My advice to you is to get out of Mexico as soon as you are free to go."

"Free to go?" That confirmed it. They weren't getting

out of here anytime soon.

"Yes. I understand Chief Pacho has questions for you and Mr. Falconi regarding this latest incident. I understand…" He consulted the folder again. "That you have had some involvement with the previous events? And now, of course, finding this latest body…"

The blood drained from her face, leaving her skin a stiff, expressionless mask. "I am not involved in this," she said, putting as much indignation as she could muster into her voice.

"If that is so, then I am sure Chief Pacho will figure it out." Mathers spoke with optimistic emphasis. "When you are able to leave, call me at this number." He handed her a card along with her passport. "We will send a car for you."

He began to gather up his papers and her stomach turned to lead. He was not going to help them. In fact, he was leaving just as soon as he could.

"In matters of homicide we must let the local police do their job."

He came around the table and held a hand out for her to shake. She took it limply but did not stand up.

"Good-bye and good luck," was all he said, then he hustled out the door.

She sat staring out the window, her mind blank. Apparently she had lost the ability to think. A few minutes later, she saw Mathers jump into the white embassy car and tear down the driveway in a cloud of dust.

Instinctively, she knew she couldn't leave the room. Not until she'd spoken to Pacho. She'd have bet a deputy guarded the door. Her previous determination had disappeared when Mathers walked out of the room. Now she sat, shoulders slumped and waited for whatever would happen next.

Finally, Chief Pacho came in. He said nothing, just

took his place on the other side of the desk and opened his folder of papers.

That was all it took for her anger to flare. She needed some papers. Any papers. Just so she was not always out-papered by these bureaucrats.

"Señora Mallow," Pacho began.

"Chief Pacho," she replied in even tones. It was time to turn the tables. Time to take charge. "What is going on in your town? We came here on vacation and find our lives endangered. Bodies floating everywhere. Mr. Falconi and I had hoped to give the town some good publicity—you do know we're writing a piece for *Travelers Magazine*? But at this rate it's going to be very difficult to write a positive review." Her shoulders shook, but she put her hands on her hips. It wasn't as intimidating sitting in the chair as it would have been if she'd been standing, but better than folding them in her lap.

The Chief raised his eyebrows in surprise but did not jump to his own defense. Finally, he said, "We are working on it, Señora Mallow. We are working on it. But here you are again, in the middle of the investigation. A coincidence? I find that hard to believe."

"Obviously, someone is out to get us," she countered. "Or we are being set up, or…" She ran out of reasons. "Something."

When he did not respond, her nerves forced her to continue. "What reason would I have to kill these people? I don't even know them. Who was the second victim anyway? Did you get the body out of the water? I hope it isn't anyone we know. Or knew. Or anyone from the village."

"I do not yet know the identity of the victim," Pacho said. Her stomach heaved. That confirmed her memories of the body. Unidentifiable. A shudder ran through her.

"What were you doing at the dock, Señora Mallow?"

Recent events had pushed her to the point where she suspected Pacho as much as Rocky did, and was determined not to give anything away. He was not going to pin this on her. "We were walking back from the ruins."

"And what were you doing at the ruins."

"We had just come back from Tulum, by taxi."

"Why did you go to Tulum?"

He was a bulldog. She tried not to pause and think, but she did not want to tell him they had been to Akam's store until it was absolutely necessary. "We did some shopping."

"What did you buy, Señora Mallow?"

"I bought a flashlight," she said, and frowned, suddenly wondering what had become of it.

"Is this it?" He pulled a bag out of his briefcase.

"Yes. Thank you." She reached for the bag but stopped before touching it. "Unless you want to keep it as evidence."

He paused a beat. She hoped he was registering her objection. "That won't be necessary."

She took the small bag and waited as seconds ticked by. Maybe he was waiting for her to blurt out something else, but she'd pulled herself together and was determined to say nothing. Two could play at this game.

Finally, he cleared his throat and said, "You can go now, Señora Mallow, but stay near the hacienda. I'm not finished with you yet."

She sat for a minute considering what this might mean, then stood up and walked to the door, her back stiff. With her hand on the knob, she turned to him. "When will I get my jaguar back?"

Chief Pacho shook his head. "I'm sorry, Señora, I really don't know."

She shot him a scathing look and left the room.

When she closed the office door behind her, the steel went out of her spine. She could hardly hold herself erect. Her irritation was real, but fear had sucked all the energy out of her and she did not have the strength to maintain her anger.

The lobby was empty. Rocky was nowhere to be seen. Neither were any of the other tour members, so she walked through the empty dining room and out to the terrace bar.

The light had faded to an eerie twilight. A menacing purple cloud blanketed the sky. The sharp scent of ozone hung in the air.

Salvador was behind the bar. The day had been interminable. It had to be cocktail hour by now, and whether it was or not, she was ready for a drink.

She climbed up onto a stool. "Hit me Sal. Make it tequila."

He frowned in concern. "That bad?"

She sighed. "That bad."

He poured the pale liquor into a tall narrow shot glass and set the glass on the counter in front of her. She eyed the golden liquid warily, then picked up the shot glass and took a sip. A shudder ripped through her. Her eyes watered and she squeezed them shut as the liquor burned its way down her throat.

"You don't like it?"

She shook her head and pushed the glass to the side. "Too harsh."

Rocky slid into the seat beside her. "For me? Thanks, I could use it."

"Go for it."

Salvador smiled at her as he got Rocky a beer. "We have ways with tequila, you know."

"What do you mean?"

"We infuse it with many interesting flavors, to smooth the taste. Fresa, coco, chilé."

Rocky's eyebrows perked up. "Chilé?"

Salvador grinned. "Maybe chilé for you, Señor, but I have other flavors for the lady."

He put three tequila glasses on the counter and into each one poured a spoonful of liquid, each a different color, from a row of bottles that sat on a shelf against the back wall of the bar.

The first was translucent rose. Salvador pushed it toward Bernadette.

"Fresa," he said, looking to Rocky for help.

"Strawberry."

She picked up the glass, tired of being a wimp in front of these two, and brought the slim jigger to her mouth. She wet her lips with the rosy liquid. It wasn't sweet, but a strong undercurrent of strawberries cut the harshness of the liquor.

"I like it," she said and drank it all, licking her lips as she put down the empty glass.

"Then try this one," he said, pushing the second glass toward her.

Reaching more eagerly for it this time, she asked. "What is it?"

"Canela."

"Cinnamon," Rocky supplied, smiling as he sipped from his own glass.

She took a bigger first sip this time, but found the dusky, slightly acidic flavor not as pleasant as the strawberry. She winced and shook her head.

Salvador smiled. "You'll like this one I am sure." Brown beans swirled on the bottom of the third bottle as he poured. "Café."

She reached eagerly for the glass and tossed back the tiny shot. She smiled as the perfect, smooth coffee notes caressed her taste buds. "That's the one. Hit me Sal."

He filled her glass and she settled back, feeling mellower already as the heat of the tequila spread through her veins.

"So how did it go?" she asked Rocky. Okay, so she wanted to have the same story after all.

His face, previously relaxed, snapped shut into his I-don't-want-to-talk-about-it expression. "Just what happened," he said stiffly. "We were walking back to the hotel and saw something in the water. We walked out on the dock, just to see what it was. How about you?"

She looked at him closely. Perhaps he did not want to talk in front of Salvador. She had to admit he might be right. The staff were so friendly, she had a hard time thinking of them as possible bad guys. Even Salvador had begun to grow on her. But perhaps they should limit their discussions to the privacy of their rooms.

Hank's arrival put any more discussion on hold and soon the rest of the group followed him into the bar. She was relieved to see everyone accounted for, although they were all unusually subdued. The Morrises settled at their regular table in the dining room and pulled out their deck of playing cards.

Salvador's shift was apparently over, and Jose replaced him behind the bar. Then Luis came out of the kitchen to tell everyone that dinner would be delayed.

As the week had progressed, Luis had become increasingly agitated until now he was barely functioning, could hardly look them in the eye. He tried to help at the bar but after getting two orders wrong, Jose sent him back to the kitchen.

Dinner was probably late because of the latest development. The body. Because of the latest body. Bernadette took her tequila and moved to one of the small tables on the terrace where she could be alone to think.

Deep down inside, she was convinced that all the events of the week were somehow related: camo-man and the temple, Caruthers' murder, the jaguar statues, the attack in the jungle at dawn, Rocky's missing camera and now this disturbing second body in the lagoon. To say nothing of her episodes and jaguar dreams.

Slowly she drank the tequila, repeatedly going over the list, but she couldn't see any connection. No connection at all.

Friday, Day 6

"The sky was overcast and portended the coming of another Norte. The wind swept over the ruined building, so that in places we were obliged to cling to the branches to save ourselves from falling."

J.L. Stephens, <u>Incidents of Travel in Yucatán, 1842</u>

<u>Chapter 39</u>

Rocky hardly slept at all that night. His mind was running like a hamster on a wheel, going over the events of the week, searching for the links. He couldn't see the connection and it was driving him crazy.

When he got to the dining room, Bernadette hadn't come down. It was quiet. Too quiet. The approaching storm added to the escalating tension, the clouds emitting a greenish light that made it feel more like dusk than early-morning. A faint breeze had sprung up in the last hour, but it wasn't enough to clear the air that hung over the hacienda, heavy as a wet dishrag, making it difficult to breathe.

By the time Rocky was on his second cup of coffee, he could see that the Cultural Tour had completely unravelled. There was no schedule anymore; people were coming and going on their own timetable.

Eloise and Celeste had gone to their room. Lying by the pool under a leaden sky obviously held no appeal. They had spent the previous day and evening in Tulum and that seemed to have appeased their party appetite for the time being.

Just as well, Rocky thought. At this rate, none of them were getting out of Ox B'alam any time soon. They were all waiting to see if they could leave the next morning as planned, or if Pacho would insist they stay. At this point, Rocky had to admit that Pacho would be justified in keeping them here.

Arthur had excused himself immediately after breakfast, leaving in such a rush that he left his book behind again. It still sat by his place at the table.

The Morrises had retired to their regular corner table for gin rummy.

Finally, Bernadette entered the dining room. She went to the buffet and returned to the table with a small plate of food. Luis brought her coffee and she thanked him, then picked at the food, not really eating. She looked better this morning, though. Finding the body had been rough on her. After the ordeal she'd looked completely drained.

Then, after Pacho and the jerk from the embassy had finished with her, she had ordered a tequila and taken it to a table on the terrace where she sat alone until dinner. He remembered his vow the first night to get her drinking tequila but was sorry it had taken such a grisly scene to make it happen. He would have gone over and sat with her then, but she'd looked like she wanted to be alone. Anyway, there'd been nothing to say.

At dinner her face had been pinched with worry. He had tried to talk to her afterwards, but in answer to his question, "Are you okay?" she'd smiled weakly and said, "Sure".

Shortly after that, she had gone up to bed.

She must have felt him watching her now, though, because she looked up and gave him a tired smile.

His stomach clenched, and his train of thought flew

out the window. He gave his head a shake. *Oh, no. Not Bernadette.* Good way to complicate a working relationship. He never had these problems working with Shuster.

He blinked, trying to force his mind back to the question at hand, but it didn't work. He hated the way Pacho seemed to be singling her out, but he hid his frustration. He had learned long ago how to keep his face expressionless, how to not give himself or his thoughts away.

Bernadette caught his eye from across the table and a frown puckered her forehead. With a jolt he realized she knew exactly what he was thinking. He was losing his edge. He glanced around the table. Luckily, she seemed to be the only one. She smiled wanly and went back to picking at her breakfast.

He should be able to work this out. Police work was all about procedure. It wasn't magic; you just track down leads until the pieces fall into place. Bernadette, on the other hand, seemed to be out in la-la land half the time, then stumbled over dead bodies.

Okay, to be fair, she'd only found one body, but there were the other coincidences, things that shouldn't happen in a murder investigation, like the matching jaguar statues. He had to admit, she'd handled the pressure well so far.

When Meredith and Annie got up from the breakfast table to go, Manuel joined him, Bernadette and Hank at the table.

Luis asked if anyone wanted anything more. They ordered another pot of coffee. As he cleared away the plates, his hands shook so badly that the dishes rattled. Rocky brushed against him as he reached out to catch a cup as it fell from the top of the pile, and Luis jumped as if he'd received an electric shock.

"I'm sorry," he mumbled, and made a dash for the

kitchen.

Rocky frowned. Luis had something on his mind. Hard to believe he was connected with the murders, but something was missing from the puzzle. Something that held the key to the whole investigation. Luis was keeping something from them. He would find a time to talk to him later.

Manuel didn't look much better. "I am sorry too," he said. "I will refund the tour fee and will try to get my father to refund the hotel portion, too."

"I'm not planning to write about the murders," Bernadette assured him. "I'll try to give the article a positive spin. It would help, though, if they found the killer."

It was the first time Rocky had seen Manuel since Pacho had left the day before, so it was his first chance to question him.

"Have you seen Annie's map?" he asked.

Manuel nodded. "It is from the reconstruction that started here more than twenty years ago."

"It was very interesting. We all had a look," Rocky said. "There was one building we didn't remember from our tour of the ruins with you, though. It was marked, 'Temple Number Eight'."

Manuel's eyes widened, but he didn't look away, so Rocky continued. "Yesterday Bernadette and I went back to the ruins. We found a path that led from the ballcourt back towards the hacienda."

Manuel looked stricken. He nodded but didn't respond, so Rocky continued. "We think we found the temple. It looked like it might still be in use. There was a padlock on the door."

Manuel's gaze dropped to the table, but he offered no comment. Rocky felt Bernadette's eyes on his face as he asked, "Who are the Black Jaguars, Manuel?"

Manuel's gaze flew up to meet Rocky's and he drew

a sharp breath. "Who told you about the Jaguars?"

Rocky felt his heart beat speed up as one more piece of the puzzle fell into place.

"Someone mentioned them the other night," he said. "Is it a religious organization?"

Manuel sighed and looked back down at the table, trying, it seemed, to arrange his thoughts. Then slowly he began to speak.

"The Black Jaguars take care of the people in the community, as they have for hundreds of years. A century ago, the Mexican government pushed the Maya people to this corner of Mexico and then left us virtually alone to govern ourselves. Here, in the isolated communities, the cycles of the old gods and the new Christian religion have mixed together. Both are very important in everyday life. Both the old ways and the new are revered.

"Since before any can remember, the Jaguars have met at the Temple of the Jaguar at Old Ox B'alam. For years they met in secret as first one conqueror then another took control of our land. They took their name from the Black Jaguar god, Ek B'alam because, in ancient times, he took care of the Maya people. Today the Black Jaguars try to do the same."

Everyone was silent, absorbing the information, and after a few minutes Manuel continued.

"From time to time we find relics in the ruins, although not much is left after hundreds of years of looting. Forty years ago, my people were living in dark days. There was no work, no money, crops were failing and the people were hungry. Then they found the statue of the Ek B'alam. It is not large, but it is ancient, and the villagers took it as a sign that he had returned to watch over his people.

"And, in fact, from that time on things did improve. The hotels were built in Cancun and slowly life in the villages got easier with new jobs, more food. Roads and electricity came to the village as well as new schools for the children. I was one of the lucky ones who went not only to elementary school but all the way to college, something unheard of in my father's day.

"In recent years, the men of the Black Jaguar have become stronger and have been able to do even more for the community. We thank Ek B'alam for his help, but is it a religion? You be the judge."

Silence hung in the room, everyone's eyes on Manuel. When he did not continue, Rocky probed gently. "What's happening now, Manuel?"

His eyes dropped to the table again. "Recently, someone has found our meeting house beneath the Temple of the Jaguar and has stolen some of our religious relics." Manuel looked up and his voice dropped to a whisper. "First it was an incense burner, then a sacred knife. Now, a few days ago, the statue of B'alam. The people of the village are very frightened. He is their protector and they fear it portends a return to dark days. With the murders, they are afraid they have already begun." Rocky could see the desperation in Manuel's eyes. "We trust Chief Pacho to find the statue. Then maybe this madness will end."

This was more information than Rocky had bargained for. Now his job was to separate the substance of what Manuel had said from the myth. Or maybe, in this case, that would not be possible.

A movement in the lobby caught Rocky's eye as Chief Pacho and his deputy walked into the hacienda.

Here we go again.

Chapter 40

Bernadette's heart sank when Chief Pacho walked into the lobby. She glanced at Rocky, but he was watching the lobby too, where the two police officers had stopped at the front desk to talk to Señor Ferrara. She had not seen the Chief since their interview the previous afternoon and she hoped he had come to tell them that they had identified the second body, not to question her again.

The others soon noticed the officers and silence settled over the little group in the dining room as they watched and waited. Finally, the Chief entered the dining room, steps labored, shoulders bowed as if he bore a great burden. The weight of the murders, so troubling to the local people, must be doubly hard on the Chief. From what Manuel had just said, he was the one who, in his duties as the Chief of Police, the villagers looked to for protection.

He stopped a few feet inside the door and announced, "We have discovered the identity of the second dead man. It is Ricardo Gonzales, from the souvenir park and yes, we feel certain it was murder."

Bernadette was not surprised. In some way, she had already known. They knew he was missing; she and Rocky had been looking for him all day yesterday. She frowned as she tried to remember why. *The earrings.* Souvenirs to take home. Time was running out and she had thought she would have to find something else.

She caught herself, horrified by what she was thinking. A man is dead, and she was thinking about shopping? She struggled to pull herself together.

Rocky was no help. As usual, he had slipped his dark glasses over his eyes and was sitting back in his chair.

Had he known it was Ricardo when they found the body? He must have had his suspicions too, although, when they found Ricardo's booth deserted, he'd said he thought Ricardo had run. Thought he was guilty of murdering Caruthers.

And what exactly was the connection between Caruthers and Ricardo? And if Ricardo killed Caruthers…then who killed Ricardo? And why?

Rocky spoke up. "How did you identify him?"

Chief Pacho hesitated, then said, "By his rings."

Bernadette's stomach flipped and slithered back into place as she remembered the rings on the hand that covered her mouth during the pre-dawn, jungle attack.

Rocky stood up. "Well, if you need us for further questioning, we will be in the hotel all day. Coming Mallow?"

It was not really a question. She struggled to her feet. "Yes, I think I'll go up to my room and lie down."

Rocky followed her out of the dining room and up the stairs. At the red police tape on Caruthers' door she turned to her room, but Rocky grabbed her hand and pulled her across the hall to his door. He dropped her hand while he opened the door with his key, then reached for her again and pulled her inside.

Although it was barely noon, hardly any light penetrated the heavy cloud cover outside the window and the atmosphere in the room was like dusk. Bernadette sank wearily into the chair.

Rocky ran a hand over his face. "Grisly."

They were silent for a moment, then he swung onto his bed, back against the wall in what she'd come to recognize as his thinking position. "Quite the story Manuel told us. It explains the temple. Sounds like the Black Jaguars are sort of a religious brotherhood combined with a local service club. But that doesn't really explain what's going on."

Bernadette sat stiffly in the chair. "The locals must be terrified. It's not just the murders. These people have struggled for so long to keep their culture alive and now someone is stealing their few remaining artifacts. No, not artifacts. Icons. They are more than artifacts to them."

They looked at each other in silence for a moment. "So," she said. "Who dun-it?"

Rocky blew out a frustrated breath. "I don't know. For a while there I thought it was Ricardo, but right now my money's on Arthur. He has a connection with Ricardo, Akam and could have had one with Caruthers, for all we know."

"And he had an unnatural interest in my jaguar."

"I'm even beginning to think Luis might be involved. He has no poker face and he's been so jumpy lately."

Bernadette frowned. "Not Luis. Can you really picture Luis killing someone with a knife?"

Rocky sighed. "Not really."

"Well, let's think. What is the connection between Ricardo and Caruthers?"

"I'm not sure yet," Rocky said. "But we did find that receipt from Ricardo's shop in Caruthers' trash. That is not so unusual though. They'd find one in your room too."

Bernadette blanched. What if Pacho insisted on searching her room? Fear dug its claws into her chest at the thought of being any further implicated in the murders, but she fought to control her panic. Yes, she had a receipt, but she had the earrings to show for her purchase. It was, however, one more damning connection between her and Caruthers.

The question was, what had Caruthers bought from Ricardo.

"The jaguar statue," she breathed.

Rocky looked at her, a questioning frown on his face.

"Caruthers bought his jaguar from Ricardo," she said excitedly. "Then Ricardo sold the second statue to Akam. It makes total sense."

Then she remembered the rings. "And I think Ricardo was the man who grabbed me in the jungle the morning we were attacked. I remember the rings on his fingers pressing into my face when he covered my mouth."

Rocky mulled that over for a minute. "Yes, maybe, but that still doesn't explain who murdered Ricardo. Maybe whoever he was with in the jungle." He picked up the remote and turned on the television, then sat back on the bed.

Bernadette nodded thoughtfully. "The man in the ball cap he was with in the bar."

Rocky pulled his computer onto his lap. "Say Caruthers did buy the statue from Ricardo, and that Ricardo was the 'Mexican' man who sold the other statue to Akam."

A menu popped up on the screen and he ran the cursor down to 'Tulum'. A moment later the first shots of the Castillo at the Tulum archeological site began to scroll by. "That doesn't explain who the murderer is, or why he killed those two men."

They sat in silence, mulling over the questions as Rocky's pictures flashed before their eyes.

The pueblo. Lunch at Charlie's. The wall of glass bottles.

"There must be a third party," Rocky mused. "Someone wasn't happy with something those two did."

Eloise, hamming it up for the camera. Street scene, street scene. Akam's window.

Bernadette sucked in a breath when she saw it and grabbed Rocky's arm. "Wait. Go back a few shots."

Rocky sighed in exasperation. "I've been over these pictures a hundred times. There's nothing to see." But he backed up a few frames anyway.

"There, stop," she said sharply. It was the photo of Eloise, the busy street slightly blurry in the background. "Can you zoom in on that background at all?"

"Not on the TV," Rocky said, and the television screen went black. "But I can do it on my laptop."

Bernadette climbed up on the bed beside him and watched as he opened Photoshop and brought the same photograph up on the screen of his laptop.

"Zoom in," she said urgently.

He enlarged it once, then again until the sign on Akam's window blurrily filled the screen.

"Can you make it clearer?" she asked.

Rocky hit a combination of keys and the image on the screen sharpened slightly. "I have a better one of the sign," he said.

"That's not what I want to see. Scroll across to the people on the street." He ran to the left and found two faces. Female. Looked like tourists.

"The other way."

He panned across the window again and stopped at a figure coming out of the entrance to Akam's shop, looking straight at the camera.

"Sal," she breathed.

"Unmistakable."

They sat in silence, contemplating the implications of what they saw on the screen. The man looked straight at the camera; he must have seen Rocky take the shot.

Outside the hacienda window, lightening flashed over the treetops. Seconds later, a tentative knock sounded on the door.

Bernadette's eyes snapped to the door as if it was magnetic, then she and Rocky both jumped off the bed. Rocky quickly closed his laptop and headed for the door. Bernadette was right behind him.

Luis waited in the corridor, anxiety etched on his face, his hands clasped behind his back.

"Luis," Rocky said. "What can I do for you?"

"Señor Rocky," Luis began. He looked so upset, Bernadette was afraid he would burst into tears. "I have to tell you, but you must believe me when I say, I did not steal it." Slowly, he brought his hands out from behind his back. He was clutching Rocky's missing camera.

"Where did you get this?" Rocky took the camera and turned it over in his hands, examining it carefully. Luis stepped back, eyes wide, shaking his head from side to side.

Bernadette took his arm and drew him into the room, glanced out to make sure the corridor was empty, then shut the door. Luis dropped into the chair and put his head in his hands.

"I do believe you," Rocky said firmly. "Just tell me where you found it."

"At the bungalow, but that is all I can tell you." He looked pleadingly up at Rocky. "It is worth my life to tell you more."

"Who took it, Luis?" Rocky asked, his voice deep and serious, his tone doing nothing to calm the man's fears.

"I should not have gone into his room. He will be so angry."

Bernadette could see Rocky was losing patience, so she crouched beside Luis's chair. "Just tell us. We can help you."

Fear and the desire to tell all battled across his face until finally he blurted, "Salvador hid it in his room. Yes, he is my cousin, but I did not meet him until four months ago. I have suspected for some time that he is not honest. He comes and goes at strange times and has money he cannot explain. He just laughs and says if I stick with him, maybe I will get rich too. I laughed with him because I am afraid, but then I watched.

"I saw him come into the bungalow with the camera. He does not know what I saw. Then I feel bad when I see you, Señor Rocky, so I bring it to you. But now I am afraid of what Salvador will do to me if he finds out."

Bernadette's heart went out to the young man whose conscience and fear were fighting it out in front of her.

"Thank you, Luis," Rocky said. "We'll talk to Pacho together."

He ushered Luis out of the room, saying, "I'll meet you downstairs in five minutes. Just try to stay out of Sal's way."

Luis looked relieved. "Chief Pacho is gone, but it is easy to stay away from Salvador today. He has taken the day off."

"Don't worry. We'll find Pacho and work this whole thing out," Bernadette said.

Rocky closed the door behind Luis, then got down on his knees and fished the empty camera case out from under the bed and carefully put his camera away.

"So," she said, struggling to fit the new information into the pattern. "If Salvador was at Akam's shop that day, he must have been the one who sold my jaguar to Akam –"

"Then it stands to reason Salvador sold the other one to Caruthers. Akam said Caruthers came in to have it authenticated. He must have been pissed to find out his relic wasn't as old and valuable as he thought."

"He certainly looked angry when he came back here that evening." She thought for a moment. "I wonder what he paid for it."

"Probably more than the three hundred pesos on Ricardo's receipt. Sounds like Sal had a pretty good con going here. Using Ricardo as a middle man."

"Until Caruthers threatened to break it up."

Rocky's eyes narrowed. "If it is Sal, he has to be pretty shaken up by now. His scam about to be exposed, two murders on his plate. Always assuming he is responsible for both deaths. I wonder what his beef with Ricardo was."

"I don't know." Her eyes widened. "Maybe Sal was the man with Ricardo at the Diablo." Then she frowned, not sure where Rocky stood on Pacho. "Shouldn't we go to the police with this?"

"Soon," Rocky said. "I don't feel I have quite enough evidence yet. We need something concrete." He shook his head. "In the meantime, I guess I should go down and deal with Luis."

Bernadette grabbed her day pack and followed him down to the lobby. They knew it was Salvador, but where was he now? And how did Rocky plan to prove it?

Chapter 41

Once in the lobby, Rocky heard Luis say to a distraught Meredith. "We will tell Manuel."

"Tell him what?" Rocky asked.

"Annie is missing," Meredith cried, frantically wringing her hands.

Rocky went cold inside.

Meredith's slim frame shook visibly, and Bernadette put a reassuring arm around the woman's shoulders. "We'll search the hotel."

Manuel and Hank walked into the lobby. "Search for what?" Manuel asked.

"For Annie," Bernadette said, transferring Meredith to Hank's capable hands.

"I've looked everywhere," Meredith said shakily. "She's just not here. Where would she go?"

"Anyone else missing?" Rocky asked.

"As far as I know, everyone is here," Manuel said, a desperate edge creeping into his voice.

Rocky could see that Manuel was falling apart. Someone had to take charge. "Where's Arthur?"

No one knew. Then a voice piped up from the dining room. "He went out, about half an hour ago."

The group in the lobby looked at each other in surprise and then turned as one in the direction of the voice. Rocky charged into the dining room with the rest of the group close behind.

Mrs. Morris looked up from her regular table in the corner of the dining room where she and her husband were playing gin rummy. "Arthur left about half an hour ago."

"Was he alone?" Rocky asked,

"Yes, he was alone, but he was going to meet

Salvador at the ruins. Although what they were doing there in this weather, I don't know." Mrs. Morris looked at her cards for a moment, then discarded.

"How do you know they were meeting there?" Rocky asked doggedly, trying to pull her attention back to her story. He could feel Bernadette beside him, quivering with the need to do something quickly, but first they had to get all the information.

"We heard them talking at the bar before breakfast. Salvador gave Arthur a piece of paper. Some kind of directions."

"The girl went too," Mr. Morris added. "Followed him into the bushes on the other side of the pool."

"Annie?" Rocky asked sharply.

"Yup."

"Followed who?" Bernadette asked.

"Arthur. He'd been over here talking to us but kept looking at his watch. Kind of rude if you ask me."

Mrs. Morris nodded. "He had to meet Sal."

"And what about Annie?" Bernadette asked.

"Well, after Arthur left, the girl suddenly came out of the dining room and followed him. She looked sort of sneaky, peeking around the corner before she went."

Bernadette picked up Arthur's book from where it lay on the breakfast table. A piece of paper fell out and she caught it as it floated to the table.

"Rocky," she said, studying the paper.

He walked over and looked at the page in her hands. It was a crudely drawn map of the ruins with the route they'd discovered the day before from the hacienda to the temple marked in red.

"I need the van," Rocky said to Manuel, who rushed to the office. A moment later, he met them in the lobby and handed over the keys.

Bernadette opened her mouth and sucked in a breath, obviously getting ready to say something. Probably to demand she come along.

There was no time to argue. Grabbing her hand, he pulled her behind him out the door. She could keep watch from the parking lot and call Manuel if he didn't return.

Once outside, he let go of her hand and they raced to the van. It might already be too late. Climbing into the driver's seat, he jammed the key in the ignition. The engine sprang to life, the wheels spitting up gravel as they roared away from the hacienda before Bernadette could even close her door.

The van shot down the driveway and at the lagoon road he cranked the wheel to the right. Bernadette flew against the door, then righted herself without comment and buckled in.

Raindrops spattered the windscreen. Rocky took the dirt road along the lagoon at full speed, Bernadette clinging to the handle on the dash as the van bounced around like a carnival ride.

"What are you going to do?" she shouted over the noise of the road, the wind and the rain.

"I don't know. Whatever I have to. We can't leave Annie alone with Arthur and Sal."

At the entrance to the ruins, he slammed on the brakes and threw the car into park. "Stay here. Don't move."

"I'm coming with you."

"No, you're not. The last thing I need is to worry about you."

Bernadette crossed her arms stubbornly across her chest. "I can take care of myself."

He didn't bother to reply, just reached across her to open the glove compartment and rummaged around inside. Manuel had something for every emergency— except this.

He pulled out a flashlight. "I wish I had a gun." He

slammed the compartment shut and jumped out of the van.

Halfway to the entrance gate he stopped, doubled back and knocked on her window. She was pissed and seemed to take forever to roll it down.

"Got your phone?"

She shook her head. "I don't have a signal."

He shoved his cell phone into her hand. "Stay in the truck. If I'm not back in ten minutes push seven on speed dial and tell Manuel we need back up."

He turned on his heel and headed for the gate, setting off down the wide main trail at a jog, rain spitting at his face.

Annie must have followed Arthur along the jungle path behind the back lagoon. *Impulsive idiot.* Sure, she felt strongly about the sale of illegal artifacts—*removing them from their home, bla, bla, bla*—but she had no idea what she was getting into. Sal must be desperate by now. There was no telling what he might do.

Rocky's chest tightened. A woman had died on his watch years ago and it had haunted him ever since. It was why he'd left his previous life behind. It couldn't happen again. Putting his head down, he charged into the storm.

Branches swirled around him and the driving rain soon soaked him to the skin. He barely noticed. One thought consumed him: he had to get there in time.

Making the turn to the ballcourt a minute later, he raced between the tall stone walls, quickly approaching the false dead end. Head down, he barreled through the shield of branches and jogged down the narrow path.

A form lay across the trail, blocking his way and for a moment fear grabbed him like a cold hand at his throat. But it wasn't Annie. Instead, a man dressed in camouflage lay unconscious and bleeding from a gash on his head. Rocky knelt beside him and put two fingers on the carotid artery in his neck. His pulse was steady and so was his breathing.

Rocky took a deep breath and tried to slow his racing heart.

Probably a guard, but for which side? If Sal could overcome this burly guy, Annie didn't have a chance. *Per favore Dio,* let her have the sense to hide outside.

Lightning flashed and Rocky realized how vulnerable he was kneeling in the path. He jumped to his feet. Branches whipped in the wind, screening any movement if someone was hiding in the forest. Obviously, someone had been this way since the previous day when he and Bernadette had discovered the temple—someone desperate enough to knock out the guard—and he had no way of knowing if they'd been alone.

He left the man lying on the path and took to the forest in case there was another guard at the temple. Moving silently from tree to tree, senses alert, he kept low, stealthy as a cat, creeping up to the standing stela that marked the edge of the temple grounds.

Hiding behind the rock, he wiped the rain from his eyes and took one last look around, but the noise of the wind and buffeting branches obscured all other sounds.

The narrow entrance to the temple gaped open. Someone had torn the vines away. He flashed his light into the empty antechamber. It could be a trap, but what choice did he have? He had to find out if Annie was in there.

He crept into the rock cavity, voices echoing from beyond the wooden door. Arthur's high-pitched voice pleaded to let Annie go. The stupid girl was arguing back.

Then the sound of a smack, skin-to-skin, ricocheted off the rock walls and Annie cried out.

The blood rushed to Rocky's head. His vision turned red and his breath came in spurts. His thoughts narrowed to a pin-point focus and with a roar he burst through the door.

Chapter 42

As soon as Rocky disappeared through the gate to the ruins, Bernadette jumped out of the van.

No bloody way she was staying in the van!

The storm created an eerie twilight. Flying raindrops stung her face. She glanced over her shoulder as thunder rumbled nearby.

Darting across the main trail, she saw Rocky running not far ahead. He'd send her back if he saw her, so she deked to the zip-line tower and jogged down the narrow escape-route they'd followed the day before. Every now and then she caught sight of him through the trees, running on the parallel path.

When their paths diverged, she broke into a run. She reached the intersection with the path from the ballcourt and ducked behind a tall Guano Palm seconds before Rocky charged out of the intersecting trail and crashed through the camouflaged opening to the temple path.

Sneaking up to the path, she peaked through the battered screen of leaves and saw Rocky kneeling on the ground not far down the trail.

The rain was falling in blinding sheets, and she wiped it from her eyes. Thunder crashed nearby, and she glanced back at the ballcourt as a flash of lightning illuminated a nightmarish tableau, harshly outlining the hoops at the top of the tall stone walls.

She'd only glanced away for a second, but when she looked back down the path to the temple, Rocky was gone.

Here she was, practically at the temple door, without a plan. She patted her pockets and groaned. She'd left Rocky's phone in the van. Her one job and she'd blown it. She pulled her phone out of her shoulder bag but, as usual, didn't get a signal. She dropped it back into her bag and pulled out her flashlight.

Stark possibilities flooded her mind. Maybe the Jaguars were guarding the temple. Or maybe a gang, a smuggling ring, used it to store illegal artifacts before moving them out of the country. If she ran into camo-man now, she wasn't sure which side he'd be on.

Salvador was a snake—no, a chameleon, hiding in plain sight. That smile, those eyes. She'd been right all along. When would she learn to trust her gut?

And now he had Annie. That thought generated a rush of adrenalin that gave her the courage to push through the screen of wet branches onto the temple path. The sight of a lump on the path at the spot where Rocky had knelt stopped her in her tracks. Another body.

Please, don't let it be Annie.

She crept down the path toward the body. She sheltered behind a tree, careful not to touch the bark, and peered out at the lump on the ground. Relief left her knees weak when she saw that whoever it was on the ground was clearly much larger than Annie.

A wave of fear followed close behind. Who was it, then? What if he was dead?

Or what if he wasn't?

Clutching her flashlight like a club, she forced herself to approach the motionless form.

It was camo-man, unconscious on the ground. She knelt beside him and put a tentative hand on his throat. Not dead, but out cold.

She was sure—almost sure—Rocky hadn't done this. For a moment she felt paralyzed—two people dead, two people missing, and now this. Plus, Annie was missing.

That lit a fire under her again and she took off down the trail.

It wasn't far to the temple when you knew the way,

and minutes later she was on one knee behind the standing stone. Breathing hard, she wiped the rain from her eyes and peeked out at the temple.

The curtain of vines at the entrance had been torn away and she blew out a breath of relief to see Rocky crouched inside the tunnel. Just as she stepped out from behind the stone to get his attention, he let out a war hoop and charged inside.

Through the open door, she caught a brief glimpse of a shadowy figure in a torch-lit chamber, then the door slammed shut. Jumping behind the stela, she flattened herself against the rock and prayed she hadn't been seen.

What the hell was he doing? Jamming her flashlight into her bag, she crept from fern to low palm, up to the temple, then flattened against the foundation wall, the stones slick with rain under her hands. A mumble of voices drifted out of the entrance way, but that was all she could hear over the sounds of the storm and the thundering of her pulse in her ears. Inching her way toward the opening, the voices became louder, but she still couldn't make out the words.

She poked her head around the corner. A thin sliver of light outlined the door at the end of the short corridor. The door had swung shut after Rocky's explosive entrance but had not caught, bouncing back open, just a crack, leaving an inch of flickering light.

Hunched over, she crept into the antechamber. Sounds from inside the temple were clearly audible now, grunts and the smack of a fist on skin, sounds of a fight ricocheting off the hard rock walls.

Through the crack in the door, she saw dark figures struggle back and forth, in and out of her view.

Thud. Crunch. At the feminine whimper, Bernadette's heart seemed to stop. Pressure built in her ears at her helplessness until she felt like her head would explode.

Salvador barked, "What are you doing here? Who's

with you?"

"No one." Rocky's voice, slurring the words.

Another sickening punch, and Sal said, "Put him over there. Tie him up."

He had an accomplice.

Not an accomplice—it was Arthur. He backed into view, huffing and puffing as he dragged Rocky over and dropped him against the wall, a foot from the door. Blood smeared Rocky's cheek and trickled from a gash on his forehead. and Bernadette swallowed a gasp when she saw his black and bloody eye. He looked unconscious, slumped with his chin on his chest, eyes closed.

But Arthur couldn't move Rocky alone. Rocky had to be helping. Relief washed over her, and her heart began to beat again. He must be okay.

A length of rope flew across the dirt floor of the chamber. Arthur stared at it blankly.

"Now," Sal shouted. He sounded frantic, like he could lose control at any minute. Arthur picked up the rope, his hands shaking like the palm fronds in the wind, and timidly pushed Rocky onto his side, away from the door, giving Bernadette a good view of Rocky's wrists as he wrapped the length of rope around and around.

A knife flew out of nowhere, clattered across the floor and lay gleaming darkly in the flickering light. "Cut it," Sal ordered.

Arthur grabbed the knife and awkwardly sawed at the rope. Surely he could put that knife to better use, unless he really was Sal's accomplice.

Finally he cut through the rope, then stood zombie-like, holding the knife, awaiting instructions.

Rocky slumped against the wall not two feet from the door. Bernadette's hands drifted toward him, wanting to reach out and untie his hands, but sanity prevailed and she stopped just in time. She needed a better plan than that. And fast. If Sal had already killed Ricardo and Caruthers, he wouldn't hesitate to use that knife again. He had nothing to lose.

Suddenly Annie hit the ground, on her knees beside Rocky. She cried out in pain and Bernadette thought she saw Rocky flinch. Her breath hitched. He was playing possum.

"Tie her up," Sal ordered. "I have to think."

As Arthur worked the remaining rope around Annie's wrists, Salvador paced. The sound of his footsteps walking back and forth like a caged animal echoed off the stone walls. For a split second, she caught a glimpse of him at the far end of his run—and froze when she saw the gun in his hand.

Annie whimpered, begging Arthur to let her go.

"Shut her up," Sal ordered, and a dirty cloth sailed across the room.

Arthur quickly covered Annie's mouth with the cloth. Then he stood up, turned and froze. Sal stepped into Bernadette's sightline, the gun aimed at Arthur's chest.

"The price has gone up. The statue is now twice the price."

"I don't have that much," Arthur squeaked.

Bernadette's eyes flashed back to Rocky, leaning against the chamber wall not two feet away. Annie sat on the floor on his far side, arms tied behind her back, rag stuffed in her mouth, eyes wide with terror.

Whose side was Arthur on? Was this a fight between partners?

"Don't try to play me for a fool," Sal yelled, clearly losing control.

Even if Arthur was an innocent bystander, Sal could not let him leave with the statue. In the end, Sal would have to kill them all. He had no choice.

Arthur must have reached the same conclusion. He thrust a wallet at Sal.

"I don't care. Take the money. It's all I have."

Sal grabbed the wallet and walked out of Bernadette's sightline. She heard him counting under his breath on the other side of the door.

Rocky's head rolled in her direction and he blinked once in recognition. Letting his head fall away from her, he rolled his body slightly to expose his hands bound behind his back.

He lifted one finger, just a fraction of an inch, pointing at the door—or at her. She couldn't tell which.

"What are you going to do with them?" Arthur asked, a tremor in his voice.

Bernadette kept her eyes on Rocky, watching for another sign. If that had been a sign. Then he stuck up his thumb. *What the hell does that mean?*

Sal said, "It's none of your business. Just remember, you are part of this now. Keep quiet or you will be next."

He sounded close. Too close. She could hear the stutter of nerves mixed with an underlying ruthlessness. A deadly combination.

Rocky's head was still slumped away, but his middle finger suddenly stuck out, joining the other two. It was a signal. He was counting. That was three. He only had five fingers—what did he want?

No time to think. She had to act.

Four. She stood up and threw her shoulder bag across her back.

"You stupid idiot," Salvador spat, so close, on the far side of the door.

Five. She threw her full body-weight against the door, praying it was the right thing to do.

Chapter 43

Thunk! The heavy slab door hit something solid on the other side. Bernadette rammed the door again. Pain shot through her shoulder, but this time the door swung open and she flew across the temple.

She had one brief second to register the scene. *Smokey flames. Shadows dancing over stone. Ancient drawings of animals painted on rock walls. A mosaic black jaguar slinking across the wall over a stone altar. On the alter, a wooden cross.*

She swung back towards the door, coming face to face with Salvador. Blood streamed from his nose over his snarling lips. His one hand flew to his face. The gun swung wildly in the other.

She looked for a weapon and with both hands, grabbed the heavy wooden cross.

On the floor, Rocky rolled onto his back, his legs scissoring around Sal's knees. He jerked back, pulling Sal's feet out from under him.

Salvador crashed sideways against the jagged rock wall, then slid down and hit the floor with a thud.

Without thinking, Bernadette swung the cross. It connected with his head with a sickening *crack*. Sal didn't move.

In the middle of the room, Arthur stood like a statue, clutching a bundle of cloth in his hands. Bernadette set the cross back on the altar and fell to her knees beside Rocky, her fingers fumbling with the ropes that bound his hands.

"Faster," he said.

Half a minute later the rope fell away and together they started on Annie's restraints.

"Get the gun," Rocky ordered.

Bernadette spun around and saw the gun lying by

Sal's feet. She had never touched a gun in her life, but she reached out, her hand hovering over the cold, hard steel. A dark resonance pulsed around it.

"For Christ sake." Rocky's hand snaked beneath hers and grabbed the gun. He sprang to his feet, checked the safety and stuck the weapon in the band of his pants.

Sal was still out cold, and although Bernadette was relieved to see a pulse beating in his neck, that meant he could wake up at any minute. They had to get out of there.

Adrenalin pumping, she jumped to her feet to see to Annie. The girl was standing, but her eyes stared blindly from dark sockets.

Bernadette pulled the cloth from her mouth. "Are you all right?"

Annie barely nodded in response. She seemed to be in shock.

Bernadette turned back to Rocky and winced to see the blood dripping down the side of his face. The cut on his temple and the swelling purple balloon around his eye hadn't stopped him, though. He was on his knees, using their bindings to tie Salvador's hands and feet.

"That'll hold him for a while," he said as he jumped to his feet.

Sal was already beginning to stir. Taking the rag out of Bernadette's hands, Rocky stuck it in Sal's mouth. "Let's go. Did you call for backup?"

Her eyes widened.

"God, Bernadette!"

There was no time to explain about the phone—men's voices could be heard outside the door. How many were there? Whose side were they on?

Rocky slammed and bolted the temple door. "Let's hope there's another way out."

Arthur finally shook himself out of his stupor and pointed to the back wall. "When we got here, Salvador came out of that crevasse in the rock."

Rocky took Annie by the arm and Bernadette followed them to the rear of the chamber where a vertical shadow on the wall turned out to be a slit in the rock.

Rocky and Annie squeezed through first. Bernadette hesitated, peering into the darkness, but a thump on the door made up her mind. Glancing over her shoulder, she saw Arthur stumbling after her, clutching the bundle to his chest. Then she slipped through the fissure in the rock.

It was dark on the other side. Underworld dark. Fishing her flashlight out of her bag, she swung the beam down the long wall of the narrow cavern, illuminating a line of painted warriors who marched beside them.

"Oh, my God," Arthur breathed in her ear, his eyes fixed on the images.

"Later, Arthur." She took his arm and dragged him through the cave, her light raking the ground for snakes or bats or God knows what else might live in this unearthly hole in the ground.

Ahead, Rocky's voice rang out, distant and hollow. "Keep up." Then his light snuffed out.

At the far end of the chamber, a faint glow emanated from a chasm in the floor, causing her shadow to dance on the ceiling above as she peered into the hole. She swung her beam down and it reflected on the shining surface of water six feet below.

Rocky's cryptic encouragement echoed up. "Not deep."

Bernadette looked desperately around for an alternative route, her light bouncing around the upper chamber, revealing a few broken pieces of pottery and a pile of unidentifiable bones but no other way out. Holding her flashlight high, she sat on the edge and dropped into the hole.

Surprisingly cold water swirled around her calves as it raced down the tunnel. She could clearly see the beam of Rocky's torch far ahead. Shining her light back up through the opening, it reflected off the spheres of Arthur's glasses where his face, a ghostly white mask, peered down.

"Come on," she ordered. "We're getting behind." Arthur was like an anchor around her ankle, holding her back. Once she found Rocky, she'd cut Arthur loose. Until then, though, she didn't want to be alone.

Arthur's face vanished, but a moment later he jumped down beside her, splashing her with icy water. Her shriek echoed down the tunnel.

Suddenly, she remembered what Manuel had said about animals using these tunnels for passage—jaguars, snakes, even crocodiles. Fear gripped her heart with an icy claw, but she forced herself to quash that nightmare before it could take hold.

In that brief, intense moment of fear, she'd lost her sense of direction. Rocky's light had vanished, and she didn't have any idea which way he'd gone. She shone her light in first one direction then the other down the rocky corridor. They had to move, but she didn't know which was worse, her fear of Salvador or the primal fear of wandering forever, lost in the dark underground maze.

Then a light appeared far down the tunnel, seeming to drop from the ceiling. Blowing out a breath she hadn't known she'd been holding, she followed the current toward the light.

Twenty feet down the tunnel, Rocky hung upside down from an opening overhead, shining the beam up on his battered face and grinning ghoulishly. "Hurry up."

As she sloshed toward him through the moving water, her teeth began to chatter. The corridor narrowed and the frigid water rose to her waist. Struggling to stay on her feet, she reached out for the wall. Her hand landed on something soft and warm. She screamed and stepped back, cracking her shoulder against the opposite wall.

"Quiet," Rocky called in a loud whisper.

Grunting through clenched teeth, she continued toward him through the water, trying not to touch the walls.

A few more feet and the tunnel widened considerably. Now the water was only ankle deep and she ran, splashing awkwardly, to where Rocky's arm hung down, ready to pull her up. She stuffed her light into her bag and, standing directly under the opening, reached up for his hand.

Then she saw it in his flashlight's glow. Swimming upstream toward her, a snake cut through the surface of the water, its long narrow body undulating against the current.

Her heart exploded in her chest. Her fingertips brushed Rocky's as the snake swam through her legs, but she couldn't grasp his hand. Then the solid body wound around her ankles and Bernadette froze in terror.

Bile rose in her throat, and her scream came out as a hoarse roar. She thrashed in the water, the snake struggling against her bare legs, holding her down. Rocky's hand stretched out to her, half an inch away. She was living her worst nightmare, and fear held her frozen.

Rocky hitched forward and grabbed her wrist. Straining upward, she found his strong forearm with her other hand. With a herculean effort, he pulled her up.

She cleared the water, but the snake came with her, tangled around her ankles. She swallowed a shriek, gave one strong kick, and was free.

Scrambling for a footing on the rough rock wall, her arms, stomach and bare thighs scraped the sharp limestone edge of the hole as she clambered into the warm dry cavern above. Her body shook as relief flooded through her, and she flopped on her back on the ground, struggling to regain her breath.

When Arthur handed his bundle up to Rocky, Bernadette sat up and took it from him. Then Rocky helped Arthur up, too.

Once he was on dry ground, Arthur adjusted his filthy, torn jacket and reached for the package. "I'll take that."

"I don't think so," Rocky said, taking the bundle from Bernadette and hefting the wad of rags in one hand. "It's heavy. What is it?"

"None of your business. Give it back. I paid for it. It's mine." Arthur's words came out as more of a whine, as if he knew he'd lost his treasure for good.

"You might have paid for it, but whatever it is, I don't think it's rightfully yours." Rocky offered the bundle to Bernadette. "Will it fit in your bag?"

"I think so." She tried, and it did, but only if she left the bag open.

The cavern smelled nasty. Bernadette shone her light over the walls. This cave was much larger with a cathedral-high ceiling where sparkling eyes glittered back from the darkness. *Bats.*

Suddenly the narrower passages felt like the safer option.

A faint glow, made bright by comparison to the stygian cavern they were in, emanated from a point where the cavern narrowed. Rocky must have seen it too because her beam picked him out already halfway there, with Annie stumbling behind.

"It's a T," Rocky said, when she reached his side. A craggy corridor crossed the narrow neck of the cavern at right angles. He flashed his light first one way then the other. To the left, not far down the corridor, the lights picked out a wooden post holding up the ceiling. The first piece of wood they'd seen since the cross in the temple, it looked newly cut, still sporting branches and twigs that thickened with leaves near the ceiling.

As they headed toward it, Bernadette could see that the post had its own ghostly light source, an eerie glow that radiated onto the passage from the upper branches. She stopped a few feet away.

Rocky walked right up to it, playing his beam on the rubble at the base of the wooden column. "Looks like the ceiling might have started to cave in and they brought this in to prop it up." Casting his light on the bark of the post, he reached out to touch it. "Or…"

"Don't touch it," Arthur squealed. "It's a Poisonwood tree."

He was right. In the light of the flashlights, Bernadette suddenly recognized the mottled bark.

"That's really too bad," Rocky said, shining the light back up into the branches near the ceiling. "Because I think this tree is alive. It rooted in the floor and has grown up through a hole in the ceiling, reaching for light. There, at the top, where it finally gets out in the open, the branches are thicker and block out most of the light, but that light is the sky."

Bernadette almost collapsed with relief at the thought of imminent escape.

"It would be easy to shinny up if it wasn't toxic. I should be all right." He indicated his jeans and long-sleeved shirt. "But you can't risk it." He ran his light over her bare legs. "Not like that."

She looked at the tree, then over her shoulder into the darkness behind them, listening to the faint echo of distant voices.

"I'll be okay," she said huskily, running her hands down her bare arms as she considered the toxic tree in front of her. If it meant getting out of this dark, endless tunnel, she'd risk it.

"Well, burn or no burn, I'm going up," Arthur said,

working the cuffs of his shirt down over his hands and starting to climb the broken branches of the trunk like a ladder.

Arthur was already half way up the tree when Annie suddenly seemed to grasp the fact that this was their way out. She started climbing at top speed, shielding her hands in a haphazard way with her shirtsleeves.

Besides being exposed to the sap, Bernadette had the dead weight of Arthur's parcel swinging from her shoulder. She shifted it uneasily. Not what she needed while climbing a Poisonwood.

Rocky lifted the bag off Bernadette's shoulder. "I'll take the bag and go with Annie. Then I'll throw my clothes down for you."

Thin broken branches stuck out around the tree up as far as the ceiling, which had to be at least fifteen feet high. After that, the branches grew thickly where the tree hit daylight above.

Arthur climbed like a monkey. Maybe the fear of Salvador waking up and coming after them fueled his flight. Annie and Rocky were close behind.

Bernadette stood in the dim chamber watching them go. Grunts and swearing filtered down as they disappeared into the upper branches of the tree.

Chapter 44

Alone in the dim cavern, Bernadette shifted nervously from foot to foot, hoping the antidote tree grew nearby—not that she'd recognize it if she saw it—hoping that Rocky would hurry up and throw down his clothes. Hoping that she would get out in time.

Straining to hear any sound of pursuers, she thought she heard faint noises echoing through the tunnel. Then Rocky's clothes fell on her from above. Laying the flashlight on the ground, she fumbled to pull on his shirt, leaving the long sleeves to trail over her hands.

Now she definitely heard voices echoing through the darkness. Reaching for the pants, she hopped on one foot as she tried to get them over her sneakers. Finally, she sank to the ground, tugging on first one leg, then the other. Jumping to her feet, she grabbed the flashlight and tucked it into the waist of the jeans. Wrapping the shirtsleeves around her hands, she reached for the trunk of the tree.

The voices behind her became clearer with every foot she climbed. The shirt sleeves slowed her down and she fumbled for each handhold, but she didn't dare risk bare hands on the bark.

Small branches and twigs, stunted in the darkness, provided handholds and footing. Halfway up, one twig broke under her foot, the sound, like the crack of a rifle, echoing down the tunnel. Her heart jack-hammered in her chest as she hung by one mittened hand from a scrawny branch, her shoulder ringing with pain, her legs cycling wildly in search of a foothold.

Finally finding her footing, she stopped long enough to take one deep, calming breath, and then continued to climb.

She could hear the voices clearly now and figured her pursuers were out of the water and onto this level. She grabbed another branch, increasing her speed as if the tree was on fire behind her.

Thick, leafy branches at the top slowed her down, forcing her to pick her way carefully. She grasped a stout branch, using the last of her strength to haul herself up.

Her head slammed into the rock ceiling of the cave. Grinding her teeth, she blinked away the stars that circled in her head.

"Rocky?" No answer.

She continued to climb toward the light. A branch scraped her cheek. The sap instantly began to sting, but all she could do was push through the burning branches and hope the antidote waited on the other side.

Where was Rocky's strong arm now when she needed him most?

Five feet of limestone made up the cavern roof, but at last her head broke through the opening into the fresh, moist air. She took a deep, shuddering breath and pushed herself away from the tree trunk, groping behind her for the edge of the rim, easing herself back until she was sitting, legs dangling inside the hole. The rain felt like freedom and she raised her burning face to meet it.

Then rough hands yanked her unceremoniously up from her seat.

"Rocky—?"

The hands spun her around. She was face to face with Chief Pacho, surrounded by a group of twenty-or-so men. Her eyes searched the circle for Rocky. Two big men had him, one holding each arm. Wearing only a t-shirt and boxers, the rain ran in rivulets through the tangle of black hair that hung over his battered face. But she was relieved to see him on his feet, head held high.

Around them trees and bushes grew out of the roof of the mound, just like on hundreds of other collapsed buildings in the ancient site. No one would notice the poison tree growing out of the hole—unless they already knew it was there. Pacho must have known.

Her eyes flew around the circle again. Not police. They were Jaguars.

Panic made it hard to breathe. What was the brotherhood really for? What would they do to meddling outsiders? Which side was Pacho really on? Her eyes desperately sought Rocky's. She longed to talk to him, but clearly that was out of the question.

Annie. She searched the chaotic scene again and saw one man holding her arm, but it looked more like for support than confinement. Arthur was in the custody of two other men.

The Chief held out her bag, Arthur's swaddled parcel poking out the top.

"Yours?"

"Yes. It's mine." *Shit! Wrong answer*. She stumbled to clarify. "I mean, the bag is mine, but the package is Arthur's."

"You were with him," Chief Pacho said.

"No. Well, yes. But just at the end."

What was the right thing to say? Who were these men? It would help to know which side they were on. Maybe Salvador was a Jaguar too. Just because Pacho was the police, that didn't mean he wasn't corrupt, especially in such a small town. And here in the jungle, no one would ever know what really happened...

Rocky spoke up. "Take us back to the station and we'll answer all of your questions."

Chief Pacho turned to him and his eyes narrowed. Then he snorted his agreement and led the way off the mound.

* * *

Bernadette rode back to town with Annie in the back of the police SUV. She hoped it was in deference to her sex, not because she was the primary suspect in the crime. Whatever they considered the crime to be. So far, Pacho had not charged her with anything, which had to be a good thing. But she longed to talk to Rocky, so they could present a united front. Probably exactly what the police were hoping to avoid.

The town square was full of pickup trucks and people. Mostly men. The police station turned out to be the bright blue stucco building on the square. Although still worried, Bernadette was relieved to get out of the jungle. She and Annie were hustled out of the car, sandwiched between deputies and led across the square toward the station. Her cheek was on fire and she lifted her face to the rain, letting it ease pain of the Poisonwood burn.

A pickup truck pulled in right behind them. Rocky sat in the back between two guards, his t-shirt and underwear plastered to his body by the rain.

Halfway across the square, Bernadette stopped and turned to Chief Pacho. "Please, can I have a minute?"

Even though she wore her own clothes underneath, it caused quite a stir when she peeled Rocky's clothes off right there in the square full of village men. Handing the clothes to the deputy, she said, "Please let him get dressed."

The deputy handed Rocky his clothes, then Bernadette turned and entered the station.

Chapter 45

The police station looked like the jail in an old western, one big room with a cell in the corner. Overhead, a lazy ceiling fan creaked as it stirred the humid air. An imposing mahogany desk stood in the center of the room. Polished to a high sheen, it was obviously Chief Pacho's pride and joy.

A kitchenette occupied one corner of the building and Bernadette breathed a private sigh of relief to see Mama Rosa at the stove, stirring something in a pot. One look at Bernadette's face, and the elder lashed out in Mayan at the Chief.

He, in turn, barked an order at his deputy who had just come in the door. The deputy turned on his heel and went back out into the rain. Beside Bernadette, Annie shivered uncontrollably. The old woman hurried into a back room and returned with a blanket which she wrapped around the girl's shoulders.

Moments later, the deputy returned with a handful of stringy red bark. He handed it to Mama Rosa who ground it between her palms, then gently placed the poultice on Bernadette's burning cheek. The embers immediately began to cool, and Bernadette brought up her hand to hold it in place. Despite the heat in the room, she was soaked through and shivering too. Closing her eyes, she took a quiet moment to pull herself together.

A soft hand landed on her shoulder and she opened her eyes to see Mama Rosa offering her a cup of hot Mexican cocoa. She inhaled the soothing aroma of chocolate and spice, content just to breathe it in. Nothing had ever smelled as good. She covered the old woman's hand with her own for a moment in thanks.

The Chief sat behind his giant desk, his attention

focussed on the bundle sitting on top. He removed it from her bag with a delicacy she would not have suspected he possessed. It made a quiet thud as he set the bundle on the desk, then he proceeded to unwrap it.

Carefully, he unwound the dirty rags, exposing a magnificent obsidian jaguar. Its jade eyes stared regally out of black stone that seemed to glow from within with a greenish light. Similar to her cat but larger with rounder, less streamlined proportions, it was obviously very old, and more resembled the mosaic over the altar in the temple or the jaguar throne at Chichén Itzá.

The sight of the statue brought Annie back to life and she grabbed Bernadette's hand.

The Chief examined the relic intently and when he seemed convinced it had come to no harm, he sighed deeply and turned to Bernadette. "Mrs. Mallow, do you have your passport with you?"

"No. It's back at the hotel."

"You will give it to us later," he said with a wave of his hand. Then he glanced at his deputy, who was writing furiously, to make sure he was getting it all down. The deputy nodded.

"Ms. Mallow, please tell me what you were doing at Old Ox B'alam today and how you came to be in possession of the statue of B'alam."

The Chief's impassive face gave nothing away. Bernadette's mind ranged back over the past week and she tried to pull together her overall impression of the man. She couldn't be certain, but despite everything Rocky had said about corruption in police departments and everything she had heard about Mexican police, Chief Pacho seemed to be doing his best. Manuel believed in him and that was a mark in his favor. And surely Mama Rosa wouldn't be here if Pacho wasn't one of the good guys.

There was only one thing to do. Trust her gut and

take a chance on the man.

So she began to tell the story, starting back when they first arrived in Ox B'alam. She told him how she had noticed Arthur's unhealthy interest in Mayan artifacts and how she had bought her jaguar in Tulum; how she and Rocky were attacked and chased through the jungle in the pre-dawn darkness and how Salvador stole Rocky's camera.

She explained how they found Ricardo, dead, in the lagoon—the public version, no sense stressing her credibility—about Annie's map and finding the Jaguar Temple.

Then she related the events of that day. The photo of Salvador leaving Akam's. Luis's recovery of Rocky's camera. And finally, the discovery that Arthur and Salvador were missing and the mission to rescue Annie.

When she finished, Pacho sat in silence for several minutes, considering her story. Finally, he asked, "Why would you follow them to the temple?"

"We were worried about Annie. Two men were already dead."

The Chief turned to Annie for the first time. "And why did you go after Mr. Bickenbaum?"

Annie had finished the cocoa Mama Rosa had put in her hand and her shaking had subsided. She looked directly at Chief Pacho with a resurgence of her old spunk. "I knew he was after a relic. I heard him talking to Salvador, planning a rendezvous, so I followed him."

Pacho looked at her calmly, then said, "A remarkably foolish thing to do. Why would you care?"

"Whatever he was buying belong to the people of the village," Annie said, indignant spots of color coming to her cheeks.

For the first time in hours, Bernadette smiled. "Arthur loves antiquities. He has the fever."

Pacho nodded sadly. "Ah, yes. The fever."

Then she told him about finding camo-man unconscious outside the temple and Salvador holding Rocky and Annie at gunpoint.

"You saw him with the gun?"

"Yes. I saw him."

Now fully revived, Annie jumped in with both feet. "I saw him too. He tied me up and stuck a filthy rag in my mouth."

"What happened to the gun?" the Chief asked.

Bernadette drew a sharp breath as she remembered Rocky sticking it in the waistband of his pants. "Rocky took it—but he didn't use it."

The Chief sat in silence for a moment, then asked, "Where is Salvador now?"

"In the temple. We knocked him out and tied him up. Someone was coming, we didn't know who—thought maybe his accomplice—so we grabbed the gun, bolted the door and ran."

She held the Chief's eyes for a moment, then said, "And by the way, how did you know we were at the temple? I never did call for backup."

The Chief held her eyes a moment longer. She had the feeling he was trying to decide how much to tell her.

"Jorje, who you call 'camo-man', called us on his cell phone when he came to."

"What was he doing there?" She knew one of these questions would go too far but figured she might as well keep going until they did.

The Chief considered her question, then said, "Jorje is a temple guardian. He and many others. It is our land and our historic temple where we still meet and worship. It is not for outsiders. Our mistake was initiating Salvador. He is a cousin of one of the village men, but he is not one of us."

"So," she said, squinting as she tried to put it all together, wishing Rocky were here. "Are you one of them? A Black Jaguar?"

Pacho frowned. "What do you know about the Jaguars?"

Mama Rosa materialized by his side and put her hand on his arm. "He is the Chief," she said simply.

With a flash of clarity, Bernadette remembered then what Manuel had said about Pacho being their leader and protector. Pacho wasn't just the Chief of Police; he was also the Village Chief. And the Chief of the Jaguars.

There was only one thing left to do. Rising from her chair, she walked over to the desk. The back of the jaguar felt cool and sleek under her hand as she ran it along the length of the cat. "Please, both of you, return this to the villagers for us."

Chief Pacho regarded her seriously and then smiled, probably the first time she'd seen him smile in the entire horrendous week. She smiled back, and he held out his hand to shake.

Mama Rosa just nodded as if she'd known all along that everything would turn out right.

The Chief painstakingly re-wrapped the cat, then gently lowered the bundle into his desk drawer and locked it. He was putting the key in his shirt pocket when a deputy burst through the door.

The deputy glanced at her and then gave the Chief a short message in Mayan. Pacho stood up and marched to the door. He looked outside and gave an order to the man, who immediately raced back outside.

"My deputy will take you and Miss Richards back to your hotel to retrieve your passports," Pacho said. "You will wait there. That is all for now."

As they walked across the crowded square to the police car, a scuffle drew her attention. Two deputies dragged a man from the back seat of a car. It was Arthur, his suit even dirtier and more torn than before. Perhaps he had put up a fight or had met with vigilante justice.

Either way, she was glad to see he was still on his feet, although he didn't acknowledge her presence when he passed not ten feet away as the men escorted him into the station.

Bernadette walked to the waiting police car. Rocky, dressed but under armed guard, was still in the pickup. She smiled for the first time in—she couldn't remember how long. Even though he stood in the back of a truck in the square, exposed to the rain, blood covering one side of his face, he had managed to find his sunglasses and put them on.

He nodded in her direction but didn't return her smile.

The deputy opened the back-seat door of the police car for Bernadette and just as she bent to get in, Chief Pacho's voice boomed across the square. "Detective Falconi. Would you come inside?"

Halfway into the police car, she stopped. *What?* She jumped out and met Rocky's eyes over the roof of the SUV, her eyebrows so high, her eyes felt the strain.

"Detective?"

Chapter 46

By the time Bernadette got back to the hacienda with Annie it was mid-afternoon. The rain had almost stopped and far to the east, the sky over Tulum was clearing. She decided to take the streak of blue on the horizon as a good omen.

Meredith met them at the door, burst into tears at the sight of her daughter and swept her into a hug. Annie, with the resilience of youth, seemed fully recovered and although Meredith whisked her up to their room, Bernadette doubted Annie would be out of the action for long.

Bernadette went up to her own room and showered quickly. She was running out of clean, dry clothes, but maybe now they could leave tomorrow as planned.

Somewhat surprisingly, she was no longer looking forward to going home. Just a few days ago, when tension was burning a hole in her stomach, she couldn't wait to get away. But now that it was all over, she would have liked to stay for a few more days, if just to unwind.

She'd feel better when Rocky got back to the hacienda. She pulled her dress out of the closet one more time and gave it a shake. You could hardly see the dirt and stains. The print had been a good choice for this week in the jungle. She should make a note of that for her next trip. If there was a next trip. This one had been a disaster from the word go and although none of it had been her fault, she wondered if Rocky would even consider going on another assignment with her.

As she towel-dried her hair, she promised herself that regardless of whether there would be another assignment or not, she would not let anyone down. She would hand in the best story she could write. But would it be good enough?

Of course, there were other photographers, but darn it, given half a chance she and Rocky would make a good team. They *had* made a good team, back there at the temple. He'd needed her help and together they'd pulled it off. She just hoped he saw it that way.

He'd looked pissed off when she'd seen him last, at the police station.

Detective. She couldn't help grinning. Who'da guessed? Then she groaned aloud, smacking her palm on her forehead as she remembered the talk she'd had with him at the restaurant, when she asked him about his run-ins with the police.

And he had let her believe he had a record. Why hadn't he mentioned he'd been a cop? Surely if there was ever a time for the topic to arise it was this week, with one murder right on the heels of another. He didn't look like any police officer she'd ever seen though, with the earring peeking out of that wavy black hair. And those dusky, probing eyes.

She gave herself a shake. Enough of that. Grinning at herself in the mirror, she put on a dash of lipstick, grabbed her passport and went down to the lobby. The deputy looked at it briefly and gave it back. Obviously just a formality.

Half an hour later, she sat drinking coffee at the long dining room table, filling in the rest of the members of the Cultural Tour on the afternoon's events.

The storm was spent, the rain just a faint tattoo on the terrace roof. The electrical charge in the air had dissipated too, and Bernadette had a feeling the episodes were over, for now. She still felt the jittery after-effects of all that adrenalin though: empty but somehow at the same time excited.

Her eyes kept returning to the hacienda entrance, hoping Rocky would walk through the door. They had scarcely exchanged two words since he had left her in the van in the ruins' parking lot hours ago. She wanted to talk over everything that had happened since.

Her heartbeat picked up when a police car pulled up in front of the hacienda door. Rocky jumped out, then leaned down to say something to Deputy Perez, who grinned and waved goodbye.

The dining room fell silent when he sauntered in, wet and dirty, sunglasses on. Someone had stitched up his eyebrow and put a patch on his cheek. He took off his glasses and a gasp went through the room. His left eye had blossomed into a first-class black eye, worthy of any prizefighter.

Bernadette rose from her chair. "Oh, Rocky."

He gave a self-conscious laugh. "Just a scratch."

Her bag hung over his shoulder and he lifted it off with two hands, placing it gently on the table in front of her.

"Thank you," she said. "I'd forgotten about it." But when she pulled it toward her and felt the weight, she looked up at him in excitement.

"Is it—?"

Not waiting for an answer, she ripped open the bag. Inside, wrapped in newspaper and tucked into a plastic bag, was her jaguar, looking sleek and sexy.

"Thank you," she breathed.

He grinned. "I'm just the messenger. Pacho sent it."

Then he looked down at the table. "What are we drinking? Coffee? I don't think so. I could use a shot of tequila."

* * *

Bernadette was waiting with the rest of the group when, a short time later, clean and dressed in fresh clothes, Rocky joined them at the bar.

"They found Salvador in the temple," he told them between tequila shots. "Turned out there was a warrant for his arrest in Cancun on suspicion of murder, among other things. So, he was hiding out here, selling fake relics to members of the Cultural Tour. He got the sculptures from his home up north and Pacho figures Ricardo probably helped him, maybe giving the buyers fake receipts to help them get the pieces out of the country. The irony is, the fake receipts reflect the true value of the statues more accurately than the amount the buyers actually paid."

"Arthur really wanted that statue from the temple," Bernadette said.

"Yeah, well, that was the real thing." Rocky shook his head. "You should have seen his face when he realized he wasn't getting it back."

His eyes flashed to hers, tentatively. She knew he was remembering what Pacho had said in the square, and she was kind of enjoying seeing him squirm. She thought he didn't want her to mention it here, but after Pacho announced it like that, it would be all over town in no time. And that included the hacienda.

"It would have been breaking the law for Arthur to take the statue out of Mexico," Annie said.

"But that isn't worth dying for," Meredith said pointedly.

"Besides which," Hank added, "it would have been immoral for Arthur to keep the sculpture when it means so much to these people."

Bernadette ran her tongue around her lips, tasting remnants of the coffee flavored tequila. The hairs on her arms stood on end and she looked up to find Rocky's gaze on her lips. Her stomach clenched, just a bit, and a delightful shiver ran down her back.

She had never been the type to give in to a last-night fling. Too bad. She would go back to her life with her son and her job in Vancouver, and Rocky would go back to his jealous girlfriend in San Francisco. Tomorrow it would all be over.

She wasn't sure if she was ready.

Saturday, Day 7

"Though happy it was their fortune to wander among these crumbling memorials of a once powerful and mysterious people, they almost mourned that their lot had not been cast a century sooner, when, as they believed, all these edifices were entire."

J.L. Stephens, Incidents of Travel in Yucatán, 1842

Chapter 47

Rocky lay flat on his back in bed staring at the ceiling. He was often sleepless on the last night of a trip, but never like this.

Then again, he had never been on a trip like this before. He had become complacent with the traveling—thought he'd seen it all—but this trip had been full of firsts.

First zip-line, he thought with a grin. The grin faded when he remembered the murders. They had stirred up feelings he'd thought he'd left behind when he left the force but, when Annie was in trouble, it all came flooding back. For better and for worse.

He put that aside to think about later.

And this time there was Bernadette. His heartbeat picked up. Shuster she wasn't, but he had discovered there were better things than traveling the world with another disgruntled middle-aged man.

When the sky began to pale, he jumped out of bed and pulled together the equipment he would need for his last shots of the jungle dawn. Looking out his window, he smiled when he recognized the figure silhouetted against the watery light at the far pergola.

She was sitting on a lounge under the bougainvillea, watching the mist rise off the water when he arrived at the small back lagoon.

She looked up and smiled. "*Hola*," she said softly. With her long bare legs curled beneath her on the lounge, the first beam of sunlight glanced over the hacienda roof, setting her hair on fire.

The mist was quickly dissipating; this moment of light wouldn't last long. Rocky set up his equipment beside her and focused on the patch of sunlight striking the far shore, soft and golden, with the backdrop of the primordial jungle.

He took a few wide shots, then zoomed in on the shoreline, not fifty feet away, to wait for the next dawn visitor. The forest became unnaturally silent. Rocky realized he too was holding his breath when, across the lagoon, sleek and swarthy, a cat stole out of the jungle. Ek B'alam, the Night Sun God, a black jaguar come to drink before disappearing from the light of day.

The spots on his dusky coat were the same deep chocolate as the shadows that had hidden him seconds before. Moving stealthily, low to the ground, his powerful shoulders rolled, and his back muscles flexed as he slunk into the shaft of sunlight that struck a large rock sloping down to the water's edge.

Rocky's eye was on the viewfinder and his hand on the zoom lens, focusing in tight on the big cat's face as he lowered his head to drink. The haze had almost disappeared, just a few misty tendrils rose from the surface of the water. Rocky zoomed out and took another shot.

The cat was huge: seven feet from nose to tail, two hundred pounds of raw muscle. He hadn't spotted them yet, had not caught their scent.

Rocky flashed a look at Bernadette. Her eyes were wide, fixed on the far shore. Although the width of the lagoon lay between them, the cat could cross that in a heartbeat. Adrenalin raced through his veins—but more exhilaration than fear.

Seconds ticked by. Then, like an irritated house cat, he waved his long, sinuous tail once and drank again. Rocky snapped another shot, but the cat heard the click and his gaze swung directly to them. Rocky heard Bernadette catch a sharp breath.

Through the long lens of the camera, he stared into the jaguar's eyes. Orange. Calm. Wary.

Click.

In one swift, fluid motion the jaguar rose. Rocky's heart pounded, his hands gripped the tripod. He had used it as a weapon before and he would do it again.

The cat turned his head toward them and snarled, lips curling back to show his fangs. Then he let loose a roar that started deep in his chest and echoed through the still jungle. Rocky felt the sound to the tips of his toes and an involuntary shudder ripped through him as the lagoon between them shrank to the size of a puddle.

But the cat kept on moving. Rocky blinked, and it had vanished into the tangled vegetation.

"There," Bernadette said softly, pointing down the far shore.

He saw a movement in the shadows, but it could have been the wind. The jaguar was gone.

Slowly the jungle came to life: a monkey in the trees sent an 'all clear' signal; a bird trilled an early morning song. Rocky sank bonelessly down on a lounge beside Bernadette.

Bernadette let out a long breath. "Did that really happen?" she whispered.

"You bet," Rocky said and held up the camera. "And I got the shot." He turned to face her with a grin. "So, partner, we did good."

"You think so?" She tried to be cool but was thrilled to hear him say it.

"I do. Sal is on his way to the penitentiary, at the very least. Arthur's going to lose all the money he'd planned to spend on the statue to the fines he'll have to pay, and hopefully he got a good enough scare that he won't ever try that again."

"And Ek B'alam is back in the temple, where he belongs," Bernadette finished with satisfaction.

"But next time..." He lowered his brows and glared in a way that didn't scare her anymore. "When I tell you to stay put and call for back up, I want you to do it."

A wave of pleasure ran through her. So there would be a next time. "I have one question," she said. "Why on earth did you rush the temple door?"

Rocky looked away for a moment, back across the lagoon. "Salvador was arguing with Annie when I got there, and then I heard him hit her. I knew he wouldn't stop there. You saw what he did to me. He was freaking out and looking for a punching bag."

"So you rushed him, even though he had a gun?"

"I didn't know he had a gun. I thought it was a knife."

She squinted one eye, her look saying, *'and the difference is?'*

Rocky looked away again and mumbled, "Sometimes when a guy takes it out on a woman, I just lose it."

"Well, I hope I can help you out again sometime," she said, knowing that would get him but holding back the smile.

He scowled. "I would have gotten out, once the *backup* arrived."

Then he shuddered. "Anyway, the thought of sleeping with the crocs would have got me out of there.

But I'm glad you are so darned intuitive, Mallow. I wasn't sure you would get my signal."

She tried to be cool, but a flush washed her cheeks. "The fingers? I wasn't sure what you meant, but I had no time to think. I just had to go with my gut."

"Well, I'm glad you did."

A silence bloomed, and she was quick to seize her chance. "So, Detective. . ."

Rocky growled. "I don't know where he got that."

"Background check? I'm sure he did one on all of us." Rocky didn't respond. Okay. She would dig if she had to. "Is that detective as in *Detective Sam Spade*, or as in *Police Detective Falconi*?"

He huffed out a breath, "I was on the force, for a while."

"Why did you leave?"

"Didn't suit me."

"And being a photographer does?"

"To a tee."

"That mark on your back is a gunshot wound, isn't it?"

"Childhood injury," he insisted, but his frown told her otherwise.

She decided to give him a break. After all, there was always next time.

They sat in silence for a few moments, enjoying the cool of the morning. "It really is lovely here," Bernadette said. "I wish we'd had more time to enjoy it."

"Do you have to go home today?"

The question took her by surprise. "Yes. Don't you?"

"Thought I might stop at Cancun for a week. Catch some rays, relax on the beach."

"With Eloise and Celeste?"

"The *other* end. It's a long beach."

Bernadette laughed, then said thoughtfully. "It hasn't really been a rest, has it?"

"No. I could use a week off right about now." He waited a beat. "How about you?"

Although he said it casually, her pulse kicked up. A week ago, she wouldn't have considered it, but now a tingle ran through her as she considered changing her plans and taking a few days in Cancun. What would be the harm? He'd called her his partner. He probably meant two partners kicking back together. And if he didn't…?

He looked particularly disreputable today with the black eye and bandages. Obviously fresh from a fight. It all just added to his tough-guy mystique—as if that needed any further enhancement. His hair was pulled back into a stubby ponytail, his one good eye smoldering at her, awaiting an answer.

Rocky was the most exciting man she had met in a long time. Maybe ever. If she accepted, it would be a week to remember—she was sure of that. This week had already been more, much more, than she had expected. In so many ways. Not just the travel and a new job, but also the heart-stopping adventure. And Rocky.

A small sigh escaped. He had a girlfriend, and Bernadette would never be the woman who tore them apart. And hopefully Rocky wasn't that kind of guy. She had her job to go back to, and she'd spoken to Colin last evening and he was excited that she was coming home. She couldn't disappoint him.

"Mmmm, I'd love to, but my son is waiting for me at home. I'm going to end up with one of those garish airport sombreros after all."

Their eyes met with a flash of understanding.

"Too bad," Rocky said. "Maybe next time."

Epilogue

Back in Vancouver, the summer breeze fluttered the curtains by Bernadette's desk, blowing her papers onto the floor. She gathered them up, tapped them into a neat pile and reached for her obsidian jaguar. Cool and sleek under her hand, it made a great paperweight on a windy day. Her hand lingered, as it often did, on his muscular back and her mind drifted back to the last morning in Mexico, when Ek B'alam had paid them a visit.

Jen loved the article she'd written on her return. It would be coming out in the next issue of *Travelers Magazine*, accompanying Rocky's photographs. He had sent her a few pictures as mementos, and Hank had sent a couple of her and Rocky together.

They'd been in touch a few times by email. Rocky had landed them a couple of other articles on side aspects of the trip and she'd landed one for them with *Archaeology* magazine. They'd been in contact to coordinate their efforts, their communication always friendly, always professional. She told herself a good working relationship was a gift. It had never been anything more.

But while it lasted, it had been the most exciting week of her life.

Her cell phone rang, interrupting her reverie. She reached for it, paused as her hand tingled, and smiled. Then she picked up the phone. "Hi, Jen."

"Bernadette. I hope your passport's up to date…"

* * * * * * *

Dear readers,

This book is the product of my imagination following a vacation in the Yucatán peninsula of Mexico. Rocky, Bernadette, and all the other characters in the book are entirely fictional and not based on any people, living or dead.

The Maya have many Jaguar myths and legends, and while I have not attempted to write a treatise on Maya culture, I did do quite a bit of research for the book, including wonderful visits to many archaeological sites in the Yucatan. Then, as fiction writers often do, I took what I needed from them to make my story work. But,

- B'alam does mean Jaguar in the Mayan language.
- Ek B'alam means Black Jaguar.
- Ox B'alam means Jaguar paw.
- And the Night Sun God is often represented by the black jaguar.

If you want to do more research into the Mayan culture, there are many wonderful books available on the subject.

Thank you for reading Bernadette and Rocky's first adventure.

You can find out more about the series and
a map of Ek B'alam at my website,
www.JudithHudsonAuthor.com
or follow Rocky and Bernadette on **Pinterest**, at
https://www.pinterest.ca/judithhudsonauthor/rocky-and-bernadette-adventures/

Watch for their next escapade, when Bernadette and Rocky travel to Italy.

J.M. Hudson

Copyright

© Judith Hudson, 2018
Published by Tall Trees Books,
June 2018
Cover designed by Rosey Hudson
ISBN: 978-1-7752022-5-7

Made in the USA
Columbia, SC
18 July 2018